"You're a dangerous man to know, Detective," Robin told him.

He released her hand and sat back, smiling a bitter smile. "Yeah, I can be that," he admitted. "If I find out you're jerking me around, you can count on it."

Mitch knew the value of intimidation and was in no way opposed to using it when the time was right. So why did it make him feel so rotten, playing the big, bad cop with Robin? He knew she hadn't killed James Andrews, but he did sense she was hiding something. Why didn't he feel justified in shaking her up a little?

Dear Reader,

As the year winds to a close, I hope you'll let Silhouette Intimate Moments bring some excitement to your holiday season. You certainly won't want to miss the latest of THE OKLAHOMA ALL-GIRL BRANDS, Maggie Shayne's *Secrets and Lies*. Think it would be fun to be queen for a day? Not for Melusine Brand, who has to impersonate a missing "princess" and evade a pack of trained killers, all the while pretending to be passionately married to the one man she can't stand—and can't help loving.

Join Justine Davis for the finale of our ROMANCING THE CROWN continuity, *The Prince's Wedding*, as the heir to the Montebellan throne takes a cowgirl—and their baby— home to meet the royal family. You'll also want to read the latest entries in two ongoing miniseries: Marie Ferrarella's *Undercover M.D.*, part of THE BACHELORS OF BLAIR MEMORIAL, and Sara Orwig's *One Tough Cowboy*, which brings STALLION PASS over from Silhouette Desire. We've also got two dynamite stand-alones: Lyn Stone's *In Harm's Way* and Jill Shalvis's *Serving Up Trouble*. In other words, you'll want all six of this month's offerings— and you'll also want to come back next month, when Silhouette Intimate Moments continues the tradition of providing you with six of the best and most exciting contemporary romances money can buy.

Happy holidays!

Leslie J. Wainger
Executive Senior Editor

Please address questions and book requests to:
Silhouette Reader Service
U.S.: 3010 Walden Ave., P.O. Box 1325, Buffalo, NY 14269
Canadian: P.O. Box 609, Fort Erie, Ont. L2A 5X3

In Harm's Way
LYN STONE

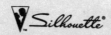

INTIMATE MOMENTS™

Published by Silhouette Books

America's Publisher of Contemporary Romance

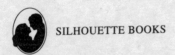 SILHOUETTE BOOKS

ISBN 0-373-27263-4

IN HARM'S WAY

Copyright © 2002 by Lynda Stone

Visit Silhouette at www.eHarlequin.com

Printed in U.S.A.

Books by Lyn Stone

Silhouette Intimate Moments

Beauty and the Badge #952
Live-In Lover #1055
In Harm's Way #1193

Harlequin Historicals

The Wicked Truth #358
The Arrangement #389
The Wilder Wedding #413
The Knight's Bride #445
Bride of Trouville #467
One Christmas Night #487
　"Ian's Gift"
My Lady's Choice #511

LYN STONE

loves creating pictures with words. Paints, too. Her love affair with writing and art began in the third grade, when she won a school-wide prize for her colorful poster for book week. She spent the prize money on books, one of which was *Little Women*.

She rewrote the ending so that Jo marries her childhood sweetheart. That's because Lyn had a childhood sweetheart herself and wanted to marry him when she grew up. She did. And now she is living her "happily-ever-after" in north Alabama with the same guy. She and Allen have traveled the world, had two children, four grandchildren and experienced some wild adventures along the way.

Whether writing romantic historicals or contemporary fiction, Lyn insists on including elements of humor, mystery and danger. Perhaps because that other book she purchased all those years ago was a Nancy Drew mystery.

This book is dedicated to
Alice and Richard Edge,
a beautiful, gracious lady and
a true Southern gentleman.

Chapter 1

"So, what's your take on it, Kick? You think she did him?" Mitch Winton asked his partner in a low voice as he studied the woman in question just visible through the doorway to the bedroom.

The woman sat on the edge of the bed, her hands clasped in her lap, back ramrod straight. Mitch couldn't see her face. She kept it turned away, probably so she wouldn't have to look at the body again. One of the uniforms stood just inside the room with her.

Kick Taylor nodded. "She did it all right. No reason to think otherwise."

"You question her yet?"

"Just the prelim I got on tape. This one's a real ice queen. Cool as they come, not giving us squat."

"Let me hear what she's got to say."

Kick hesitated, then handed Mitch the small tape recorder. "Not much to it. She's been sitting like that since I got here. Davis and Mackie said she's been in there the whole time. Didn't even come out to answer the door when they responded."

"She phone it in?"

"Affirmative."

Mitch sighed. Why couldn't he have just said yes? "So how'd we get on call tonight? Did I check the wrong roster?"

"Smith's baby's due anytime. I volunteered to switch with him and Williams."

"He asked?" Mitch would be surprised if he had.

"No, I offered. Sorry I forgot to tell you. It won't mess up your vacation, though. I can handle this one myself."

There were perils in being gung ho, Mitch thought to himself. The captain had teamed them up a few months back when Kick had transferred from Vice, hoping Mitch could tamp down a little of Kick's enthusiasm. He was a case hog. Still, there was no way he could have known about this one before it happened.

Homicide detectives were supposed to appear a little jaded, at least experienced. It didn't give any of the principals involved a warm, fuzzy feeling if one of the people in charge acted as if they were working their first murder and their whole career depended on an immediate arrest. It was a whole lot different from Vice where Kick had spent his last five years.

"You're looking too cool for words," Mitch commented as he squatted and visually examined the dead man. White male, on the green side of forty, about six feet tall, exceptionally well dressed, probably considered good-looking without that hole in the center of his forehead. "Love the tie."

"You talking to him or me?" Kick asked, methodically inching his way around the body counterclockwise, looking for traces of evidence like he was employed by forensics.

"You. The ducks are a nice touch."

"Thanks," Kick replied, smoothing a palm over his expensive neckwear, offering no explanation for what he was doing so well turned out this close to midnight on a Wednesday. He was a night owl and there was plenty to do in Nashville all night long. Probably got called in off a hot date.

Mitch admitted to a little envy. He had just about forgotten what a date was like. He'd been sound asleep when the phone rang. He suddenly felt very over-the-hill for thirty-six. Homicide was a bitch at any time, especially the middle of the night. Another hour and he would have been off the clock for two whole weeks.

"The weapon," his partner said, pointing to a Beretta lying on the floor near the body.

"I guessed," Mitch said dryly. One of the techs was getting ready to bag it. "Anyone hear the shot?" Mitch asked.

"Haven't had a chance to ask yet. Why don't you go on home?"

Mitch snorted. "What? And miss all this fun?"

The print lifters were busy dusting things while Kick measured a stain he'd found near the coffee table. The medical examiner would be arriving shortly to take charge of the body. Mitch knew there wasn't much he could discover here that Kick and the M.E. wouldn't.

Again he glanced through the door at the witness, or suspect, or whatever she would turn out to be. She hadn't moved. Or relaxed. "She live here?"

"Nope, but she is still the missus. Says she just flew down from the Big Apple. Andrews must have been expecting her. Wine's in the fridge, glasses were out, little napkins, nuts and stuff. All scattered now, of course, but he had it ready at one time."

"Looks pretty straightforward," Mitch said. "Not much

question about cause of death. Single shot to the head. No sign of a break-in?"

"Nope. He opened the door and let her in."

"Maybe he let someone else in first? Let's try to keep an open mind here."

Kick snorted. "Don't you be fooled just because she's a looker. Pretty fingers can pull triggers, too, y'know."

"You want to stick one of those fingers in a light socket right now and save the state a trial? How about some proof first, huh?" Mitch felt obliged to point out that the investigation was not complete. Kick was acting as if he had the case sewn up.

"I'm working on it, okay?" Kick snapped.

Mitch ignored his attitude and returned to examining the body. "Died where he fell, looks like."

Kick mumbled an agreement, engrossed in an address book he'd found in the drawer under the phone. "Captain was looking for you this afternoon after you left. Wanted to see you before you took off. Something about that shooting I guess. The guy still alive?"

"Last I heard." Mitch glanced around at the living room. "Whoever did this left a big enough mess, didn't they? You got things covered?"

"Absolutely. You can go ahead and leave." Kick inclined his head toward the woman in the bedroom. "I'll take her in soon as I get through here."

"I'll do it," Mitch said. "I stopped off and got an unmarked in case you'd apprehended somebody."

Kick frowned at him. "And let you play Sir Galahad to Princess Sureshot? Not hardly. I'm transporting, Mitch, *and* interrogating her."

"No, you're going to stay here and question the neighbors," Mitch informed him firmly, unsure why he was pulling rank on Kick. He had never done that before, and it bothered him to do it now. But his partner was being too close-minded about this whole deal. He had already decided they had their shooter. Mitch just wanted to make sure Kick wasn't taking the easy way out.

"Checked her for powder and printed her yet?"

Kick looked up, his lips tightening. "Not yet."

Mitch called Abe Sinclair over and quietly ordered him to do a quick paraffin test on Mrs. Andrews to detect whether she had any gunpowder residue on her hands and then get her prints. He wanted all the bases covered.

Then Mitch moved away from the body, got as isolated as he could in the middle of a busy crime scene and turned on the recorder. He put it to his ear and listened to Kick's curt demand that Mrs. Andrews tell in her own words what had transpired. Following was the brief statement she had given. Very brief.

He could see her better from where he stood now. Abe was in there now, doing his thing with paraffin. She appeared almost oblivious to the process. Classic profile. Perfect hair. Lovely. She was thin, no, slender. Beautifully dressed in a beige suit and gold earrings. Tasteful. Cool, just as Kick had said.

From this distance she didn't look all that upset about what was going on. At any rate, she wasn't sobbing her heart out, not that that meant anything necessarily. Could be in shock.

Her voice on the tape was soft and cultured, but with almost no inflection. A pleasant-sounding computer robot came to mind. She referred to the victim by name, not using the *we* pronoun that would indicate they'd had a happy relationship. Of course, if she'd killed him, she would want to disassociate herself, not think of him as half of her couple.

As he listened, she made it clear she had touched the body while checking for signs of life. Or maybe to explain away any forensic evidence that might turn up later. She admitted she had touched the gun before she thought what she was doing.

When the tape ran silent, he clicked Stop, stuck the recorder in his pocket and entered the bedroom. With a jerk of his thumb, he ordered Abe and the officer who'd been keeping watch over her to leave them alone.

"Mrs. Andrews?" he greeted her. "I'm Detective Winton. You're the one who discovered the body?" He sat on the edge of the chair located about three feet from the bed, so that he faced her.

"Yes," she whispered. Then she looked up at him with beautiful, dark-fringed blue eyes that badly needed to weep. He knew better than to feel sympathy for her. You didn't last long in this business if you couldn't stay detached. This was the hardest part of the job, but it usually wasn't quite this hard.

He had seen faces filled with sorrow more times than he could count, but he couldn't recall one that had moved him quite the way hers did now. Why was that? Instant attraction, yeah. But it seemed more than that, something he couldn't get a handle on and name.

Getting thunderstruck by a woman was a new experience for Mitch and he didn't much like it. His defenses wouldn't go up like they were supposed to. He probably should let Kick take over right now, but he couldn't make himself do that. Not when she was looking up at him with those soulful eyes, as if she was depending on him to get this right. And not when Kick was ready to hang her on the spot.

Mitch prided himself on judging character. Women seemed easier to read than men. Their emotions were usually closer to the surface, somehow more accessible. That was a sexist view, he knew, but he'd found it to be true, anyway.

Either Robin Andrews cared for that man on the floor and was grieving, or she had delivered the shot that killed him and was terribly sorry about it. "Did you kill your husband, Mrs. Andrews?" The question had slipped right out of his mouth before he could catch it.

Damn. Mitch almost pounded his head with his fist. He wasn't supposed to put that to her yet. She hadn't been read her rights, unless Kick had done it off tape, which was almost surely not the case.

Mitch hoped she wouldn't confess right now. If he was being perfectly honest, he hoped to hell she didn't have cause to confess at all. It surely would cut down on the workload if he could just haul her in and not have to track down some unknown, but for some inexplicable reason he just didn't want her to have done it. The thought rattled him.

Women were perfectly capable of murder. However, as a man brought up to revere women, he had to keep reminding himself of that. Finding it hard to believe that the gentler sex would do such a thing was his one huge hang-up and he worked hard at concealing it and compensating for it. But he didn't want to overcompensate. It was a problem.

He wished to hell another team had caught this one. He obviously needed a good night's sleep.

Robin couldn't believe this was happening. "No. I didn't kill him. I'm the one who notified the police," she explained.

"Sorry. Won't get you off the hook." The detective shrugged as if he didn't care one way or the other. "Sometimes a perpetrator will call in the crime, tryin' to throw off suspicion," he continued in that maddeningly slow drawl of his. "But we'll get around to that in a little while. For now let's just clear up a few things. Minor points, really."

He pulled a small black notebook out of his pocket and smiled at her when he successfully located the ballpoint pen to go with it. Had Columbo started out like this? Robin wondered.

She hated his Southern accent. It poured out like thick molasses. Sinfully rich and dark. It made her want to finish his sentences for him. When he spoke in sentences.

Robin riveted all of her attention on him simply because it was something to think about other than what had happened in the next room. She couldn't deal with that yet.

Her first thought was that this man didn't look official. He hadn't shaved. His dark-brown hair needed a trim, and he must have thrown on yesterday's wrinkled clothes. He wore khaki slacks, a UT pullover and a windbreaker. He wasn't even wearing socks, just scuffed leather deck shoes. He looked entirely too casual, too rumpled and laid-back for a detective. Since he didn't look official, Robin didn't trust him to act officially. She didn't have much trust in men, anyway. Certainly not this one.

Worst of all he had a smile and an attitude that were working hard to make her drop her guard and lean on him. She quickly realized just which way she would fall if she did that.

"Did you see anybody when you came into the building? In the parking area? Driving away?"

"No," she answered simply, in the second or so that he provided between each of his questions. He looked and sounded lazy. Or maybe only tired. Suddenly Robin was horribly afraid this man was going to lock her up just because she was handy instead of pursuing the person who had really killed James.

She shuddered, took a deep breath and clasped her arms tightly across her chest. James was dead, *murdered,* lying lifeless in the next room. The chilling horror of it made her shiver again, but she couldn't put it out of her mind for more than a few minutes no matter how hard she tried. *He* was not going to let her.

"You say you flew in from New York just to visit your husband?" the detective asked.

Robin didn't want to talk about her reasons for being here. She didn't want to talk at all. Shouldn't he be ordering people out to look for James's murderer? Setting up roadblocks or whatever they did down here to catch a criminal? If they all moved and talked at this man's speed, it was a miracle they ever got anything done.

"Mrs. Andrews?" he prompted, more firmly this time. "Why did you come here?"

"To visit," she said, her words more clipped than usual.

"Does that mean you have one of those, ah, long-distance—" he paused to make a little questioning gesture with one hand "—what do you call 'em?"

"Separations," Robin supplied. "James and I have been separated for almost a year."

He frowned and made a note. "Okay. Were you on friendly terms with your husband, Ms. Andrews?"

"Yes," she said with an emphatic nod. "James and I had been friends for several years before we decided to get married. After about six months he and I both agreed it was a mistake. He transferred to Nashville right after we separated, and I stayed in New York. His company has an office here."

"Yeah, Townsend, Inc., you said. So what are you doing here visiting him if you're not together any longer?"

Robin explained, "He called me at home last week and asked if I planned to fly down to Florida to visit my mother. I usually go for her birthday and he was aware of that. He wanted me to schedule my flight through Nashville and stop over so that we could talk."

"Unfinished business?" Those penetrating blue eyes focused on her like lasers.

Robin bit her lip and glanced around the room, determined

to concentrate on her answers rather than the horror that threatened to tear her apart if she let it.

James was dead. She didn't love him, but she still liked him. He might have had a weak will where other women were concerned, but she figured she was as much to blame for that as James. The spark between them had been just that, a spark, not the fire they'd first thought it was. It had gone out more quickly than it had erupted. But fortunately it hadn't destroyed their friendship.

The detective cleared his throat to get her attention. She gave it, studying his face, trying to guess what he would ask her next. This man was about to arrest her. She could feel it.

"I asked if you had unfinished business with your husband?"

"Yes, I suppose so. Also he...he wanted me to bring him something he said he'd forgotten when he moved down here. A computer disk."

"Music?"

"No. Something to do with his work in the insurance company, he said. He told me he didn't want me to mail it, because he was afraid it might get lost."

"You didn't mention that when Detective Taylor taped your preliminary interview."

She lifted one shoulder in a half shrug. "He didn't question me. He only said to tell what happened after I arrived here."

"So you brought what your husband wanted you to bring and, in addition to that favor, he planned to discuss something important with you?" he asked slyly. "Maybe he wanted to reconcile?"

"No, he didn't. James and I are just friends now." Then she remembered and corrected herself. "*Were* just friends." Her voice only broke a little.

"I wonder why you didn't get a divorce."

Robin exhaled slowly. "We discussed it several times. I thought we should. But he..." She hesitated, unsure whether she should have admitted this. "Maybe he was ready to start proceedings. He didn't say on the phone."

"And now a divorce won't be necessary," he commented, shaking his head, sounding sad, looking sad. She resented the implication he made, and hated his acting as if he were concerned. Damn him, did he have no decency? The man she was married to had just been killed. But he was doing his job, wasn't he? He had to eliminate her as a suspect.

She had to be precise, give the detective all the information he could use and suggest things he might do to establish her innocence. If she didn't do that, whoever killed James would get away with it. And she might be blamed.

She drew in another deep breath and released it carefully, trying to gain a little control over the tremor in her voice. "I took a taxi from the airport and arrived here about ten-thirty, give or take ten minutes. I'm sorry I didn't look at the clock more closely. You could verify the time with the cab company. Oh, and the plane was delayed for over an hour," she informed him, remembering that detail suddenly, thinking it might be crucial. "It was Flight 1247, American. Check the passenger list."

"Good idea. I'll do that," he agreed, as if that hadn't occurred to him before. "So you got here and..." he prompted with an expectant look.

Robin rushed to explain, "James was...was like that when I found him. The door was unlocked, the rooms were wrecked, and he was just lying there. Like that."

It felt surreal, all of it. James's death, her second recitation of the events, this detective's quiet questions in the deep, velvety voice. She looked at him again, puzzled by his unassuming manner. It was as if he did this every night. Did he? This was Nashville, not New York. Did people get killed here so regularly that it didn't faze him at all?

Robin's breath felt jerky and shallow as her gaze strayed to the door of the living room, through which she could see James. He lay sprawled facedown on the floor beside the coffee table, a dark pool of blood encircling his head. His eyes were open. A camera flashed.

She closed her own eyes tight. "Could...could they cover him? Please?"

"Sure they will. Don't you worry," he said, his words soft with faked compassion. It had to be faked. Why would he care if James lay there so exposed or that she might worry about it? He hadn't known James and didn't know her.

He went on. "As soon as they do what they have to do, they'll cover him up. Why don't you sit back on the bed a ways, ma'am. Then he won't be visible to you. It bothers you, doesn't it," he asked gently, "seein' him that way?"

Though he spoke softly, he watched her with an intensity that scraped across her exposed nerves. His words and relaxed attitude didn't match those keen, narrowed ice-blue eyes that watched her like a hawk. A circling hawk about to dive at its prey.

"Of course it bothers me! He was a good man and he's *dead*," she said, choking on the words. Robin covered her eyes with a trembling hand and shook her head. "Please, Officer Wendall—"

"It's detective, Detective Winton," he corrected without a trace of impatience. He nudged her free hand and she looked down to see him offering her a pristine, neatly ironed handkerchief with a blue *W* embroidered on one corner.

Robin blinked. She didn't know men did that anymore. Offered their handkerchiefs. Hesitantly she took it, though she had no idea why. She wasn't even crying. Her throat hurt, her heart ached and she was terrified, but her eyes felt dry as dust.

"Are you going to arrest me?" she asked. It came out a bit more sharply than she intended. Had she sounded guilty?

He smiled. It was a quick little expression of what looked like sympathy. She knew better. "Not right now," he assured her, then added, "but you do have to come downtown with me and give a written statement."

"I told you everything." She inclined her head toward the living room. "The other detective has it on tape and now you have notes." She looked at the small tablet he'd been scribbling on.

"We'll need another, more formal statement, ma'am. In more detail, and in writing this time." He held up a hand when she started to object. "I realize you have other things to do, but I know you want to help us all you can."

"Of course," she replied. What else could she say?

"Good. You'll be able to call his family, yours and anybody else you want to once we get to the precinct, but I'd appreciate it if you don't touch anything else in here. You know, like the phone over there? I need to look around a little more before we go. You just sit right there for a while longer."

She knew she had already contaminated the crime scene, even touched the gun. A stupid thing to do. How many times had she seen people do that on television and thought they were absolute idiots? Now she figured it must be a reflex or something. God, she wished she had left it alone.

She had felt James's neck for a pulse. How could she not have done that? He might have still been alive and she could have helped him. But she couldn't. He was already cold. The memory of his chilled skin made her fingers twitch.

Then she'd grabbed the phone in the living room to call for help. To make matters worse, she had rushed into the bedroom to get away from the terrible sight of death and wait for the police to arrive.

The covers had been torn off the bed and she was sitting on the bare mattress, so hopefully she hadn't disturbed much in here. There would be fibers from her clothing, she guessed. She glanced at the satiny surface of the bedding. Could they take fingerprints from this? Why hadn't she just backed out of the apartment and called from an outside phone?

As many times as she had seen it happen on TV and in movies, watched stupid people walk in after a murder and handle the very things that would incriminate them, it had never once occurred to her that she shouldn't touch anything until after the fact.

She looked at her hands with the traces of wax residue on both sides. Why had they done that? Had the policeman said why? He had mumbled something about the fingerprinting, she thought.

There was also blood on her hands. James's blood. On her hands. From the carpet where she had knelt beside him.

Suddenly Robin felt sick, ready to throw up. There was little time to debate whether she would destroy evidence in the bathroom. Better there than in here. She jumped up, rushed for the toilet and heaved until she couldn't. Since she hadn't eaten anything after breakfast yesterday, there was nothing in her stomach to lose.

Robin straightened, brushed her hair back behind her ears and turned to wash her face. The sight of James's bottle of favorite aftershave sitting there on the counter top was the trigger. She saw it, sank to her knees, clutched the detective's handkerchief to her face and wept uncontrollably for the man she had once thought she loved.

James shouldn't be dead. He was only thirty-seven, too young to die, only six years older than she. Who would do such a thing to him? To anyone? He wasn't bad. He didn't deserve this.

She recovered from her crying jag, washed her face, scrubbed the blood off her hands and sat down on the closed seat of the commode to wait. Her legs felt too unsteady to carry her back into the bedroom just then.

After what seemed an eternity, the detective approached the open door of the bathroom. "Are you okay?"

"No," she whispered, shaking her head. "No, I'm not okay."

He came closer and frowned down at her with what looked like worry, then brushed her bangs off her forehead with the tip of one long finger. She should have avoided his touch. It was inappropriate, certainly, but it seemed oddly comforting and not in any way threatening or suggestive.

At that moment the thought reoccurred that he was very dangerous. Handsome men almost always were in one way or another, and she rarely met one she liked. Usually she could figure them out, however. Not this one, not this detective.

He was being nice to her, but only sporadically. He believed she had killed James. She could see it in his eyes and tell from his questions.

If he considered her guilty of murder, why would he bother to pretend concern? To win her trust, Robin supposed. To trick her somehow. Yes, that must be what he was doing. She had to be very careful.

"Let's go on downtown now and get you a good shot of caffeine. I could use some of that myself. It won't take long to do the statement, I promise."

Gently he took her by her elbow and helped her stand, his grip steadying rather than forceful. He slid the strap of her purse, which she had left lying on the bed, over her shoulder. Then he escorted her out through the trashed bedroom and the dreadful scene of the murder, remaining between her and James's body, so she couldn't see it, even peripherally. No matter what else he might do later, she did thank him for that small kindness. He could have made her look again.

She wondered where her suitcase and laptop computer were, but was afraid to ask. Robin guessed they would both have to be searched before she was able to retrieve them.

She wondered if the detective had searched her small shoulder bag while she was in the bathroom. Winton, she reminded herself. Detective Winton. She must try to remember his name.

The upstairs apartment opened to a breezeway with stairs back and front that connected the two buildings of the fourplex. Neighbors in nightclothes stood in their doorways, observing as she and Detective Winton exited the building. He led her straight to a light-colored sedan parked beneath the streetlight.

An ambulance had pulled up on the sidewalk, lights flashing, back doors open, waiting. There were a number of uniformed police and several other vehicles forming a kind of perimeter around the building's entrance. Beyond the semicircle of authorities, a news team interviewed people within the small crowd that had gathered.

Robin wished she had rented a car, and that she could get into it now, drive back to the airport and fly on to Florida. There was nothing she wanted more than to dismiss this entire night like a bad dream.

When Winton opened the back door of his car, she obediently slid in and suddenly found herself caged. Though it was unmarked on the outside, he was definitely driving a police vehicle, complete with the barrier to protect the driver and front-seat occupant from the criminals they transported. Without even trying them, she knew the back doors would only open from the outside.

He had not handcuffed her, but she was definitely a suspect, Robin realized. The only suspect. Were they even considering that anyone else might have done it?

Chapter 2

Mitch hated this part of his job, but he was damned good at it. His interrogation techniques worked, and his instincts had been honed by twelve years on the force, the last four as a detective. If he couldn't drag a confession out of a suspect in her condition, then she was, by God, not guilty.

"Are you booking me? Should I call a lawyer?" she asked after they'd entered the precinct.

Oh, great. Now she was going to lawyer up. "If you want to call one, that's fine, but you're not under arrest. All I want to do is get on record what took place. It's standard procedure."

Mitch didn't want to hang around here the rest of the night waiting for her attorney to show up and then be advised he'd have to either arrest her or turn her loose. He was ready to get down to business. "We'll be in room three," he notified Nick Simon, who was manning the desk.

He took Robin Andrews's arm and guided her down the hall. He hoped her written statement and the following interrogation didn't turn up anything new and he could simply release her.

Mitch didn't want her to be guilty, and truthfully didn't think she was, but she had a lot going against her. She had possible motive and opportunity. She had been at the scene, had the victim's blood on her hands and prints on the weapon.

She was the spouse and the most likely perpetrator according to statistics, he reminded himself. Sure, she'd phoned it in herself, but as he had told her earlier, she could have done that to try to divert suspicion.

Mitch supposed it could be a crime of passion. A shot to the head. Weapon dropped on the floor by his body. The apartment had been trashed.

That last aspect bothered Mitch a little, however. The mess wasn't exactly consistent with the tossing an angry wife might do after shooting her husband in a fit of anger. It looked more like a quick, frantic search. Maybe she'd been looking for something. But if she'd found it, where had she put it? And if she hadn't found it, why had she called 911 and just sat there on the victim's bed until they arrived?

Oh well, he would take her statement, read it, then do his best to find holes and inconsistencies.

Robin Andrews was an exquisite woman, a pale, slender blonde with aristocratic features, who, in spite of her height of around five-ten, appeared to be as fragile as thin crystal. But he couldn't allow that to color his opinion of her one way or the other. He should be the last man on earth to be taken in by beauty and a look of vulnerability. Given a fit of rage, she could have shot her husband.

But she didn't. You know she didn't, said the insistent voice in his head. Gut instinct aside, Mitch intended to bend over backward to counteract that feeling, to leave no doubt about her innocence or guilt when he was finished with her.

"This way," he directed, releasing her arm and pointing to the door at the end of the hall. She preceded him wordlessly and hurriedly, obviously wanting it to be over. He could tell by her body language that she was terribly afraid. The question was *why?* Fear that she'd be railroaded for a crime she hadn't committed, or fear that she would let something incriminating slip out?

She had made no further mention of a lawyer.

He took his time seating her in the uncomfortable straight-back chair. "Just take it easy, Mrs. Andrews, and we'll get this out of the way as soon as we can. Don't you be nervous now. I'll be back in just a minute."

Mitch went down the hall to the coffee room and poured two cups of sludge that had been steeping for several hours by the smell of it. He loaded both cups with sugar and powdered creamer, then returned to the interrogation room.

"Here you go," he said, placing one of the cups in front of her. She just stared at it, wide-eyed, then slowly cupped both hands around it, probably seeking warmth. The air-conditioning was working overtime.

Her long, elegant fingers were free of the blood now, but their tips still bore faint traces of the ink used to fingerprint her again when they'd first arrived. This time they'd taken three sets, for local, state and FBI use. He'd told her that was so they could distinguish her prints from any others that shouldn't be there at the scene. The explanation hadn't reassured her.

He had explained what the paraffin test was for and she had seemed almost eager to have that done again, assuring him they wouldn't find any gunpowder on her anywhere. Of course, she might be under the impression water and soap would have washed it off.

Mirandizing her would probably scare her to death, but it was necessary. Kick might have neglected to do it. Mitch had to do this by the book in the event she broke down during questioning and admitted to the murder. So he began, trying not to sound too gruff. "You have the right to remain silent..."

She hung on his every word, nodding, and in the end, decided against calling an attorney or having one appointed.

The woman didn't know any lawyers in Nashville. As far as he knew, she didn't know anyone south of the Mason-Dixon line other than her dead husband and her mother in Florida.

Calling for legal counsel was the smart thing for her to do, and he had no right to prevent it or even discourage it.

"Do you want me to get a lawyer for you, Ms. Andrews?"

She glanced up at him and swallowed hard, meeting his eyes with a bravado he knew she was faking. "Are you sure I'm not under arrest?"

"No, ma'am, not under arrest, but you are in custody for questioning at the moment, so if you think you might say something that could incriminate you during this interview, you'd be wise to have legal counsel present."

It was a mind trick, of course. He couldn't, by law, say as much, but the implication was there. *Ask for a lawyer and look guilty as hell. Waive the right and take your chance on outwitting the law.* Mitch hated games, but he knew how to play them.

"No, I don't believe I need an attorney," she said, just as he'd expected her to. "I haven't anything to hide, Detective Winton. Ask me anything you want to know. I'll cooperate fully."

He smiled at her, part of the act to put her at ease. Or was it? Reaching into the drawer of the gray metal table, he withdrew a tablet of lined blank forms and a ballpoint pen. When he had filled out the top portion, he slid the pad across the table to her and handed her the pen.

"Just write down everything you remember happening from the time you arrived at the airport."

She eyed him warily and then stared at the writing instruments. "All right." She picked up the ballpoint.

He watched her gather her thoughts, knowing that would be like herding butterflies at the moment. She was sleep deprived, barely over a case of shock and she was scared. He felt cruel for putting her through this, but he had no choice.

In the end, after she had written her statement and he had filled in the gaps by questioning her further, Mitch's instinct assured him once again that she'd had nothing to do with Andrews's death.

He had tried every trick he knew, even assuring her he could well understand how an estranged wife might fly off the handle and do something she would never consider doing without provocation. She'd looked at him as if he'd lost his mind, advocating murder that way. He had preyed on her conscience. Apparently it was clean as a whistle. Or nonexistent. He had accused her outright. She had stuck to her story like Scotch brand cellophane tape and, in an uncharacteristic flare of anger, flat-out demanded that he stop wasting time and get out there and find whoever had killed James Andrews.

If he was wrong about her innocence and she had killed the man, the physical evidence would have to point it out, because she had perfectly logical and believable answers to all his questions and accusations. Her reactions were totally consistent with those of an innocent. So she was that.

Or she was very, very clever.

They would have to keep her around until all the evidence was evaluated, of course, but at the moment there was nothing that would justify placing Robin Andrews under arrest.

The tests on her hands showed no powder residue consistent with her discharging a weapon. Her prints were on it, but not in a configuration that would indicate she had gripped it in a firing position. She could have worn gloves, disposed of them, then touched the gun. But where were the gloves? And where was the blood spatter she would have gotten from shooting Andrews at such close range? On someone else, of course. She hadn't done it. He was convinced. Almost.

In the meantime he and Kick had a murderer to catch.

Kick would be interviewing the neighbors as instructed. Tomorrow he would start running down all of the victim's contacts, checking his finances, looking for enemies. They would both be on it. The caseload was low right now and they could give it full attention.

But it was very early morning, not even daylight, and he couldn't just cut Robin Andrews loose to fend for herself in the shape she was in. She didn't even know her way around town. He had an idea.

"Do you have a place to stay?" he asked her. "You know, you can't leave town until we wrap this up, and you sure can't stay at your husband's apartment."

Her eyes grew large, the shadows under them emphasizing their redness, and she was biting her lip again, shaking her head, looking confused.

"No, no I hadn't planned to stay there. Even before..." Her voice drifted off, then strengthened. "James promised to arrange for a hotel, but I'm afraid I don't know which one he chose."

She was too tired to think straight, totally wiped out and barely hanging on to her composure. Mitch had the absurd desire to hug her and tell her that everything would be all right. He'd been fighting that urge since the minute he first laid eyes on her. But everything might *not* be all right, and he had no business hugging her even if he knew it would.

"Come on with me," he said, rounding the table and reaching for her arm. "I'll find you a place to crash. Trust me to do that?"

She looked up at him like a little lost girl and nodded. He knew she didn't trust him any further than she could pick him up and throw him, but she was too frightened to say so. She was afraid he would take offense and lock her up. He could read her right now as clearly as the big print on a wanted poster.

It reassured him that she was exactly what she appeared to be, a frightened woman in a terrible situation over which she had little, if any, control. His early training kicked in big-time, totally overriding anything he'd ever learned at the police academy or later on the job.

Treat every woman with the respect you show your mother and your sisters. The golden rule applies here, Mitch. Every female you meet is some mother's daughter. Mitch could hear his father's words of wisdom as clearly as if the man were standing there looking over Mitch's shoulder at Robin Andrews. What would Pop think of her? She certainly was unlike any woman Mitch had invited to dinner so far. The thought made him want to smile.

"You should get a little rest before you phone your mother," he told her. "It's still too early, anyway. Give me the address and I can get a local minister or family friend in the city where they live to go and tell your husband's family if you like."

She fumbled inside her purse for a small address book, riffled through the pages and handed it to him, open. "James only has a half sister. If you could get someone to inform her personally, that probably would be better than if I called. We've exchanged Christmas cards, but I've never actually met her."

"Consider it done. Will your mother be badly upset? Maybe we should send a minister or priest to tell her. I know how mothers can be," he said.

"She'll worry about me, I suppose, but she didn't know James very well, so there shouldn't be any grief involved. I'll call her."

She *supposed* her mother would worry? Very interesting. And Mitch couldn't imagine marrying anyone when you didn't know their family. His own had always been such a large part of his life, he rarely made a move they didn't know about. All their advice and interference might be a little over-bearing at times, but Mitch was as guilty of that as they were. That's what families were for. *His,* anyway.

Captain Hunford was waiting in the hallway when they exited the interrogation room. Mitch had known someone had been observing through the one-way mirror. He had sensed it even while he was working.

"Hey, Cap'n. What're you doing down here at this hour?" The three of them walked down the hall to the bullpen. The lighting seemed eerie and uneven with the flickering of screen savers on the computers. The desks were deserted, their surfaces stacked with case files and the usual assortment of pens, coffee cups and the occasional family pictures.

"Taylor called and filled me in when he first arrived at the scene," Hunford said in a tired, gravelly voice. "I couldn't get back to sleep."

"This is Robin Andrews," Mitch said by way of introduction. "Wife of the victim. Ms. Andrews, Captain Hunford."

"Ma'am," the captain said with a nod, his only acknowledgement of her. He looked at Mitch. "Since you're here, I need to see you for a few minutes," he ordered, leaving no room for delay or argument.

Hunford was okay, maybe a little too conscious of public

opinion at times, but Mitch supposed the boss had to be. The man had been on the job nearly twenty years now and obviously knew what he was doing. Judging by his expression, this was probably going to be one of those times when Mitch wouldn't think so.

Mitch spared a look at the woman and saw she was almost asleep on her feet. "Wait out here," he told her after he had guided her to a chair beside one of the vacant desks. "I'll be back in a few minutes."

He crossed the room, glanced over his shoulder to make sure she wasn't leaving, then entered Hunford's office and closed the door.

Mitch briefly detailed the findings on the prints and lack of powder residue. "So, what do you think?" Mitch asked. "You hear the entire interview in there?"

"Most of it. There's not enough for an indictment. Not yet, anyway. I'll read what you got from her earlier and get with Taylor on it. I was looking for you this afternoon. You're on suspension, pending an inquiry."

Mitch blew out a frustrated breath and ran a hand over his face. "The review board? About yesterday," Mitch guessed.

"You know to expect it, Winton, any time you fire that weapon. You shot that boy in the arm and the leg. The doctors say he might have a permanent limp."

Mitch rolled his eyes. "He's damned lucky he won't have a permanent *nap*. He shot two people right there in the restaurant before I took him down."

"I know. You did what you had to do." Hunford leaned back in his chair, his palms flattened on the desktop. He stared at them and frowned. "But his victims didn't die. And the kid you shot—"

"—was thirty-one years old and holding a smokin' nine-millimeter," Mitch finished. "I identified myself and he turned on me. When a guy's that hyped on coke, you can't talk him down, sir. You try, you die. I could have killed him and been justified—and you know it."

"Just the same, I'll need your badge and piece. You were planning to be gone for a couple of weeks, anyway, so it's not like you'll miss it. Take your vacation, let the review board do their thing, and we'll get this ironed out soon as you get back. Don't worry, I'll go to the mat for you. You know that."

Mitch nodded. It wasn't like he had a choice here.

He unclipped the badge from his belt and tossed it on Hunford's desk. Then he reached under his jacket and removed his department-issue Glock. His backup pistol rested comfortingly against his ankle. With a weary sigh, he unloaded the official weapon and carefully laid it on top of the desk blotter.

"There you go. Hey, you don't mind if I give Taylor a little unofficial help on the Andrews homicide, do you?"

Hunford pursed his lips and thought for a minute. "I thought you were going fishing?"

"Hadn't decided. I'd rather hang around, do what I can. I'm still on the payroll, right?"

"Well, yeah. If you do lend Taylor a hand, be discreet about it. I mean, *very* low profile. You got that? Suspended is supposed to *mean* suspended."

"Okay. If that's all, I'm outa here," Mitch said, heading for the door.

"You taking her to a hotel?" the captain asked, inclining his head toward the glass wall through which they both could see Robin.

"No. She might have to be in town for a good while and that could get expensive. Thought maybe I'd try to find something a little more reasonable for her. Sandy's apartment is empty."

Hunford raised one bushy brow. "That'd keep her handy, I guess. You think she's a flight risk?"

Mitch shrugged. "Maybe, maybe not. I don't mind keeping an eye on her for a while."

Hunford studied him for a minute. "Might not be a bad idea if you or somebody did that." He held up his finger again. "And, Winton?"

"Yessir?"

"Don't shoot anybody else if you can help it. And for goodness sake, don't get personally involved with the suspect."

"You ever known me to do that kind of thing?" He hid his exasperation and left before he said something he shouldn't.

Don't get personally involved with the suspect? However, the boss did have an excellent reason to issue such a warning, Mitch admitted to himself. He just hadn't thought his interest was that obvious. Hell, he'd just been polite to her. There were no longing looks or unnecessary touching in that interview room. Nothing suggestive at all. He'd been very careful of that.

As he approached Robin Andrews now, Mitch was struck anew by that fawnlike vulnerability wrapped in such a deceptive package of striking sophistication. He knew he was going to have to watch himself as closely as he watched her.

The way she looked, she shouldn't need to fear anything. The world should lay itself at her feet and wait to be walked on. But the outer package was camouflage, Mitch knew. Inside there was a young woman who needed someone to take care of her. To care about her. He could do that temporarily without going off the deep end.

Mitch puffed out an exasperated breath, stuck his hands in his pockets and shook his head. Even knowing what he might have to face later, he still couldn't bring himself to send her out into a strange city all alone.

"Let's go, Ms. Andrews," he said, accepting the inevitable. He wouldn't get involved, damn it. Not exactly. He'd just make sure she had a place to stay. Nobody could argue she needed that, and there was no one else who would see about it.

"I know where there's a furnished apartment. One bedroom with a kitchenette in an old Victorian," he told her. "Actually, a friend of mine left me the key, and plans to be away for the next couple of months. You could sort of sublet if you're interested. There wouldn't be a lease or anything to fool with. Rent's next to nothing. Much less than a hotel will be if this runs on for a week or so."

It would be considerably longer than a week, almost surely, but he didn't have the heart to tell her that now.

"No, thank you. I would prefer a hotel. The expense is no problem," she said.

Mitch smiled. "I'd feel better knowing you were in a safe place. The Captain said I should make sure you were okay until we catch the shooter."

She still looked doubtful.

"Come on, it's a nice apartment. Cozy. How 'bout it?"

"All right, thank you. That would be fine," she murmured. "Does this mean you believe me when I say I had nothing to do with James's death?"

"It means that after I complete the report and hand it over, I'm off the case. Detective Taylor, that young sergeant you met earlier, will be in charge. Right now, I'm just trying to get you settled."

She got up and adjusted the strap of her expensive leather handbag over her shoulder. "I don't know how to thank you, Detective Winton."

"Don't mention it," he answered with a fatalistic shrug. "And you might as well call me Mitch if we're going to be neighbors."

"Neighbors?" she repeated with a look of concern.

"That's right," he confirmed. He opened the door for her, and they walked side by side through the parking area to his old brown Bronco.

The rigid set of her shoulders slackened, and she sighed with relief when she saw they were not returning to the unmarked car he'd used to bring her there. He opened the front passenger door and she got in. Thought she was home free, he guessed, and wished to God it were true.

No, he was not behaving professionally by wishing that, but figured he had better be fully aware of it so that he could act accordingly. He was attracted to her, felt protective toward her and, consequently, had the overwhelming urge to prove her innocence. His objectivity, if he'd ever had any with regard to her, was completely shot to hell.

Traffic was almost nonexistent in the wee hours. Mitch automatically kept a check on their surroundings and the rearview mirror. The habit was so ingrained it was annoying sometimes. Most of the time he did it without even thinking.

"Nashville looks like a nice city judging by the little I've seen of it," she said softly. "I've never been here before."

Mitch glanced over, taking in her profile. She was wearing a small, sad smile, probably thinking about her husband and what he'd told her about the town. She needed distracting. "You stated your occupation is graphic designer. What exactly do you do design?"

"Web pages for businesses," she answered. "I've always been fascinated with computers."

"Sounds like a perfect job for you, then," he said, wishing he knew more about computers so he could discuss them intelligently. "I know how to log on at work and access the info I need, that's about it. You know, I actually **had** you pegged as a model?"

"I used to be, but I outgrew it." From her curt answer, Mitch concluded she definitely didn't want to elaborate.

"Thanks for trying to take my mind off...things," she said. "You're very kind for a stranger."

"'I have always depended on the kindness of strangers,'" he quoted. "Blanche DuBois, *Streetcar Named Desire*."

"Oh, come on," she said, with a surprised little laugh. "She was such a wimp!"

"I didn't mean to imply that about you. What you said just reminded me of the phrase. You like old movies?"

"Sometimes. Books are better."

"I guess," he said, bringing that particular conversation to a dead end. He rarely had time to read, other than for additional training or information. He liked to, but if he couldn't sit down with a book and finish it in one sitting, he didn't pick one up.

"So," he said, broaching another subject as he turned onto the loop and snaked his way around the city, "I guess New Yorkers keep to a much faster pace than we do down here."

"Evidently," she said dryly without elaborating.

Mitch smiled. "Never rush when we can take our time. Never run unless somebody's chasing us."

He heard a short laugh of surprise, then a soft little "Sorry. I did sound condescending, didn't I?"

"No problem. Being underestimated works mostly to our advantage. Mine, anyway."

"I'll certainly keep that in mind," she said, but without any asperity.

Mitch hadn't meant it as a warning. Or had he? Was he subconsciously trying to prepare her for the fact that he wouldn't cut her any slack if she was lying about killing Andrews? This second-guessing himself was driving him nuts.

"Will you be all right?" he asked, shoving his self-analysis to the back burner. "Financially, I mean. What about your work?"

"I can function just as well from here, assuming I can have my laptop back."

"Back? Where is it?"

"It's at James's apartment. So is my suitcase," she said.

Mitch bumped the steering wheel with the heel of his hand. "I should have thought about that. We can go for your things first."

He moved into the lane to take the next exit, intending to reverse their direction. "They're probably finished checking them out."

"Wait!" she said, reaching out, almost touching his arm. Then she drew back. "Could...could we not go back there just now?"

He understood. "Sure. I'll call and have one of the guys bring them to you or I'll go pick them up."

"Thank you."

The ensuing silence extended and became uncomfortable. He was usually a pretty good conversationalist, but for the life of him, Mitch couldn't think of anything else to talk about that didn't involve discussing some aspect of the murder. He had nothing at all in common with a woman like Robin Andrews.

Instinctively he knew she was going to hate the apartment. He could imagine her world, envision her living in mono-chromatic, uncluttered splendor in some New York high-rise. Where he was going to put her, she'd think she had landed on another planet, or at least in a former century. But it was the best he could do for her under the circumstances. She would just have to get used to it.

"Are you hungry?" he asked, figuring he couldn't go wrong applying the lowest common denominator. Everybody need-ed food.

She considered for a minute. "I could probably eat, yes. Fruit or something light."

"How do you feel about waffles?"

"Ambivalent," she said, sounding resigned.

Mitch sighed. Damned if he was going shopping all over town for yogurt, fresh fruit or whatever this time of night. She could eat what he ate or go hungry.

"Waffles it is, then," he said.

He had a feeling Robin Andrews was going to have trouble adapting outside her natural habitat. All the more reason to get the Andrews case solved as soon as possible and send her back to New York where she belonged.

Chapter 3

Robin slid into a booth at the diner. Detective Winton—Mitch, since he had insisted on first names—took the side facing the door. She remembered reading once that gunfighters of the Old West had done that.

He smiled when he handed her a plastic-coated menu and held the pleasant expression as he looked up at the waitress. "Hey, Mabel. How's it goin'?"

The heavyset blond with frizzy hair grinned back and popped her gum. "Great. Y'all want coffee?" She wrinkled her nose at Robin and said with mock confidentiality, "This rascal's on my list. He ain't been in here for weeks. You musta been keepin' him real busy lately."

Mitch cleared his throat to regain the waitress's attention. "Just bring us the coffee, Mabel. Got any of that country ham I like?"

"You betcha." The waitress thumbed a page off the top of her order pad, scribbled, paused and asked, "Your usual with it?"

"Yes, ma'am. You want eggs with yours?" He raised a brow at Robin.

She declined and placed the menu on the table. "No eggs, no ham. Just a waffle. And a glass of water."

Mabel laughed and winked. "You ain't gotta watch that figure, hon. Bet he'll watch it for you." She scooped up the menus and wriggled off behind the bar. Robin winced at the way Mabel screamed the order through the opening to the kitchen in back. So all Southern belles weren't soft spoken.

"The cook's a little hard of hearing," Mitch explained. He clasped his hands on the table next to the rolled-up napkin that held his flatware. "I guess this place is out of the ordinary for you, huh?"

It seemed to amuse him, bringing her to a restaurant like this. Robin was determined not to react the way he obviously expected. She had eaten in worse places, though not often.

Dylan's Diner looked like a fifties diner that hadn't been refurbished since its creation. More antique than retro. A bar ran the length of the place, its chrome stools topped with mottled red leather cushions. Old photos of Elvis, Dolly, and others she didn't recognize dotted the walls in a haphazard arrangement. An old-fashioned jukebox stood at the far end of the room in front of the rest rooms.

The booths were in fairly good shape. Blinds covered the windows that began at table level and nearly reached the ceiling. Thankfully they were closed, so Robin didn't have to see the neighborhood outside. It had looked rather seedy driving through it.

"Sorry, but there aren't too many eating places open this time of the morning, at least not on the way to where we're

going. Dylan's plays host to the night crawlers in this area."
He shrugged. "I'm one of 'em when I pull night duty."

"This is fine," Robin said, gingerly unwinding her fork,
spoon and a serrated steak knife from their paper wrapping
and arranging them in a proper place setting. The utensils appeared to be clean, she noted with relief. "I'm really not that
choosy."

"Good sport, aren't you?" He shrugged out of his windbreaker and laid it in the corner of the booth. "Beaner is a fair
cook. The food's good here, trust me."

Robin sighed. He kept saying that. *Trust me.* If he only
knew how impossible that was, that she would put her trust
in any man. Or any one else, for that matter. It was good that
he didn't seem to expect an avowal of it. Maybe it was only
a figure of speech with him.

"How far is it to this apartment you mentioned?" she asked,
wondering if she would be required to stay in this particular
area with its unkempt houses interspersed with run-down
storefronts.

He didn't answer her. His full attention was suddenly riveted on the entrance. Robin had heard the door open and
close, felt the draft.

She started to look over her shoulder and see who had
come in when Mitch grasped her hands, squeezed and whispered. "Trouble! Lie down, Robin. Sideways in the seat and
slide under the table. Do it *now!*" He shoved her hands off the
table sending her flatware clattering to the floor. She followed.

Robin didn't even think about protesting. She did exactly
as ordered, curling herself around the sturdy chrome pedestal.
Mitch was grappling with his ankle which was mere inches
from her face. He pulled a gun from a small holster strapped
to his leg.

Oh, God, it was a robbery! That had been her first thought

when he warned her to duck out of sight, and she'd been right. All those years in New York and never a bit of trouble, and now... She heard Mabel scream and scooted as near the wall as she could.

"Drop it, cop, or I'll blow her away," said a deep voice.

A clunk sounded on top of the table above Robin.

"Move back," the voice shouted. "To the back of the room."

Robin watched Mitch's legs and feet as he slowly backed out of her limited line of vision.

Desperate for something to defend herself, Robin searched the floor for the steak knife, but couldn't find it. She grasped the fork. Her breath rushed in and out between clenched teeth and she felt sick.

When a head appeared wearing a ski mask, Robin yelped. A large and rather dirty hand reached under the table, attempting to grab her foot, the closest part of her to the aisle. He was cursing, saying something, but the words wouldn't register. In terror that he would drag her out before she could stop him, Robin struck. She stabbed the fork into his hand. The tines disappeared into hairy flesh and the resulting roar was deafening.

All hell broke loose, and she couldn't see a thing but the blur of tangled legs. Mitch Winton had attacked. That much was obvious.

Robin twisted around, feeling beneath her for the knife. She couldn't simply wait to see what happened. That robber could kill Mitch and drag her from beneath the table and...

She thought she heard sirens above the grunts and curses and the smack of fists against flesh. Several shots rang out and glass broke. Tires screeched outside, blue light bounced around the room like a strobe. *The police!* Thank God! She heard the thunder of footsteps, cursing, doors slamming.

"It's safe. You can come out now." Mitch was crouching on the floor beside the booth, peering at her.

Robin wriggled around the table support and grasped the hand he offered to help her out. "Are...are they gone?" she asked, scanning the diner as they stood.

"They ran out the back." He took the steak knife from her, placed it on the table, then picked up his pistol. Bracing his right foot on the booth seat, he replaced the gun in its holster and snapped the flap.

"Shouldn't you...go after them or something?"

He shook his head and indicated she should sit down. Her legs were so shaky, she nearly fell. "The cops are pursuing. Excuse me a minute."

Robin watched as Mitch went over to the bar and leaned over it. "You okay down there, Mabel?"

"That bastard shot my winder," she complained, her voice rising as she got up off the floor. Her hair was a worse mess than before, and there was coffee all over the front of her white shirt and red nylon apron. "Broke my coffeepot, too." Then her gaze jerked toward Robin. "Y'all didn't get hurt, did ya?"

"No, we're fine. That silent alarm works pretty good," Mitch commented. "Quick thinking, Mabel. You're a peach."

"Thank you for tellin' me I needed the thing." She brushed herself off with a towel and smiled over the counter at Mitch, then at Robin. There were tears in her eyes, and she sniffed. "Y'all will have to wait a little bit until I get another carafe out of the back and get some more coffee goin'."

"Don't worry about the order," Mitch told her gently. "You look a little shaky. Why don't you just relax and catch your breath."

"Don't leave!" whined Mabel, reaching out toward Mitch with a trembling hand. "Don't go now."

Mitch took it and smiled at her. "I won't go yet, Mabel. But you go on and take a break, huh? Powder your nose and fix your hair. I'll be here when you get back."

She nodded and sidled down the back of the bar, around it and toward the door marked Ladies.

Robin knew how poor Mabel felt. Right now she wanted Mitch Winton and his gun as close by as they could get. He seemed to know that and came over to join her in the booth.

"You're a scrapper. I wouldn't have guessed it." His chuckle was warm, approving. "Surprised the hell out of him, plowing that fork through his hand. Glad you were on my side."

Robin stared at him, not sure whether she was upset at his apparent calm or reassured by it. She glanced at the door. "They might come back."

He laughed outright at that, then grimaced, grasping his side.

"You're hurt!" Robin cried, sliding out of the booth.

"No, no, sit back down. I took a kick to the ribs. Nothing serious. Either those guys really were as big as they looked or I'm gettin' soft in my old age."

"They could have shot you!" she cried. "What did you mean rushing them that way?"

He sighed and leaned back, his fingers still exploring the site of his injury. "You made him so mad with that fork, I was afraid he would shoot you if I didn't move on him right then. They heard the siren and split before I could do much."

Robin raked her hair back behind her ears, shook her head and gave a deflated sigh. "James's death and now a robbery. What next?"

He leaned forward over the table and peered into her eyes. "Robin, he went straight for you. Once he had threatened Mabel, he never even looked at her again. His buddy was standing lookout at the door. Neither one asked for the contents of the register. Never demanded my wallet. They knew I was a cop, knew my name, but I've never seen them before. I think they knew who you are, too. It was your purse they were after. Didn't you hear him?"

"No, I wasn't really listening." Robin frowned down at the thin strap that lay securely around her neck and across her body, the leather rectangle resting against her hip. "My purse? But why? Do I look rich?"

Mitch smiled. "As a matter of fact you do, but I don't think it was your money he was after. It was something else. What do you have in there?"

She lifted the purse onto the table and opened it. "Powder, lipstick." Robin listed the items as she emptied the contents piece by piece. "Credit cards, address book, a bit of cash, James's CD, a small brush, old theater ticket stubs and," she said, plunking down a little spray can, "pepper spray." She frowned and scoffed. "I should have remembered that. I completely forgot I had it. All I could think about was locating the knife."

Mitch picked up the spray container and turned it around several times, then shot her a questioning look. "Somehow, I don't believe this was what he was looking for, do you?"

She surveyed the pile of stuff. "The CD, you think? What could anyone possibly want with that?"

"Your husband wanted it badly enough to have you bring it all the way from New York instead of mailing it."

"Maybe you're right," she admitted, meeting his gaze. She shoved it toward him. "You take it. Keep it."

"No," he said, returning it to her. "Hang on to it until we can have a look at what's on it."

Mabel returned from the ladies' room, obviously relieved that Mitch was still around. "Be just a minute," she said, pushing through the door to the kitchen. "I'll get that coffee carafe."

Robin exhaled and rested her forehead on her hand. "Could we leave, please?"

"No, not yet. We still have to eat, and I don't think Mabel's up to winging it with only ol' Beaner in the back for company. We'd better hang around until Bill and Eddie come back or send word that they caught the bad boys."

Robin resigned herself. "Somehow I always thought of Nashville as a rather tranquil city full of musicians."

He laughed. "If that were the case, I'd be playing backup guitar and bemoaning the fact that I can't sing."

"You can't sing?" she asked, eager for any diversion.

"Well, I *can,* but you wouldn't want to hear it. Trust me."

There it was again. Maybe it *was* only a figure of speech, his saying that so often. If someone was after James's disk and was willing to go after it with guns, she knew she had to trust someone. Mitch Winton certainly seemed the likeliest candidate in town.

Dawn was about to break when they were finally able to leave the diner. Mitch kept stealing glances at Robin, wondering when she would crash. She seemed to have gotten her second wind by the time Bill and Eddie had come back to interview them about the supposed robbery. The poor girl must have had it up to her ears with cops by this time.

She had separated the miniblinds with one finger and was looking out the window now, probably marveling at how hospitable Nashville and its occupants had been to her since her arrival.

"Why didn't you tell the officers your theory about the disk?" she asked, breaking the silence.

He turned onto the off-ramp leading to his neighborhood. "Because it's only that. A theory. Besides, they would have wanted to take it with them, see what was on it." He smiled. "I thought we might do that."

She remained quiet then, so he turned on the radio. "Fiddle with the stations there and see what you can find," he suggested, really wanting to see what she would settle on. Her taste in music might tell him a little more about her. Was she really as highbrow as she looked, or was there a closet blues fan inside that slick exterior?

She parked it on the local news, listening intently. When the newscast was over and no mention was made of her husband's murder, she clicked the radio off. A small frown marred her almost perfect features.

They were almost perfect, but not quite. Mitch had noted, a little belatedly, that her chin was a shade too prominent, gave her an almost haughty look. Her nose would have been cuter, would have made her more appealing and approachable, if it had tilted up just slightly, but it was straight as a die. Too aristocratic. Looked as if it had been straightened on purpose.

That made him wonder if she really had enhanced herself with surgery anywhere. Her breasts looked smallish and were probably real. She said she had modeled and small was necessary with braless fashions, he guessed. She might not be absolutely perfect but came a little too close to it for Mitch to believe it was all real. Oh well, models had to use what they had and improve it if they could, he reckoned. It was a business, and he couldn't fault her for it if she'd resorted to that.

"Nice nose," he commented. "Mind if I ask what it cost? Mine's been broken twice and I'd sure like the name of a good doctor, one who wouldn't do a Michael Jackson on me and make me look like Janet."

She laughed, sounding surprised. "You think I've had my nose done?"

Mitch shot her a smile. "Looks great."

"Thank you. I was born with this nose," she informed him.

"Don't be insulted," he said. "I just wondered."

"Are you able to breathe well?" she asked.

"Sure, no problem." Other than when she looked at him a certain way and stole his breath.

"Then leave your nose alone. It fits your face." Then she added grudgingly, "Not because you broke it. It's a nice nose...and face."

She liked his face. Mitch mumbled his thanks and focused on his driving, not enjoying the little thrill that ran through him when she gave him that compliment. He had to get over this growing obsession with the woman, his need to know everything there was to know about her. Jeez, what did it matter whether she'd had her nose done? What was it to him? Nothing, that's what.

What did that say about him, that he was getting so wrapped up in her this quickly? His objectivity was shot to pieces, had been since the minute she turned those baby blues on him in that bedroom at the crime scene. He needed to get a grip. Problem was, he wanted to get a grip on her.

That ol' bugaboo, sexual attraction, of course. It had never hit him quite this square in the gut, however, and he was having trouble straightening up. The blow to the ribs he'd taken in the diner didn't even compare. He pressed on the injury just to make it hurt, just to feel something that would counteract what she was making him feel.

Her hand covered his. "Broken?" she asked with a look of tender concern. The touch of her hand on his set his nerve endings jangling.

"Nah. Just bruised. You should see the other guy," he quipped.

Her breath huffed out and she removed her hand. "I hope I never do! Do you really think they'll try again? If it is the disk they were after?"

Mitch shrugged, relieved that they were on less intimate ground. "Could be. You don't have to worry about that right now. No one knows where we're going except the chief, and we aren't being followed."

She swiveled and glanced out the back window. "You're certain?"

"Absolutely."

A few moments later she had leaned her head back against the headrest and closed her eyes. It was all he could do not to pull the car over just so he could sit there and watch her sleep for a while.

Mitch sat up straighter behind the wheel and clutched it tighter than necessary, reminding himself that Robin Andrews was still the primary suspect in a murder case. Not only should he avoid getting involved with her on any level other than making sure she didn't skip town, he should not let her bravery back there at the diner impress him so much.

So she had a healthy sense of self-preservation. So what?

He drove on, deliberately listing all the reasons Robin might have had to shoot that man she had married.

Had Andrews cheated on her? For whatever reason, he'd left her there in New York to fend for herself. And he might have gotten her mixed up in something shady by asking her to bring him that disk. The murderer had been looking for something in that apartment, something not found yet. And those guys who attacked them in Dylan's were definitely after whatever Robin had. Maybe she knew more about that than she admitted.

Surely she wasn't capable of murder. But she sure hadn't hesitated to plant that fork in the perp's hand tonight. Maybe she hadn't hesitated to plant a bullet in James Andrews's brain a little earlier in the evening.

The best he could do was keep an eye on her, get to know her as well as he could and try to determine the extent of her guilt. Or, best case, prove she was innocent.

* * *

"Well, this is it," the detective told her as Robin became aware of their surroundings.

Streetlights cast their glow over shadowy houses with gingerbread trim. They stood like a double row of old-fashioned sisters, each unique yet bearing a family resemblance. Some were spruced up beautifully, but a few carried the marks of age and neglect. Ancient oaks spread their branches over small, neat yards as well as most of the street. "Peaceful," she muttered.

"Quiet, anyway," he agreed, opening his door and getting out. He came around and opened hers.

A gentleman to the bone, she thought, wondering what kind of cop that made him. Other than the intensity of those eyes, he seemed almost too deferential to be true. He frightened her with all of this courtesy.

Robin tried to shake off the fear, chalking it up to watching too much television and its stereotyping of lawmen from the South. Good ol' boys who had laws of their own. God, she hoped that had no basis in fact.

She took the hand he offered to help her out of the Bronco. It was warm and strong, his touch too casual to signify anything other than a gesture of assistance. But Robin felt the power of it, nonetheless, the tingling awareness that this man could destroy her if he wished.

He had given her fair warning. She would never make the mistake of underestimating Detective Mitch Winton.

There was no concrete reason to believe his attitude was a deception. If he was trying to lure her into trusting him enough to confess she'd killed James, he'd have a long damned wait for either her trust or an admission of guilt.

She knew she should have gone to a hotel. He'd said he lived near here, hadn't he? What had she been thinking? Her brain was so foggy from stress and lack of sleep, she hadn't been thinking at all. First thing in the morning she would find another place to stay. She would call a taxi and have it take her downtown.

Depending on the very person who had nearly arrested her for murder—and still might do so—was worse than absurd. Yet she couldn't afford to alienate him completely. Making him angry was the last thing she should do.

He led her up the walkway and the brick steps of the house. The wide front porch with its draping ferns and off-white wicker rocking chairs seemed to welcome her.

Fishing his key ring out of his pocket, he unlocked the door and entered before her. When he had switched on the lights, Robin stepped inside, taking in the gaudy floral wallpaper and large, gold-leaf mirror hanging over a marble-topped rosewood hall table. He immediately ushered her toward a sturdy, curved staircase. "Second floor."

She made a note to examine the small paintings hanging in the stairwell later when she could focus properly. They appeared to be very old pastoral scenes. Everything looked old. Ancient.

Again he unlocked a door and turned on the lights.

"Make yourself at home. There's the bedroom through there. Since she took practically everything but the kitchen sink with her, Sandra's things shouldn't get in your way. I expect there are some nonperishables left in the kitchen, but we'll get you supplied with whatever you like later today."

He glanced at his watch as if he had somewhere else to be, but she didn't want him to go yet.

"Exactly who is Sandra?" Robin thought he'd said a friend, another policeman, rented this place. She'd erroneously assumed it was a man.

"Sandra Cunningham," he explained. "She's at the FBI academy for a training course."

He sounded terribly proud of this person. Robin made herself smile at him. "Are you sure this *friend* won't object to my invading her space while she's away?"

"Positive she won't, but I'll call her and let her know." He backed out of the door. "Speaking of calls, if you'll excuse me, I need to make some. I'll do it from my place."

"You live close by?"

"Just next door." He looked at his watch again. "Try to get some sleep this morning and I'll check back with you around noon."

Robin turned the dead bolt after the door closed and leaned against the solid panel. She listened for his footsteps on the stairs, but didn't hear them. He must move like a cat.

She looked at the phone on the table by the window, then decided it might be best to wait until after she had slept to call her mother. Dealing with her would take energy Robin didn't have at the moment. Exhausted beyond bearing, she went straight to the bedroom and stretched out across the big brass bed.

Usually she preferred being by herself, but now almost wished Mitch Winton had stayed. She suddenly felt too alone.

Chapter 4

Mitch cradled the phone between his ear and shoulder while he shucked his shorts. He turned the taps on the old clawfoot tub and adjusted the temperature of the water, wishing he had one of those whirlpool thingamajigs attached. His muscles felt kinked and his brain was fuzzy from sleeping in the daytime.

He had gone directly to bed after leaving Robin in the next apartment and slept a good half day uninterrupted. Now his internal clock was screwed. He had to get back on track.

First he needed to find out what was going on with the case. Then he would go over and see how his houseguest was holding up.

Kick answered his cell phone on the fifth ring.

"What you got so far, Kick?" Mitch asked.

"A headache for one thing," Taylor declared, sounding like

he was in a real snit. "Hunford tells me you took the suspect home with you. What the hell are you thinking?"

Mitch grunted. "The boss thought it was a good idea."

"You should have put her up in a hotel or something. Do that today," he snapped.

"Soon as you make captain and start calling the shots," Mitch replied easily.

He stepped into the tub and lowered himself into the steaming water, holding on to the phone so he wouldn't douse it. "Anything new turn up after I left?"

Kick pouted for a few seconds before sharing. "Forensics found some red dirt stains on the rug. Hardly noticeable, but they could be important. We might want to check the lady's shoes. Victim's were clean, every pair he had."

"Anything else?"

"Yeah. His cleaning lady was in there yesterday afternoon. I found her in the address book and called to see when she'd done the place last. I guess Andrews was getting things polished up, expecting his wife. We're trying to find out if anyone else was seen coming in after the floor was vacuumed." Kick was silent for a minute. "You keeping her in your apartment?"

"The cleaning lady? No—"

"Mitch, I'm not in the mood!"

Mitch smiled to himself, enjoying the yank on Kick's chain. "She's in Sandy's apartment, across the hall."

"Taking her to your own house is *not* wise and you know it."

"Don't worry. I'm just keeping an eye on her," Mitch explained patiently. "And I figured Sandy's was a good place to do that. She wanted me to sublet for her if I could."

"Listen, Mitch," Kick said, sounding calmer, though his voice held a warning, "everything we've got so far points directly at Robin Andrews. Blood on her hands, prints on the weapon, sound motive—he wanted the divorce, she didn't. Or vice versa. And that ain't all—"

Mitch scoffed. "That's not enough to stand up. Way too circumstantial. Hunford even said so. She could never have brought the weapon in on that plane and didn't have time to get one after she arrived."

"The Beretta belonged to Andrews," Kick said. "Registered and licensed. Already there."

"Notice the results from the paraffin tests?" Mitch asked.

"She could have worn gloves."

"Then what did she do with them?"

"We're still looking."

"Why are her prints on the gun if she wore gloves?"

Kick missed a beat, then picked it up. "Touched it later. Good move. Threw you off, didn't it?"

"She's innocent," Mitch declared. "Look somewhere else."

"All right, then, how about this?" Kick asked, deadly calm now and all business. "We found a life insurance policy in the desk. The Mrs. is about to be a hundred thousand richer than she was yesterday. Is that enough?"

"Not much insurance, is it? Peanuts for a guy who's in the business." Mitch sank deeper into the hot water, closed his eyes and rested his chin on his chest. "Let me call you back, Kick. I'll check her shoes."

"You bring her shoes *in,* Mitch. That's how it's done."

"Giving me orders again, hotshot?"

He heard Kick sigh. "No, just reminding you to think with the big head and not the little one."

An hour later Mitch was back at the precinct.

"She could have scrubbed them," Kick said, staring through the plastic bag at the classic pumps with their three-inch heels. "I really think she's guilty."

"Yeah, I know. You keep saying that. Just run tests for residue." Mitch had elected to bring the shoes straight to Taylor immediately and turn them over expressly for that purpose. He wondered what Robin would do when she woke up and found herself barefoot. "Bet you my next paycheck you don't find any red dirt."

Kick scoffed. "If you live to *get* a next paycheck. It's mighty risky taking a murder suspect under your wing. Besides, you're on suspension."

"I got the okay to do this, Kick. Look, I need to get back home. You want anything else, give me a buzz." Then he remembered the computer. "By the way, I need to pick up Ms. Andrews's suitcase and laptop. Are they here?"

Kick frowned. "Where did she leave them?"

"Right by the front door, she said." He felt his heart jump when he noted Kick's tightened lips. "What?"

"I went over everything in that apartment, Mitch. No computer. No bag."

They stared at each other for a minute. "Either somebody on the investigating team has sticky fingers, which we know is not likely, or...the killer was still in the apartment when she arrived and took her stuff with him after she went into the bedroom," Mitch said.

"That's crazy," Kick said. "Maybe she's making them up. Ever think about that?"

"Maybe not. We know the shooter was after something," Mitch said. "Could be he thought Robin Andrews might have brought whatever it was with her."

Kick's eyes narrowed, but he had nothing to say. Mitch didn't mention the disk then. It seemed best at the moment to keep it to himself. Until he found out what was on the damned thing and if it was enough to kill someone over, he was not turning the disk over to Kick.

"Catch you later," he said as he turned to leave.

"Hey, wait a minute! Let's talk about this."

But Mitch didn't have time to waste arguing. Whoever took Robin's things must have realized pretty soon that they didn't have everything she'd brought with her to Nashville. The attack in the diner, the object of it being Robin's purse, meant just what he'd thought it meant.

Whoever was looking for the disk wouldn't have any idea where to find Robin at the moment. Hardly anyone knew where he lived. That was a closely kept secret, since he had made a few enemies during his time on the force. He had sent quite a few guys up the proverbial river who might paddle back down to find him after they'd served time.

Mitch was sure no one had trailed them to the neighborhood this morning. He had been alert to a possible tail after what had happened at Dylan's.

This suspension of his was coming at the worst possible time. Mitch needed to be on the Andrews case officially, where he could get things done without first having to run everything by Kick.

Going to bat for Robin against his own partner could produce some serious questions about Mitch's abilities as a detective.

For his sake, as well as her own, Robin Andrews had better be totally innocent and he'd better be able to prove it. This new development was another solid indication that she was. Somebody had stolen her computer and her suitcase.

Unless Kick was right and she hadn't brought either with her in the first place. Was she going a roundabout route to convince him someone else had been in that apartment besides her and the dead man?

* * *

Robin awoke, looked around the unfamiliar room and then squinted at her watch. It was afternoon, close to four o'clock. She felt as if someone had beaten her with a very large stick.

She got up, straightened her clothing the best she could and found the bathroom. Straight out of *Country Homes,* she thought. Ruffles and roses. Wine red and dark green on cream. Vanilla potpourri emanated from a small porcelain flower on the shelf below the mirror. Her reflection made her groan.

The makeup was history. Her hair was lank and in need of shampoo. The syrupy breakfast she'd ingested after the confrontation at Dylan's Diner had made her feel queasy and she wasn't hungry now. She figured she might as well do as Mitch Winton advised and make herself at home, at least temporarily. There didn't seem to be anything else to do since he hadn't returned.

After a long, relaxing bubble bath, she dried off, combed her wet hair into place and put back on her wrinkled clothing.

She was searching for her shoes when she heard the squeak of the doorknob as someone outside turned it. Again it turned slowly but firmly in both directions. The door was locked. It must be Mitch.

She padded to the door. There was no peephole to look through. "Yes? Who is it?"

Again the doorknob turned, sharply back and forth, this time without stealth. The door shook with the violent attempts to open it.

"I have a gun," she cried as loudly and menacingly as she could, quickly scouting the living room for anything she could use to defend herself. "And I *will* shoot!" There. She had sounded determined. Forceful.

Silence. Then the wooden stairs creaked twice.

Robin waited, ear to the door, listening, but heard nothing

further. No closing of doors, no hurried footsteps, no sound of a car engine outside. Just the silence peculiar to a quiet neighborhood with all the children at school and their parents away at work.

She dashed to the phone on the table beside the rear window to call the police. No dial tone. It was dead. Had the cop who lived here had the phone disconnected before she left?

Robin huddled in the corner, the dead receiver clutched to her chest. Her heart pounded so loudly she doubted she could hear anyone breaking through the door with an ax.

If she were at home, there would be a solid steel door, not that lovely six-panel one, hung in a century-old door frame. The whole thing would probably collapse inward with one good body slam.

At her own apartment, this scare would never have happened. Building security was so efficient, whoever tried to get inside would never have made it to the elevator.

"Stupid!" she thought suddenly, replacing the receiver. That incident at the diner had made her paranoid.

Some friend had probably come to see the woman who normally lived here, that was all. When Robin had answered instead, they became concerned someone was in here who shouldn't be. Now they had gone to notify the police that a stranger with a gun was in Sandra Cunningham's apartment. Yes, that made sense. That was it. That was what *she* would do. She looked at the phone again, knowing she was grasping at straws.

"It's broad daylight," Robin reminded herself. "And this is Nashville, not New York. The crime rate here must be low." But it wasn't exactly that, now was it? James had been murdered in his own home just last evening. And two men had burst into the diner in a robbery attempt.

No matter how much she scoffed at herself or tried to explain away the visitor, Robin could not dismiss her fear. Someone had tried to enter the apartment without knocking first. And she was alone and unarmed. What if they came back, bringing some means to get through the door?

What were they after? Was it those same men from last night, perhaps after James's disk?

Then she heard footsteps on the stairs again. This time whoever it was did not care whether she heard him! Terror mounted. She rushed through the bedroom and into the bathroom. Hurriedly she closed the door and realized there was no lock on it. "Oh, no!" she moaned.

Recalling Mitch's order to get under the table when they were accosted in the diner, Robin knew she had to find a place to hide. She yanked open the large double cabinet beneath the sink and crawled inside. God, she was too large for this! She wound her body around the pipes, wedged half underneath them, and drew up her knees so the doors would shut. It was a much tighter fit than beneath that table in the booth last night. Plus, she had nothing at all to use for a weapon now. Not even a can of hair spray.

She held her breath, trying not to gasp so loudly that she would give away her location. Her only hope was that the intruder would believe she had left the apartment.

Even inside the cabinet with the bathroom door shut, she heard the footsteps on the hardwood floors, then muffled cursing, coming closer.

Her lungs were bursting, but she dared not take a breath or she would scream her head off. The bathroom door swung open with the loud, prolonged squeak she remembered from earlier, like a sound effect from an old horror film.

Robin froze, squeezed her eyes shut and moved only her lips in silent entreaty, "Please, please, please, please..."

Both cabinet doors flew wide, and she felt the instant rush of cool air on her face and legs.

"What the *hell?*" A deep voice thundered.

Hell. With two sweet syllables. Robin unclenched her eyes, sucked in a deep breath and began to laugh.

It took considerably longer to get out of her hiding place than it had to wedge herself in. By the time she managed to crawl out, her hysteria had subsided.

She sat there on the fluffy throw rug trying to catch her breath. Mitch was kneeling beside her, brushing dust bunnies off her arms and shoulders. "Was that you before?" she demanded. "Did you try the door earlier?"

His hands stilled and his intense blue gaze fastened on her at close range. Robin's heartbeat accelerated dangerously. "No, I just got here. Tell me what happened."

She did, including her panicked response and how foolish she felt about it now.

He simply listened but didn't comment. When Robin had finished, he stood and offered her his hand to get up. While they were walking through the bedroom to the living room, he asked, "When you entered Andrews's apartment last night, did you close the door behind you?"

"No." She was certain she hadn't. "I saw James the moment I entered. I set down my bag and computer—dropped them, I think—and ran straight to him."

"Didn't you worry that the one who attacked him might still have been there?" he asked.

She lowered herself to the sofa and leaned back. He sat near her, turned sideways, facing her, intent on her answer.

Robin thought back. "No, that didn't even occur to me. At first I didn't realize what had happened. He was lying there and I saw the blood. So much of it." She shuddered. "I thought he had fallen and hit his head."

"Go on," he encouraged her. "I know this seems repetitive, but it's very important, Robin. This time I want to hear not only what actually happened, but tell me your feelings. What ran through your mind?"

She nodded. "I cried out his name as I ran over to him, then knelt down and felt for his pulse. I knew, though. I knew he was dead before I touched him. That...that round hole in his...head. That's when I saw the gun lying there on the floor and thought he had shot himself. I reached for it without thinking. Then I put it down, horrified. When I glanced up at the room and noticed the wreck someone had made of it, I thought, Not suicide."

"And then?"

"On hands and knees I scrambled over to the phone, the one on the end table, and dialed 911. My hands were shaking so I could hardly hold on to it. The woman who answered told me to stay on the line, but I couldn't. I couldn't just sit there so close to James and see him...I felt sick, but knew I couldn't leave. I had to wait for the police. So I got up and ran into the bedroom. That's where I was when they came. They told me to stay where I was. Where you found me."

"Did you hang up, Robin? Did you replace the receiver on the handset?"

She concentrated, tried to recall the exact sequence of events. "I don't think so...no, I just put it down. I think." She met his frown. "Wouldn't the police officers know? The ones who came in first?"

He squeezed her arm gently where he'd been resting his hand on it just above her elbow. "Sure, they can tell me. Could you see the door to the living room from where you were sitting, Robin?"

"I didn't look back in there," she admitted. I covered my face with my hands after I sat down. I just couldn't look."

"That's okay," he told her softly. "It's probably best that you didn't."

"But wait," she said, grasping his sleeve, hardly aware of what she was doing. "I did look, didn't I? Yes, after you came. Remember when I asked you if they would cover him? I couldn't see the front door. I'm certain I couldn't."

"I don't want to frighten you more, Robin, but I think someone was still there. The door was closed when the officers arrived."

"Yes," she said, wide-eyed with fear of what could have happened to her. "Now I remember! The policemen knocked loudly and identified themselves. I called out for them to come in. Oh, God, the murderer was there, wasn't he? He was still there, hiding, and then left before they arrived!"

He nodded. "Either behind the door or in the coat closet beside it. I think he left as soon as you went into the other room. And he took your computer and suitcase with him. That disk you have, the one James asked you to bring him? I believe that's what he thought he would find."

She watched as Mitch retrieved her purse and withdrew the plastic case from inside it. He held it up and read the colorful insert. "Classical Interludes?" he said, turning it over in his hand.

"The disk was in a clear sleeve so it wouldn't take up so much room in the safety deposit box. I was afraid it might get damaged in my purse so I placed it in that heavy plastic jewel case to protect it. I keep my CDs for the computer files in a folder so I didn't have any extra cases lying around. I took out a musical one and used that."

"He had it in a safety deposit box." Mitch's brows drew together, and his lips firmed. "He must have considered this pretty important. If I'm right, it could be something worth killing for and could give us a clue about who was so hot to have it."

If what Mitch said was true, that meant James was mixed up in something dangerous and had been even when they'd been together in New York. She simply couldn't imagine that.

She shook her head. "Believe me, James was not the type to take any risks. If you're thinking he was caught up in something that could cost him his life, you're sadly mistaken. Everything he did was so precise and well-thought-out it drove me crazy. He never entertained a spontaneous thought that I know of."

"I got the impression that he married you on impulse."

Robin sighed and looked away from his piercing glare. "No, that was strictly *my* impulse. James constructed a dedicated campaign to convince me we should. It took a year before I finally caved. The whim was mine, not his." She added without thinking, "Even the affairs he had later were deliberately arranged so that I couldn't help but find out."

"Affairs? More than one?" Mitch asked casually. Too casually for Robin not to realize he considered it crucial. She had just admitted to yet another motive he could use against her, but she had gone too far not to finish the explanation.

"Yes. Apparently marriage proved too confining for him after a while, so he made certain I had excellent reasons to end it. He admitted it to me later and apologized."

"And you accepted?" he asked in obvious disbelief. "You stayed friends with that—"

"Yes," she told him firmly, cutting off what was about to be an insult. "You see, it really was at least half my fault that it didn't work for us. I made him unhappy. In fact, I was relieved it was over between us because we could go back to the way things were before, when he was just my friend. I'm sure he was, too."

Mitch huffed. "I think he was a damned jerk."

Robin secretly agreed with him, in a way. But she had understood James better than any other man she'd ever known. He'd been weak and often selfish, but he had also been generous with his affection and praise, which she'd badly needed at the time. She knew the reasons behind his selfishness and her willingness to tolerate it until she had grown strong enough to resent it.

Simply, she and James had used each other to recover, and when that recovery finally took place, the marriage had unofficially ended. They discussed it, understood it and went on from there.

"Better the devil you know," she muttered, not even realizing she'd spoken aloud until Mitch replied.

"I don't think you knew this devil at all, Robin," he told her as he reached for her hand and brought it to his lips. "And I can almost understand if you *did* shoot him."

"So you said. But I swear I didn't do it." Fear riffled through her, chilling her to the marrow. Did he still think she had killed James? She could see accusation of some kind in his eyes. Maybe it was only that he thought her a fool for allowing James to dupe her the way he'd done.

Would Mitch Winton, a man sworn to uphold the law, actually kiss a hand he believed might have wielded a murder weapon? What kind of cop would do such a thing? One hoping she was innocent? Or determined to prove guilty by using any means available?

"You're a dangerous man to know," she told him.

He released her hand and sat back, smiling a bitter smile. "Yeah, I can be that," he admitted. "If I find out you're jerking me around, you can count on it."

Chapter 5

Mitch knew the value of intimidation and was in no way opposed to using it when the time was right. So why did it make him feel so rotten playing the big, bad cop with Robin? He knew she hadn't killed James Andrews, but he did sense she was hiding something. Why didn't he feel justified in shaking her up a little?

She broke eye contact and turned away from him. As if coming to a decision, she grabbed the disk and thrust it at him defiantly. "All right. If you must know, I looked at it."

"So you already know what's on it?" he asked as he took it from her.

At her guilty nod he asked, "So, what did you find? And be honest. I plan to pick it apart when I get to a computer."

"Well, good luck," she snapped impatiently. "There were

names of some of his clients, numbers of their insurance accounts and a few pages of notes in a foreign language."

"Interesting. What language?"

She stilled. "I don't know. You don't believe they're insurance accounts like James said, do you?"

"People aren't usually killed for a client list. What were the numbers like? How many in a sequence?"

Robin shrugged, rubbing her arms with her hands. After thinking for a minute, she shook her head. "I'm not sure. Nine beside each name, I think."

Could be Social Security numbers. Or numbered bank accounts. Or simply what they appeared to be, insurance account numbers. But there would be time to worry about that later. He stuck the disk in the pocket of his jacket.

"You'd better stay with me tonight."

She ignored the last suggestion as if he hadn't made it. "You can take me to a hotel. I'll be ready in a second." She began looking around, bending over to check under the coffee table. "Have you seen my shoes?"

"I took your shoes," he admitted.

She frowned up at him. "Why?"

"They look splendid with my beige suit. Why do you think, Robin?"

Her mouth dropped open, and she snapped it shut as she straightened and tugged down the hem of her skirt. "I'm sure I haven't a clue."

"I hope not. Kick would love it if your shoes provide one. There were traces of red dirt found on the carpet at the crime scene. Forensics will be analyzing your soles."

"All right." She curled up her toes, looking down at them as if she'd never seen them before. "So what do I do in the meantime?"

"Go barefoot," he told her. There wasn't much choice. Her

feet weren't exactly tiny, but she would never be able to wear any of his gunboats. Sandra might have left shoes in the closet, but she was a little bitty thing and wore a very small size.

Robin's feet were long and narrow. So graceful, he thought to himself, hardly able to tear his eyes away from them. But he did. It was silly to sit there ogling a woman's feet. He caught her watching him do it, too.

Her luscious lips firmed and he thought she might be about to cry. He couldn't much blame her considering the night she'd had. And her day wasn't promising to be much better. He reached out, took one of her hands and held it, offering what comfort he could without taking her in his arms the way he wanted.

"You won't need shoes to go over to my place. What you need now is food, and I've got supper on already."

"You cook?" she asked.

Mitch laughed self-consciously. "Yeah. My mama made it very clear when I moved out all those years ago that she wouldn't tolerate my freeloading every meal. She gave me lessons and a set of cookware."

Robin nodded knowingly. "I certainly can identify with that! My mother didn't want me around, either, after I stopped being the breadwinner."

"You were the breadwinner?" Mitch frowned.

"Well, I was all she had to work with after Dad left. Mother actually drove herself harder than I did. She managed my modeling career. When I quit, that also put her out of a job, so you can understand how upsetting that would be."

"No, I don't understand at all," he argued. "She threw you out?"

Robin got up and paced over to the window. "Not physically, of course. I'm a lot larger than she is. But, yes, she did want me to go, so I went. Found my own apartment. Created a new life for myself. She left New York a few weeks later and bought a place in Florida."

"And you visit on her birthday," Mitch said, watching her reactions closely. "Are you closer now?"

She turned from the window and grimaced. "You're the one who started this business about mothers. Do we need to get this in depth? We both got the boot when we went independent. What's the big deal?"

"No big deal," he said, forcing a smile, making himself abandon the subject she seemed to find difficult. "So, you gonna try my soup or what?"

She picked up her purse and slung the strap over her shoulder. "Lead on, but I warn you it might be slow going. I'm not used to going barefoot outside, even for a short distance."

Mitch already had the door open and was waiting for her to exit. "Not a problem. I'm just across the hall."

She stopped. "What?"

"There," he told her, inclining his head toward the door facing hers.

"When...when you said next door, I thought..."

He shrugged. "You assumed I meant in the next house, right? I knew you thought that, but I decided it might make you uncomfortable having me just across the hall. Does it?"

She met his gaze and hers looked distinctly wary. "No, I suppose not. No one lives...with you, I take it?"

"Nope. I live alone."

Robin was still questioning the advisability of staying with him when they reached his kitchen. The room was larger than the space allotted in Sandy's apartment for cooking.

"It smells divine in here," she commented. She plopped her purse on the counter and lifted the lid to his Crock-Pot for a closer sniff. "What is it?"

"Beef vegetable soup. Old family recipe. Please tell me you eat meat."

She nodded and trailed her long delicate fingers along the counter as she continued to explore. Mitch pretended to ignore her snooping when she peeked into the pantry.

"Who lives downstairs?" she asked.

"Except for the foyer and parlor, the first floor is mostly gutted right now and waiting for me to remodel," he told her. "I'm only renting to Sandy to help pay for the materials. Eventually, this will be a one-family dwelling again, the way it was originally intended." He fished out his large cast-iron skillet and set it on the front burner of the stove. "The kitchen down there will be huge. Lots of counter space and a big island. I'm thinking about a walk-in fridge."

She made herself comfortable on the stool at the end of the counter. "You're bringing your family here to live with you?"

"Bite your tongue." He laughed and plopped a small sack of cornmeal down beside the sink. "The Winton crew's pretty big, though. When we all do get together, we need lots of room."

"They come here often?" she asked, looking truly interested. He supposed she would be. It sounded as if she had very little family of her own. He ran hot water into the cornmeal and stirred it briskly.

"Not so much now, but I hope they'll come over a lot when I get everything finished. That's why I bought this place."

"Ever been married?" she asked.

He grinned. "No, Miss Nosy."

"Are you gay?"

"No, I'm just getting the nest ready for Miss Right."

She looked around the room as if reassessing it. "Yes, I can visualize some lucky woman filling this house with children for you. Happily-ever-afters do occur occasionally, I guess."

"No, darlin', they don't just *occur*," he said, dropping a

spoonful of cornmeal mixture into the oil-coated pan and watching it sizzle. "You have to work at them. Leave nothing to chance."

She traced a pattern on the countertop with one finger. "That's a unique perspective on marriage these days, isn't it?"

He slid the spatula underneath the patties one at a time and turned them carefully so that each one browned evenly. "Maybe, but it's worked for my folks. I expect it will for me."

When he looked up and pinned her gaze, she was smiling the saddest smile he had ever seen. "You sound dangerously optimistic."

Mitch slid the corn patties onto a paper towel he'd arranged on a plate. "If you don't expect to be happy and do everything you can to make it happen, you sure as hell won't be." He picked up one of the corn cakes and held it out to her. "Here, taste this."

She looked at it warily, then pinched off a tiny piece. Her eyes grew round as she chewed. "That...that's *good!* It's really good!"

He rolled his eyes. "Well, don't sound so all-fired shocked, will you? Mama was a good teacher."

Robin was the pickiest eater he had ever seen, Mitch decided later as he watched her studiously push aside the chunks of potato and every single butter bean in her bowl. Everything with any starch or carbs, she avoided. No wonder she was so thin. She kept taking pinches of the corn bread as if eating it constituted a serious sin she couldn't resist committing. It tickled him that he could tempt her.

He would love to tempt her in other, much more intimate ways, but knew he'd better keep his libido in check. If he had ever been this drawn to a course of foolish action, he couldn't recall it. She was off-limits and that was that.

When she pushed her plate back and sighed with pleasure,

he couldn't help but stare. Her eyes closed, her head tilted back and her lips stretched into a satisfied smile as she exhaled. God, he almost lost it. She would look just like that when she...

He shook his head to clear it, firmly dismissing the fantasy she roused. What he needed was a cold shower. An icy shower. Problem was, he didn't have a shower in the house. Just a couple of antique tubs large enough for two. Damn, he was going to have to do something to get sex off the brain.

"You want to watch a movie?" he asked, desperate for any kind of distraction. There wasn't much to do that didn't involve going out somewhere. Well, there was *something*, but that was exactly what he was trying to avoid thinking about. "How about *Monty Python*?" Pure unadulterated silliness was what they needed.

She made a face. Mitch thought it was cute. Hell, he suspected the worst she ever looked in her life was cute.

"Okay, *Attack of the Killer Tomatoes*," he said. "A true classic."

She laughed and stood up. "Let's see what else you have. Where's your collection?"

He pointed to the living room. "Go ahead and choose something. I'll just stick these dishes in the dishwasher. No, no," he protested when she began to stack hers. "Just go. I'll do this."

"My, my, Mom did train you well." She shook her finger at him playfully. "Count yourself lucky I'm not in the market, or you'd be in serious trouble, my man."

Then Robin suddenly seemed to realize she'd gotten too familiar. Her sly smile rapidly faltered. She made a wordless little gesture of embarrassment, turned and left the kitchen in a rush.

What a mass of contradictions she was, Mitch thought as he emptied her unfinished food down the disposal. One minute she was the worldly sophisticate and the next she came off like a kid who hadn't learned the most basic social graces. The real Robin was somewhere between the two extremes, he knew, but apparently she was out of her element here. With him and with the situation she found herself in. She was uncertain how to play it.

He wanted to hold her, to reassure her that he wasn't the enemy. All sexual attraction aside, he wished he could somehow put her at ease and let her know that for him to like her she didn't have to *be* any way but the way she was.

When he finished cleaning up in the kitchen and joined her in the living room, he found her curled in one corner of his overstuffed sofa watching *Casablanca*. She was clutching a pillow, her long legs tucked to one side. Her bare feet looked pale, cold.

"So you went straight for the chick flick," he said, sounding grumpy as he raked the fringed plaid throw off the back of a chair and tossed it over her legs and feet. "The only one I own. I should've known. Like all that mushy stuff, huh?" he asked with a weary sigh.

Her smile was timid, her gaze still focused on Bogey as she nodded.

"Okay." Mitch lounged in the opposite corner of the sofa, already feeling the magnetic pull toward her that was going to devil him for the duration.

She would stay here tonight, for safety's sake, and he would sleep on the sofa so he could keep watch.

First thing in the morning, they would go over to his parents' house and use Susan's computer to pull up the info on the CD. But for tonight he simply wanted to forget all about the case. He wanted to watch Robin watch this movie. And he wanted to pretend neither of them had anything more problematic than whether or not to pop popcorn.

When Bogey finally got to his "Here's lookin' at you, kid,"

thing, Robin wiped a tear off her cheek, sniffed and stuck it out to the bitter end where the hero walked away. They watched the credits roll in silence.

"She's so beautiful, isn't she?" Robin said of Ingrid Bergman.

"She's okay. You ever want to act? You've sure got the looks and the presence for it."

"Me? Act?" she asked with apparent disbelief.

But Mitch had seen that telltale flicker in her eyes and guessed that she had given it some thought at one time or another.

"I'll bet you'd be great on the big screen. What was it like modeling?" Mitch asked. "Must have been exciting, huh?"

He smiled at her, encouraging her to talk. She had a hesitant, almost self-deprecating way about her he wouldn't have expected someone in her profession to have. Former profession, he reminded himself, though he couldn't imagine she'd quit because she was losing her looks.

For a full minute she didn't answer. She sat there looking pensive, gazing across the room at nothing, lost in thought. Then she turned to him, and her eyes met his. "Grueling. Most people don't realize that it's very hard work. Long hours, uncomfortable poses. Hot lights and wind machines. Crabby photographers and—"

"Large paychecks?" he interrupted, teasing her.

Her sensuous lips twitched. "Yes, there are those."

"Seeing your picture everywhere must give you a charge. Seems like every girl's dream."

Her eyes darkened as her long lashes lowered and she glanced away, her slender fingers nervously pleating the edge of the soft wool throw he had draped over her. "More like a nightmare," she muttered with a halfhearted laugh. She didn't sound bitter, exactly, just resigned. "I'm glad it's over. I felt like a reluctant exhibitionist even when the clothes weren't that revealing. And when they were, I was mortified every minute."

"Funny, you don't strike me as shy," he commented, though that wasn't strictly true. His perception of her changed like colors viewed through a prism. One minute she would seem totally on top of things, a real cosmopolitan. The next, she reverted to wariness and uncertainty, an innocent battling the big, bad world. Right now, her weariness was obvious, her guard down, allowing him a glimpse of Robin probably seen by few.

"Would you like to go to bed, Robin?" he asked.

Her eyebrows flew up, and she looked mighty offended, though she said nothing.

Mitch realized then what he had said and it made him laugh. "Not with *me!*" he clarified. "I only meant you should feel free to turn in whenever you feel like it. It has been a busy day, and I'm a little worn-out myself."

Relief made her laugh, too. "Oh." She looked embarrassed. "It's not that I thought you were really coming on to me, but—"

"You get that a lot, don't you? Propositions? Not surprising. A man would have to be blind or dead not to get turned on by how gorgeous you are. Even I...well, we'd better not go there," he said with a wry twist of his lips. "You're safe with me."

She didn't look convinced. "Looks aren't everything, you know. What's inside a person is much more important," she stated primly, as if she'd made up the concept all by herself.

He cocked his head and shook one finger at her. "A hard lesson for guys to learn. Me included, I confess. I bet most people never get past that first impression you make, do they? I promise I'll look a little deeper, okay? If I forget, you just beat me over the head with your intelligence and your talent and I'll shape up."

Her eyes narrowed and her hands stilled. "Are you patronizing me, Detective?"

Mitch made a face. "Sounded like that, didn't it? You're a

beautiful woman, no question about it, Robin. I'd be lying if I denied noticing that." He looked her straight in the eye. "But I think there's a lot more to Robin Andrews than meets the eye."

That seemed to please her, which was exactly what he'd intended. He added, "I'd like to get to know the real you."

"Then I'm afraid you will have to wait until tomorrow. If you wouldn't mind, I think I will try to get some sleep. Where would you like me?"

Oh, God, what a loaded question. Everywhere, Mitch thought. Every which way. But he clamped the lid on his wayward thoughts and answered, "You can bunk in there in my bedroom and I'll take the sofa."

She scanned the length of it as she got up. "You're too tall for it."

"So are you," he replied with a grin. "Let me suffer. I deserve it for *almost* hitting on you, right?"

She laughed, but it was a nervous laugh. Mitch knew she didn't quite trust him to behave.

"The door locks," he told her, and watched her nod. He also didn't miss the slight exhalation that indicated relief.

"If you need anything you can't find in the bathroom— shampoo, extra towels or whatever—just let me know."

She met his gaze directly then, without a hint of fear or embarrassment. "Thanks," she said, her voice a breathy whisper.

Mitch wondered if he had misconstrued that look of hers as one of interest. Had he misread her altogether? Did she actually want him to make a play for her? Did she expect it of every man? He didn't know, but he'd bet his favorite A3 track that most every guy got around to it sooner or later.

She was under his skin. He was *smitten,* as Granny would say, and there wasn't a damned thing he could do about it but try to keep his cool and keep his hands off her.

Surprisingly, she hadn't kicked up a fuss at all when he had told her that he thought it would be wise for her to stay in his apartment for the night instead of across the hall.

He followed her to the door of the bedroom. "There are T-shirts in the top drawer over there if you want one to sleep in."

Her gaze darted away from his and she was worrying that bottom lip something fierce.

"What's the matter, Robin?" he asked.

She forced her chin up. "This is just a bit awkward. I've never slept in a man's room before. They...always came to mine."

"First time for everything," he said, ushering her on into the bedroom. He knew he ought to stay out of there. He knew it. But he didn't. "Fresh sheets are stacked on the shelf in the closet. Plenty of pillows," he said, grabbing one off the bed for himself, "I'll just take this one."

"Okay," she murmured, and turned at exactly the wrong time. Mitch found himself too close to her. Way too close. She was tall enough that their lips were scant inches apart.

All he would have to do was lower his head just a little and...

She quickly backed away and plopped down on the bed, bouncing a little. "Comfy," she said, a bit too brightly, brushing her hands over the bedspread and giving it a pat.

"Yeah, I guess. There's a half bath in there," he told her, nodding at the closed door. "The only full bath is down the hall, on your right."

"Thanks," she said, her voice almost timid.

Mitch nodded once and left in a hurry before he forgot why he wasn't supposed to kiss her. Just in time, too.

Good thing he'd had a few hours' sleep today, he thought as he retired to the sofa for the night. He sure as hell wouldn't be getting any tonight.

* * *

Robin couldn't imagine what had possessed her to speak so frankly to a virtual stranger. Maybe that was the key. She had always heard it was easier to open up to someone you didn't know.

Once James's murder was solved, she would be able to leave Nashville and there would be no reason on earth why she should ever return. She'd never see Mitch again. In her wildest flight of imagination, she could not picture him, the quintessential Southerner, venturing North to New York. Why ever should he?

It seemed he had everything any man could want right here. From the way he talked about them, his family was a great part of his life.

He must be successful at his job, though she couldn't think anyone would truly enjoy dealing with crimes of violence. Perhaps he did. Some people thrived on solving problems and puzzles, which homicides certainly could be. He must have found a way to block out the unpleasant aspects of his work or else had grown impervious to them. Robin guessed he also must have altruistic reasons for choosing to do what he did. Mitch seemed the type. Someone had to take murderers out of circulation and protect the populace.

It surprised her that, doing what he did for a living, Mitch was not a bitter man. In fact, he possessed a gentle humor and optimism she had seldom, if ever, encountered in men with comparatively innocuous occupations. Maybe it was a Southern thing.

She smiled about that as she washed her face and prepared for bed. In the medicine cabinet, Robin located a new toothbrush still in its protective plastic. There were clean, colorful towels and washcloths rolled and handily tucked on a shelf over the commode. Robin removed one and patted her face dry, inhaling the fresh, subtle scent of fabric softener.

She liked his place. Everything was clean but not scrupulously neat. A bit of clutter only made it looked lived in, comfortable. Friendly. Robin figured she must have arrived several days after the maid had been here.

Then again, maybe he did his own housework. He certainly could cook. He also did dishes. And he was infinitely proud of this house. She could see why. It would make a lovely home for some lucky woman one of these days. There was a warmth here already that beckoned a person to relax and enjoy it. Or maybe it was just Mitch's open friendliness that made it seem so.

While she felt more at ease with him than she should, considering how briefly they had known each other, he also disturbed her in some elemental way.

He caused a certain, not unpleasant tension inside her that Robin recognized as sexual. That, in itself, was highly unusual. And almost reassuring. She had begun to think she was immune. Maybe she had always tried too desperately to grasp that feeling with James. This attraction to Mitch Winton had taken her totally by surprise.

Inappropriate as it was, she should mind it, but she didn't. It would come to nothing, of course, but Robin couldn't think of a single reason she couldn't secretly enjoy it while it lasted. Mitch need never know.

It could very well be something as simple as a delayed adolescent reaction. An infatuation. She'd never had one of those, not on movie idols, rock stars or even a handsome teacher. That's what came of not attending school the way other girls did, she supposed, never interacting normally with her peers. Never really having the time to fantasize.

Well, Mitch Winton certainly did fill the bill when it came to fantasy. He was handsome in a rugged sort of way, kind when the occasion called for it, and it probably didn't hurt matters that she was under his protection. Transference, probably.

Everything about him tantalized her. There was his scent, not totally accounted for by his faintly spicy aftershave. She had to fight the urge to draw closer and breathe more deeply when she was around him. And there was the way he spoke, his voice sending a slow curl of heat through her insides like a deep draught of Irish coffee. Hot, sweet and intoxicating.

In her own defense, she did try to avoid his touch. That tingling current whenever they connected in the slightest way was altogether too enticing. If she didn't watch it, she would give herself away.

Figuratively and literally.

The thought made her frown at herself in the mirror. "Silly idiot," she muttered. "Behave."

For now she would put her reaction to Mitch into perspective and give it only the momentary attention it deserved. She had far weightier problems to deal with than a belated schoolgirl crush.

She pulled on a soft, gray T-shirt with a Marine Corps logo nearly faded out of readability on the front. It hung on her slender frame, the folds caressing her bare skin, the loose drape of the knit mocking her lack of musculature and making her dwell on thoughts of his wide shoulders and the expanse of his chest. Robin doubted she would get much rest wearing this thing.

The soft knock on the bedroom door sent her scurrying out of the bathroom to answer. When she opened it, the object of her ruminations stood there with a glass of milk in his hand.

"Here you go," he said. "My recipe for sleep. Guaranteed to work."

Robin took it and sipped when he indicated she should. It was delicious. She licked her upper lip and peered up at him. "What is it?"

"Vanilla milk. Drop or two of flavoring and a spoonful of sugar. Great, huh?" He grinned. "Mama used to add red and blue food coloring, turn it an icky shade of lavender and tell us it came from purple cows. Ever heard that rhyme?"

She frowned. The man was an alien.

"'Never saw a purple cow. Never hope to see one. But I can tell you anyhow, I'd rather see than be one,'" he recited.

"'Reflections of a Mythic Beast,' Burgess wrote it," she replied automatically.

He shook his head, laughed and tapped her nose playfully with his index finger. "Now how the hell did you know that?"

Robin shrugged. "Read it somewhere. Things stick. So what do purple cows have to do with getting to sleep?"

"Nothin' at all, smarty-pants. I just wanted an excuse to say good-night again."

She sighed, looked at the glass of milk she was holding and raised her gaze to his. "Good night, Mitch," she whispered.

A silence fraught with that delicious tension grew. Finally he moved back a step. "Sleep tight."

Robin slowly closed the door, leaned against it and shut her eyes, holding fast to her last glimpse of him in spite of knowing better. Her breath shuddered out.

She was going to have to fight this after all. And it was going to take a lot more energy than she needed to spend. She wished she could enlist his help, but that would mean she'd have to admit her foolishness. And tell him she recognized his.

Chapter 6

The day dawned cool, gray and held the promise of rain. "Mornin'. I'm a little short on groceries," Mitch said when she appeared in the kitchen fully dressed, hair perfect, apparently ready to face the day. Except for her bare feet. "Tell you what. We'll stop somewhere for breakfast, then swing by my parents' house this morning. Susan has a computer, so we can check out the disk. She can loan you some shoes. Clothes, too."

He handed her a cup of coffee. Black, as he figured she would like it.

"Susan?" she asked, sounding disgruntled. "Who is Susan?"

"My sister. She's about your size."

"I'm not wearing anyone else's clothing and shoes and that's all there is to it! I never have and do not intend to start now!"

"Aw, c'mon, don't tell me you and your girlfriends didn't used to swap clothes. Jeez, seems like there was always a house full of giggling wanna-be fashion plates around when I was growing up. Sue was the world's worst for borrowing things. She does have a lot of clothes and shoes, even now, and would be happy to share."

Robin merely looked at him as if he was making it all up. "No," she said simply with a look that shut him up.

He considered her predicament while she drank her coffee. She was dressed in what she'd worn all day yesterday and the evening before. Her suit was a mass of wrinkles, but the rest of her looked like a million bucks. Not a hair out of place. "Okay. I guess we'll have to buy you some."

She looked almost as horrified by the idea of shopping with him. He wouldn't want to disappoint her. He knew just the strip mall with a jam-up dollar store.

"Come on. Let's shop!" Then he smiled. "Bet you never thought you'd hear a guy throwin' around that kind of invitation, did you?"

With her nose in the air, she slung her purse strap over her shoulder, marched right past him and exited the apartment with all the polish of a runway model. Which made perfect sense, he reminded himself, as he followed her downstairs.

Even the color on her toenails matched her getup. No doubt about it, the girl had class to spare.

She also had a dead husband, and might even be involved up to her gorgeous neck in whatever had gotten Andrews killed. He didn't think so, but he could be wrong. Beauty, class, murder and intrigue. A detective's dream, that's what she was. Mitch admitted he was fascinated with her and couldn't help it. Not that he could afford to do anything about that, other than own up to it and make sure she didn't find out.

When she reached the front door, she stopped so abruptly he almost stumbled against her. "What's the matter?"

She peered through the etched glass sidelights that framed the door. "Do you think we'll be followed?" Her voice was nearly a whisper.

"It's possible, but I'll know it if we are and I'll deal with it," he said with conviction. "I'm pretty sure now that whoever killed Andrews was looking for that disk and still is. However, your visitor yesterday gave up way too easily to have been one of those guys from the diner, though, don't you think? It could have been a neighbor, a deliveryman, just about anybody."

She let out a breath and her shoulders sagged a little. "I hope you're right. But they could be out there now, waiting."

"Would you rather stay here? I could call Susan, have her bring the computer over. We don't have to go out." Maybe that would be best, anyway. She looked sort of shaky.

Her shoulders straightened and she took one last look out the sidelight. "No, let's do it. Let's go."

"Atta girl!" Mitch said, giving her a gentle pat on the back.

She immediately arched to escape his touch, then glanced over her shoulder with a wary expression. Well, he should have known better. She had let him hold her hand, brush the hair off her face and guide her through doorways with his hand at her back before. But that was when she had really been terrified and probably in shock. It didn't count.

Obviously, Robin Andrews was not much of a toucher and liked her space uninvaded, thank you very much. Someone must have made her overly cautious and suspicious at some time in her life. Understandable. She said she'd once been a model like it was a dirty word. Now she chose to work in isolation, on a computer, designing Web pages.

He'd bet money she never even met her clients in person. Her choice of occupation told him something about her right there. She'd pretty much given up on the human race. The male half, anyway. Well, after her friend-slash-husband screwed around on her while they were married, what could you expect? Her mother didn't sound all that terrific, either, kicking her out when she stopped making the money.

Robin badly needed to get her mind off her troubles for a while. Maybe he could give her a few more hours to rest and regroup before they got down to brass tacks.

He led the way out to his old Bronco and opened the door for her. At least she allowed him to do that. He slammed it shut and went around to the driver's side and got in.

"Hungry?" he asked.

"A little." She flashed him a tentative smile, almost like an apology. That touched him. Maybe she didn't really like being the ice princess, but just couldn't help being how she was.

"Judging by the way you ate last night, you're a fruit and yogurt girl, I bet," he said, wrinkling his nose.

She laughed timidly. "That would be good."

"No," he said with a laugh, "that wouldn't be good. That would be *healthy*. Grits would be good."

"I haven't had the pleasure."

"You never had grits? For real? Hey, unless you're passing right on through Dixie without stopping, you have got to eat grits. It's the law, and I *am* a cop!"

"All right, all right," she said, giving in to the laugh she'd been suppressing. "I'll try it. But I want something else to eat in case I don't like it."

"Them," he instructed automatically as he backed out of the driveway. "Grits are plural. You try *them*."

She cast him a doubtful look. "We don't even speak the same language, do we?"

He tossed her a grin. "I'll teach you. It's almost as easy as Greek."

They stopped at the little mall with the clothing and discount shoe store he'd been thinking about. Mitch had figured she'd be in and out of there in a flash, but he was wrong. She took so much time choosing her shoes, she might as well have been in Sak's and paying a fortune for them.

He watched, antsy as any guy would be while waiting around in a women's clothing store, as she selected several pullover shirts, three pairs of pants and a stack of what Grandma Dolly called unmentionables.

In Robin's case, these last items were skimpy little scraps of lace that Grandma would have blushed to look at. Mental images of Robin wearing what she was buying had him shifting uncomfortably as he stood waiting for her to pay.

She took it as impatience. "Sorry, I'd forgotten how much fun shopping is," she admitted as she plunked down her Visa card. "I do most of my buying online these days."

Well, that explained everything. Mitch experienced a little pang of pity for her. What in the world could make a woman give up shopping? The females in his family lived for it. Their daily Wal-Mart expeditions were a social experience.

Lord, this was worse than he'd thought.

He got no complaints when he took her to Brown's Restaurant, a buffet place near his parents' house.

The first thing she did was hit the ladies' room and change her clothes. When she emerged wearing the inexpensive yellow pullover and long skinny jeans that looked as if she'd been poured in them, she still looked like a million bucks. Yep, Robin Andrews wore clothes well. Even discount stuff looked pricey when she put it on. He wished he could stop thinking about those little lacy numbers she'd picked out to go under the rest.

"Hey, look at you!" he said as she rejoined him at the table. "Feel better?"

Her smile was pure delight. "I do. But I'm starving!"

At the buffet she piled a plate high with fruit, cottage cheese and dry toast. So much for his idea that women like her ate light.

He watched as she wolfed down a sizable breakfast in half the time it took him to eat his.

Then she polished off her juice and a cup of black coffee. "I *never* eat this much," she explained as if she'd done something wrong, "but I was so hungry."

He smiled and motioned the waitress to refill their cups.

"I suppose it's show time," she said, and picked up her spoon. With a determined look on her face, she drove it directly toward his plate, scooped up a spoonful and stuffed it in her mouth.

Mitch watched with great interest as she chewed, her expression changing with every movement of her jaw. Finally she swallowed, took another sip of coffee and sighed with pleasure. "It...rather, *they* aren't that bad, actually. Taste very like potatoes."

Mitch deadpanned. "That's because they are."

No grits, no shopping in stores and not even any hash browns in her life? Did the poor girl live in a New York cave?

Robin had to admit she liked Mitch Winton. His Southern drawl wound around her senses and made her want to relax and forget the real reason she was stuck in Nashville. The accent had irritated her at first, but then she had been upset, not herself and scared of what he might do.

Also, the mixed signals he sent had confused her. Great concern for her comfort did not compute with obvious suspicion. Now, of course, she realized he was concerned out of a natural courtesy. And he'd explained why he had to consider her a suspect. Mitch was up-front about it all, she had to give him that.

His teasing her was just a thing he did naturally, without any thought at all, she suspected. It wasn't even flirting. If he had planned to hit on her, he would have done it already.

Mitch was different from any man she had ever known, thank God. That alone was reason enough to like him.

"...so Susie spent a whole hour in the corner while Mama recovered from the frog in the lunch box. I was the angel of the family."

"Why do I doubt that?" Robin asked, laughing at his family anecdote. "You put the frog there, didn't you?"

"Me? Now that's a sexist assumption if I ever heard one. Susie handled her own frogs. It was worms she couldn't stand. But that's a whole other story."

She appreciated what he was doing, trying to get her to lighten up. It had worked, too. Robin hadn't looked behind them for a car following or worried about anything else for a good five minutes or so. The cadence of his voice and the flash of humor in his eyes when he glanced over at her put her more at ease than she had been with a man since James left New York.

Mitch pulled the Bronco into the double driveway of a modest ranch-style house set on the corner of a street in what must have been one of the older suburbs of the city. Robin tensed.

"Here we go. You're about to meet the infamous Winton crew. They're loud but fairly harmless. Looks like they're not all here, anyway."

At the thought of meeting them, Robin's composure took an immediate nosedive. She wasn't good with people. On the phone she was okay, but in person she usually just faked a haughtiness that had served her well on the runway and at parties she'd had to attend years ago. It put off conversation and kept everyone at a distance. Not since her separation from James had she been forced to socialize with a group of people, and even then he hadn't required much of that. At least he had understood that flaw of hers.

She figured she ought to explain. "Mitch, I should wait in the car. I'm not very good at—"

"Shy, huh? Don't worry, they won't let you be," he said, smiling. "Just slap on a grin and nod. They'll be your best friends. Trust me."

That again. Robin sighed as she got out and followed Mitch to the door. Instead of knocking, he opened it and walked right in. Robin hung back, appalled by the act. She had never in her entire life violated anyone's privacy by entering their home uninvited.

"Hey, where is everybody?" Mitch shouted as he barged right through the small foyer into a comfortably furnished living room. "I brought company!"

A short, gray-haired woman appeared wearing jeans and an orange sweatshirt with a University of Tennessee logo on the front. She held a rubber spatula in one hand. "Hey, baby," she said, hugging Mitch and tiptoeing to kiss his cheek. "Daddy's gone to the store. You just missed him. Y'all come on back to the kitchen. I'm right in the middle of a cake." She smiled sweetly at Robin. "Hi, honey."

"Mama, this is Robin Andrews. Robin, my mother, Patricia Winton."

"Mrs. Winton," Robin acknowledged, immediately attempting to compare the smiling stranger to her own mother. There were no comparisons. Not in looks, not in expression, not in congeniality. At a total loss, Robin said nothing further.

"Oh, call me Pat," the woman said, waving the spatula in Robin's direction as she led the way through the dining room. "All Mitch's friends do." She nodded toward the stools surrounding a large kitchen island. "Have a seat. I'll be through here in a minute and make us some coffee."

"I'll do it," Mitch offered, heading for the coffeemaker. "How're the kids doing?"

"Fine. Mack made the football team. Finally."

"Good for him. Lily's grades up any?"

"Not so's you'd notice," she said with a grimace.

Kids? How many were in this family? Robin wondered. And whose kids were they?

His mother continued. "Paula needs a good talking to, Mitch. Boy crazy." One eyebrow raised as her lips quirked to one side. She shared a knowing look with her son.

"Sic Susie on her. That'll straighten her out." He swiped a long finger along the edge of the bowl his mother was stirring as he passed by and licked the batter off his finger. "Mmm, pineapple pound cake. My favorite."

Pat Winton laughed and shot Robin a sly look. "They're *all* his favorites. He's a cake freak. You cook?"

"Mama, don't interrogate her. That's *my* job," he snapped with mock anger, then looked over his shoulder at Robin. "So, you cook?"

Robin gave a nervous little laugh, totally unused to this sort of byplay, though she did recognize it as such, and answered hesitantly. "Yes, but never cakes."

"Then you don't *cook*," he declared. "I live for cake."

"Ignore him," his mother said as she poured the batter into a tube pan and bounced the thing three times on the counter. "Settles out the bubbles," she explained when Robin startled at the racket.

"Well, well, who have we here?" said someone from the doorway.

Robin turned at the question and prepared to greet another unfamiliar face. This woman was almost as tall as Robin and about twenty pounds heavier. She had a long brown braid hanging over one shoulder and a remarkable resemblance to

Mitch. They might have been twins. Same coloring, same smile and apparently the same disposition.

"Hi, I'm Susan," the newcomer said, confirming Robin's guess. "You're the girlfriend? Mitch, warn us, will you? I would have dressed up!" She glanced down at her scruffy jeans and faded T-shirt.

Robin felt her face heat with a blush. "But...but I'm not his—"

Mitch interrupted. "This is Robin Andrews, Sue." He wasn't smiling now. "We're investigating the death of Robin's husband night before last."

Susan's smile immediately faded to a frown of compassion. She made directly for Robin and enfolded her in a firm hug. "Oh, you poor thing! I am so sorry for your loss. I know that's what the cops say all the time and it sounds so cold. But I mean it, I really do."

Robin tried very hard not to jerk away. The woman was trying to comfort her and seemed so sincere. "It...it's okay. Thanks. My husband and I were separated." That sounded so uncaring Robin winced. "But we were still friends," she added. "So thank you. I appreciate it."

Mitch's mother had come around the island and was laying a hand on her back, adding her pats to Susan's and making a sound of sympathy.

"Robin found him," Mitch said, as if to fuel the fire of their compassion.

"How awful for you!" Mrs. Winton exclaimed. "You sit right down here, honey," she ordered, backing Robin onto one of the stools. "Mitch, you ought to have told me. What do you mean coming in here and cracking jokes about cakes after all she's been through? You know better than that!"

"She's fine now," Mitch said, rescuing Robin from their clutches and putting himself between them and her. "Robin's over the shock. She's even going to help me find out who did it. Sue, we need to borrow your computer and look at a CD."

"You insensitive clod! *Men.* I swear, they all need to be shot," Susan declared with a huff of disgust.

Robin immediately forgave Susan's unwitting faux pas. She obviously referred to the entire male gender and not poor James.

"Sorry, Robin," Mitch told her with a humorless half smile. "Sue rarely reads the papers."

"It's all right," Robin said, looking down at her lap and shaking her head. "Maybe we could just...get on with it?"

"Sure!" Susan rushed to say, "Oh, sure. Come on. The computer's already set up in the den where I was working."

She led the way out of the kitchen, down the hall and into a room paneled with oak. An enormous television dominated the wall opposite a stone fireplace. In one corner sat a well-used desk with a laptop, a lamp and papers in disarray.

Susan scooped up the loose pages and set them aside, quickly exited the program she'd been working on and stepped away. "There you go. All yours. What's this all about, anyway?"

"Robin's husband asked her to bring this disk to him when she left New York," he explained. "We're thinking it might have something to do with his murder. Looks like somebody's after this info. The perp stole her computer and her suitcase while she was calling the cops."

Looking worried, Susan reached out and gave Robin's arm a quick squeeze. Surprisingly, it did lend a little comfort instead of making Robin retreat. It wasn't at all like the constant impersonal handling she'd endured during her career.

Mitch retrieved the CD from his jacket pocket, sat down in the computer chair and popped out the CD holder.

He made no move to order his sister from the room. In fact,

he had been quite open with her about why they were here. Somehow Robin had assumed he would go out of his way to shield his family from the ugliness of what had happened, make light of Robin's dilemma or simply not tell them anything.

Susan and Robin stood on either side of him, eyes focused on the screen as he worked. In moments he had opened the file and was scanning the information on the disk. He hit Print and sat back to wait until the small printer slowly ground out the page. His long, strong fingers tapped impatiently on the arm of the chair, and he was frowning.

"What is it?"

He released a sigh and nodded. "I know one of them."

"From here?" Robin asked.

"Yes, Rake Somers, and he's no candidate for sainthood. He is very bad news." Mitch closed out the file with the names and numbers.

"Those could be numbered accounts," he said as he tried unsuccessfully to open the other file. It was password protected.

"It's *Andrews* spelled backward," Robin informed him. "James always used that. Said he couldn't remember passwords and hated to write them down."

Mitch typed in the letters and the file opened. "Kept it simple, huh?" he asked, then hummed. "Guess not all the time, though. Look at that gobbledegook."

Robin glanced at the screen as Mitch scrolled down the first page. "Do you recognize what it is?"

"Cyrillic, I think. Russian. Better give the disk to Kick and let him get the experts on it. The FBI will want this." He printed what he'd found, folded the pages in thirds and handed half of them to Susan. "Put these in Dad's safe as backup." The duplicates he put in his pocket.

"Are you sure it's...Russian? What does this mean, Mitch?"

He slipped the CD back inside the music case and snapped it shut. "Looks like he might have bitten off a little more than he could chew." His gaze sought hers. "Robin, if you know anything about this, anything at all, now's definitely the time to come clean."

She stepped back. "No! I don't know anything about any of it! What makes you think I know something?"

Susan put an arm around her and pulled her close as she glared at Mitch. "You back off her, Mitch! Can't you see she's upset? What's the matter with you?"

"Her life depends on this, Susan. Or at least her freedom," he snapped. "I might be able to cut her a deal with the feds in exchange for what she knows."

Robin's breath rushed out and her knees felt wobbly. "I don't! Please, I don't know anything. James never—"

Susan led her over to the sofa and sat down, forcing Robin to join her since she hadn't let go of her shoulders. "Take it easy now," she said in a soothing voice. "Mitch is just being mean." She scowled over at him. "You say you're sorry right this minute. Can't you see she's telling the truth?"

Mitch felt like dirt, but every word of what he had told her was gospel. This could be espionage they were dealing with. At the very least, the Russian mafia.

He ambled over and took a seat on Robin's other side and leaned forward, his elbows on his knees, hands clasped between them. "Sorry, Robin, but whether you actually do know anything or not, I think you're in some deep trouble here."

His mother brought coffee in on a tray and offered them a mug. Robin refused. She still eyed the computer as if it held answers, though the CD was now in Mitch's pocket. He knew she was simply lost in thought, probably wondering what the heck James Andrews had gotten her into.

He ought to get the disk to Kick today.

"What are you thinking?" Robin asked.

Mitch answered her honestly. "Theorizing. I believe your husband was killed for that disk. He knew the person who came for it and let them in the apartment. When he didn't turn the CD over—because, of course, he didn't have it yet—the killer assumed he was holding out. The apartment probably was being searched when you arrived. The killer heard you coming up the steps and hid, then took off with your things, hoping what he was looking for was in them." Mitch patted his pocket. "Before James was killed, he could have said he was expecting the disk to arrive shortly. Then you walk in carrying a computer. That's just an educated guess, but it could've played out that way."

She shivered. "Wh-why wasn't I killed, too?"

Mitch considered. "Could be one of several reasons. Maybe they knew the contents were in Russian and that you wouldn't be able to read it or know what it was all about. Other than Andrews himself, you don't know any of the principals involved. Do you?"

She shook her head. Standing there, hugging herself, staring at the carpet, she looked so alone, Mitch could hardly bear not consoling her. He almost reached out to do that, but then she glanced up. Her eyes held that touch-me-not look. He got the impression she might fall apart if he violated it. Even Susan and his mom were keeping their distance now, watching Robin as intently as he was.

Mitch shrugged. "You might be alive only because the killer drew the line at killing a female. Something simple as that."

She managed a crooked little smile. "Or maybe he thought he couldn't take me. I'm not exactly a ninety-pound weakling."

"A regular Amazon," he replied, raking her length with an admiring gaze. She was slender but not skinny. There was a chance she was right, now that Mitch thought about it. As defenseless as she might look at the moment, Robin was only a couple of inches shy of six feet and moved with the confidence and grace of an athlete. Mitch didn't doubt she would have put up a hellacious fight for her life if anyone had attacked her after she found Andrews dead.

He smiled at her. "You might have something there, Robin. The gun was on the floor. But you said you moved it. If he didn't see it where he left it or where you put it down, he might have thought you took it into the bedroom with you. So, instead of confronting you, he simply slipped out unobserved, assuming you'd take the fall."

"Why did he drop it in the first place?" she asked.

"One of the little tricks of the trade. Saves getting caught with the weapon. Besides, if he left it there on the floor, wiped of prints, whoever found the body would probably—"

"Pick it up," she said in an awed whisper. "Of course. And I did just that, didn't I? Stupid move."

"You'd be surprised how often it happens."

Robin swallowed hard as if digesting the close call with death. Then she cleared her throat and seemed to cast off whatever grip fear had on her. Her change in stance and attitude amazed him. "So what do we do now?" she asked, her voice steady as a rock.

"Turn over the disk. Then if we can get word out there that the police already have it, we won't have to worry about anyone coming after you and trying to get it first."

His mother grasped his elbow and shook it. "You be careful, you hear? And you take care of Robin."

"You know I will, Mama. I'll give you a call tomorrow. Tell Dad I'm sorry we missed him. The kids, too."

He nodded at Susan and shot her a meaningful look. She nodded back, assuring him she would keep an eye on the folks if he was not able to drop in every day or so.

Robin offered her hand, first to his mother, then to Susan. "It was nice to meet you both," she said.

"I wish it were under better circumstances. Next visit, you'll have to stay for the cake," his mother said, regaining her smile.

She drew Robin into a quick embrace. To Mitch's surprise, Robin returned it, even though it seemed to embarrass her a little. That was Mama for you. She never met a stranger.

Mitch could tell by her eyes she had a soft spot for Robin, and that made him feel good. Robin needed affection, if anyone ever did. His mother wouldn't miss picking up on that. He was glad, because it didn't look much as though Robin was going to accept any from him.

Just as well. He had no business offering it, anyway. Hunford had given him orders not to get involved.

Chapter 7

Robin glanced back at the Winton home as Mitch pulled away from it. It wasn't a remarkable house, only a plain brick rancher like millions of others across the country. But she had always longed for what resided inside that one. Closeness. Caring. Normalcy. Acceptance. Or was what the Winton family had abnormal these days? Robin had no way of knowing, but she hoped it wasn't.

How did people come to be the way the Winton women were? Was that inborn or learned behavior?

Mitch himself could be every bit as outgoing and affectionate as his mother and sister. He had tried to be that way with her. Of course, he had a tough side, as well, she admitted. Detective Winton of the suspicious nature. He who issued dire warnings and looked as if he would follow through with them. A pretense, she thought now. An act that went along with his job. He was probably a teddy bear.

"Your mother and sister are very nice," she said.

He grinned. "Yeah. They're okay, aren't they?"

"So, you have other brothers or sisters?" Making conversation with him might take her mind off the problems she was facing.

His face darkened a little, and the worry line appeared between his brows. "A brother, Mark, who's married with two kids. Lives across town." He said the next as if he had to force the words. "I had another sister. She...died. Her children live with Mom and Dad now."

"The three she mentioned?"

"Yes. Susan, Mark and I help with them as much as we can. They're a handful. Meg, their mother, was killed five years ago."

"I'm so sorry," Robin said. "Car accident?"

He remained silent for a full minute. "No. Her ex-husband...killed her."

Robin winced. How awful! Why had she kept on with the questions when he obviously had not wanted to talk about it? She never knew when to leave well enough alone. Every time she tried to make conversation, she ruined everything. "Forgive me. I shouldn't have pried."

"Not a problem," he snapped, but Robin wasn't convinced he forgave her for bringing up the memory of his sister's death.

A muscle kept jerking in his jaw as he clenched his teeth. Robin did not ask what had happened to the ex-husband. She hoped he was locked up forever. Judging by the look on Mitch's face, she probably didn't really want to know what sort of justice was served on the man. Somehow she didn't think a jail sentence would have satisfied Mitch as brother to the victim and uncle to the motherless children.

Maybe that tough side of Mitch Winton was not a pretense after all. Robin only knew that she never wanted him to focus that menacing look on her for any reason.

Hunford had told Mitch to keep a low profile. There was the suspension. Since he'd been to the precinct only yesterday, Mitch decided to call and ask Kick to meet them somewhere.

"That was brief," Robin observed. "You didn't tell him about the disk."

Mitch merely shrugged. "Didn't want to go into it over the phone." He'd given his partner their location, and they had agreed to meet at a downtown coffee shop where they sometimes ate lunch.

Shortly after the call and before they reached their destination, Mitch noticed a black Taurus weaving through traffic behind them. It remained about the same distance away, regardless of how much or how little he accelerated. "Company," he muttered as he kept an eye on his mirrors.

If he were by himself, he wouldn't even attempt to lose them. He'd call in backup, and together they might end this thing here and now. But if something went down in a crowded coffee shop, someone might get hurt. Robin might be hurt.

"Hang on to what you got," he warned Robin a second before he whipped around two cars in the lane beside him and continued zipping in and out wherever he could. When he was far enough ahead, he took a side street and gunned the Bronco.

The old workhorse didn't look like much on the outside, but he'd souped it up enough to leave most race cars in the dust. A youth misspent hanging around racetracks definitely had educational benefits.

"We lost him," he said finally, when he was sure he was successful. When he looked over at Robin, he saw she was pale as bone china and her eyes were clenched so tight he could barely see her long lashes. "Sorry if I scared you."

She issued a shaky little hum of an answer that wasn't really a word.

"You okay?"

Her nod looked frantic and she was hugging herself again. But after a few seconds, she opened her eyes and took a deep breath, deliberately placing her hands in her lap and relaxing them. When she spoke, her voice sounded steady as a newscaster without much to report. "Yes, I'm fine."

Mitch didn't think he'd ever met a woman with that kind of control. She looked calm now, way too calm, totally at ease. "You really missed your calling," he told her. "Maybe you ought to try acting after all."

She shot him a lazy look and slowly shook her head.

He parked the car on a side street, about half a block from the coffeehouse, then got out and went around to open her door. She exited gracefully showing no hesitation at all in accompanying him wherever he led.

Java Joe's was crowded and getting more so. It was close to noon. Mitch glanced around but didn't see Kick anywhere. A window booth came vacant just as they walked in and he ushered her to it quickly. The windows were tinted so that he could see out, but they would not be visible from anyone passing by. The place was on a corner. With the wraparound windows on two sides, he had a fairly clear view up and down the main drag and also part of the way down the side street.

"Coffee?" he asked.

"Maybe some orange juice," she said as she slid in across from him.

A waitress he knew pretty well came over to take their order. She smiled down at him. "Lunch or breakfast menu?"

"No, just OJ and coffee, thanks." He wondered what had

held Kick up. He could have walked from the precinct in half the time it had taken them to drive here.

They said little, drank their coffee and juice and waited.

Suddenly Robin began to exit of her side of the booth. "Would you excuse me for a minute?" she asked.

He smiled. "The ladies' is that way," he said, pointing toward a small hallway across the room. For a minute he considered escorting her to the door and standing outside it, but knew she would probably decide not to go if he did.

He scanned the room again for anyone who looked unaccountably interested in them. Unfortunately, a number of the men in the place were accountably interested in Robin. She was an incredibly striking woman, very tall and very noticeable.

Mitch kept his own eyes on her as she wove her way through the tables and disappeared down the hallway. He kept watching in case someone got up and followed her.

Julie, the waitress who had taken their order, was delivering a loaded tray to one of the tables situated between Mitch's booth and the rest rooms.

Suddenly, she pitched forward. The entire contents slipped off her tray causing a horrendous crash. She screamed as it happened and tried to catch herself on one of the tables as she went down. It tilted, falling sideways as everyone tried to jump out of the way of splashing liquid and sliding dishes.

Had somebody tripped the girl? He leaped up and forcibly plowed his way through the commotion, needing to get to Robin, to make certain she was all right. The corridor where the bathrooms were located had an exit to the street. Why the hell hadn't he remembered that? Before he even reached the hallway, he heard Robin shrieking like the hounds of hell were attacking.

He rushed into the bathroom. She was inside one of the stalls. "Robin? It's me!" he shouted.

She stopped screaming, fumbled with the latch on the stall

door, yanked it open and rushed out to him, throwing herself into his arms.

"I should never have let you come back here alone," he said, gathering her close. "I forgot about that outside door."

She gulped. Frantic fingers curled into the front of his jacket and for a moment she just held on. Slowly her breathing evened out.

After a few seconds, as if she'd commanded herself to do it, she released him, smoothed down her clothing and swept her hair back behind her ears. She lifted her chin and met his worried gaze with one that appeared totally calm.

"A man snatched my purse," she said.

"Are you hurt?" She obviously wasn't. Mitch noted Robin's uncanny transformation and recognized the pattern that was becoming familiar. All this forced composure was making him crazy. She had to be shaking inside. Hell, *he* was.

She backed away from Mitch as he held out a hand to steady her. "I think he was just a purse snatcher. It's just a co-incidence, that's all."

"Could be." But it wasn't and they both knew it.

"What happened exactly?" he asked.

She sucked in a deep breath and propped one hand on the sink, trying to look casual, he supposed, but really to prevent collapse.

"He followed me in and grabbed me. I bit his hand, slammed my purse in his face and pushed him, then scrambled into the stall. He tried to force the door, but I had latched it. That's when I started screaming. He ran outside, I guess. Didn't you see him?"

"No, he made it out the back door." Mitch removed her hand from the counter, ignoring her jerk of protest and enclosed her fingers in his. They felt like ice. "Come on, let's get out of here. Kick should have arrived by now."

"I screamed as loud as I could," she informed him, holding her ground when he would have led her out of the room. "I know yelling 'Fire' is what they say to do, but I thought everyone might run right out the front door. I tried to draw attention to myself."

"You sure got my attention! I bet they heard you across town. You did exactly the right thing," he told her. "Are you okay now?"

"Yes, of course." She seemed very reluctant to leave the rest room, and Mitch couldn't say he blamed her. Whoever was after the disk was also after her, and she knew it. The man already had the purse when he'd tried to get the stall door open.

"Can't live in here," he told her, pasting on a smile that nearly cracked his face. "Come on, sugar, I promise we'll find you someplace safe to stay."

"Sugar?" she repeated, arching one eyebrow.

"Colloquialism," he explained with a shrug. "No offense intended."

Her cold fingers had laced through his as if behaving of their own accord. "None taken." Mitch doubted she even noticed how tightly she gripped. He hated to let go, but figured he might need that hand if someone was waiting on them outside.

He retrieved his backup weapon from his ankle holster. The .38 was small and fit comfortably in his palm, not even noticeable unless someone looked closely. Robin had watched him palm it, of course, and she *was* looking closely, like the sight of it really bothered her.

"Do you expect them to shoot at us?" she whispered as she followed him out into the hallway.

"No, but stay behind me," he ordered.

Mitch felt sure someone would be outside waiting for them to leave. The spills causing the distraction earlier had been cleared away now and everything was back to business as usual in the coffee shop. Kick was nowhere to be seen.

Backup would be welcome right about now, but Mitch didn't want to hang around any longer than necessary waiting for Kick to show up.

He led the way through the kitchen to a door that opened onto the alley. After he looked both ways and saw no one, he ordered, "Come on. Be quick about it."

They dashed across the alley and he pushed open another door, this one leading into the busy back room of a dry cleaners. The startled employees watched as Mitch dragged Robin through to the front, around the counter and out onto the sidewalk. Hanging a right, he hurried several doors down to a real estate office and entered. He pocketed his gun before anyone saw it and thought he was staging a holdup.

"May I help you?" a helmet-haired lady agent asked him.

Mitch reached for his badge and realized he no longer had it. Damn. "Yes, ma'am. We've seen one of your properties in Brentwood and need to make a deal. Now."

Her face lit up like a Christmas tree. Mitch would have said just about anything to get them into one of the inner offices without causing a fuss that might be noticed from the street. It worked. The woman immediately herded them into her office and closed the door, obviously eager to make that fat commission.

Jane Higgens, as she had introduced herself, offered them a seat, then moved behind her desk. Mitch immediately took out his cell phone and punched Kick's number. Ms. Higgens looked annoyed, and Mitch shot her a look of apology.

"Hey, Kick, where the hell are you?" Mitch demanded when he heard Kick's response.

A short silence ensued. "Stuck in traffic. Where are *you?*" Now *he* sounded annoyed.

"Trying to shake a tail. We need a safe house."

He glanced at Ms. Higgens whose ruby-red lips made a

perfect circle. Robin, on the other hand, appeared totally at ease and unconcerned, as if this were an everyday occurrence. Miss Cool. A visual lie. Her hands were fists, the knuckles white as cotton.

Kick took his time. Mitch shifted in the uncomfortable leather chair. No doubt the search was on for them, now that the perps knew the disk wasn't in Robin's purse. They'd be watching Mitch's car, his house, the precinct, probably even Kick.

"She's a suspect, Mitch, not a witness," Kick said. "I don't think she qualifies for us putting her up at the city's expense, do you? It would be hard to justify." Another interminable pause. "How about my place? You could take her there."

Mitch didn't like the idea, but beggars couldn't be choosers at this point. They needed refuge and they needed it quick.

"That'll do temporarily. Don't meet us there now. Just go back to the precinct and come home when your shift's over like you usually do. Thanks." He clicked off his phone and stowed it in his pocket.

"Ms. Higgens, I'm sorry for the deception. I'm with the police and this lady is in grave danger. We need your help."

She looked at Robin doubtfully, then back at him. "Could I see some identification, please?"

Mitch almost rolled his eyes, but caught himself in time and smiled as charmingly as he could while still looking worried. "I'm undercover and not allowed to carry ID, ma'am. Look, all we need is the back way out of here and your silence if anyone comes asking about us. Can you help me with that?"

She shrugged and sighed as she got up and headed for the door. "This way." Prancing ahead of them on her too-high heels, she ignored the curious look of the receptionist and led them through a storeroom to the alley exit.

While Mitch opened the door a crack to check whether their pursuers were out there, Ms. Higgens tucked her business card in his jacket pocket. "In case you ever really need a house...or anything," she said provocatively. The gesture did not seem business oriented.

Mitch grinned and winked at her, his peripheral vision catching Robin's expression of outrage, quickly suppressed. Jealous? he wondered. Or flabbergasted at the woman's nerve? He didn't dwell on it more than a second before checking the alley again, then taking Robin's reluctant hand and pulling her toward yet another back door.

Robin resisted the urge to huddle down out of sight in the taxi as they zipped through downtown Nashville. The back of her neck tingled as if someone had it in the sights of a gun. Her stomach contracted painfully and she felt sick. This must be what a panic attack felt like. Though she'd never had one, this seemed a logical place to start.

"Don't worry," Mitch told her.

"Right. Why should I worry?" she asked tersely, trying to quell her nerves with anger. She cast a worried look at the cab driver who seemed oblivious to the fact that dangerous people might be following his vehicle.

"We'll be fine." Still, he spent an inordinate amount of time surreptitiously watching the cars around and behind them. She also noticed that he kept one hand in his pocket, no doubt firmly fixed on that small handgun he carried.

The thing looked hardly large enough to do any damage even if he shot someone more than once. She was admittedly curious about it, never having fired a pistol. The only one she'd ever touched was the one that had killed James.

She nudged Mitch's pocket with the back of her hand. "I thought police officers carried something a bit larger."

"We usually do," he admitted, still keeping a vigilant watch on the neighboring cars and trying not to be obvious about it.

"So, where is it now?"

"Boss has it," he murmured. "Don't worry about it. I can take the eye out of a gnat at twenty yards with this little peashooter."

"I'm not worried. I merely wondered."

"You can drop the act, Robin. It's okay to be scared."

Yes, now was the time, she admitted, but she had encountered situations before that had been almost as frightening. Situations when she didn't dare show any evidence of fright. She remained silent now, furious with herself that she had somehow betrayed her fear, her weakness.

"Don't get me wrong," he explained, "I'm glad you aren't hysterical or anything, but a healthy dose of fear can keep you alive in a dicey situation. Trick yourself into thinking you're invincible, and you're toast. Remember that and don't let that pretense of yours lull you into thinking you've got things whipped. Know what I mean?"

No, she had no idea what he meant. There had been times when the pretense had saved her. Some men really got off on a woman's fear and she wasn't about to give one that satisfaction if she could possibly help it. She had slipped a little with Mitch. Just enough so that he had found her out. Now she would have to convince him that any terror she had allowed him to see had been thoroughly conquered.

The taxi finally exited the freeway and entered a residential neighborhood. Mitch had relaxed somewhat and seemed satisfied they were not being followed. He began giving the driver instructions.

They eventually pulled into the driveway of a modern split-level that looked as if it belonged on the California coast. Instead it was nestled in a very upscale suburb where each dwelling occupied at least an acre of perfect landscaping.

"Your partner lives here?" she asked, amazed that a detective, especially such a young one, owned such a place.

"Kick said one of his relatives had money and left him pretty well-off recently."

"So why is he still doing what he does?" she asked.

"Dedicated, I guess," Mitch said. Kick had gone from poor to rich practically overnight and did flaunt it a little. Still, he remained serious about the job. Sometimes *too* serious.

The man was hard to get to know. Instead of the close relationship that usually existed between partners on the force, Mitch and Kick had a sort of surface friendship. They joked around with each other the way all the guys did, but there was still a reserve there Mitch couldn't seem to break down. They'd probably never be tight the way partners ought to be. Sometimes it worked out that way, but it would be a first for Mitch.

He'd keep working on Kick, trying to loosen him up a little, find some common ground. This offering his home to Mitch when a safe place was needed seemed a sign that the kid was coming around after all.

Chapter 8

Robin started to open her door, but felt Mitch grab her arm.

"You know what?" he asked. "I think this is a really bad idea, us staying here."

"Why? You think whoever is after me might be watching Detective Taylor's house?"

He paused, looked out the window at the surrounding grounds. His eyes were narrowed, assessing the place as if he'd never seen it before. "I don't know why. Can't put my finger on it, but I just don't think this is a wise move." Without any further explanation, he raised his voice to the driver. "Let's go."

"Where to?" the cabbie asked as he turned around to drive out.

"Just drive. Out of town. Take I-65 South."

Robin watched out her window as Nashville flew by. Compared to New York, the buildings sat low on the landscape, sprawled lazily as if the city had all the room in the world to grow. Maybe it did. She had never seen the outskirts or whether anything confined it in any way. "Do you know where we're going?" she asked in a near whisper.

"I'm thinking."

She left him alone and let him do that while she tried to figure out why he hadn't taken his partner up on the invitation to stay at his house.

When they had cleared the city Mitch got his phone out again and dialed. "Calling the boss," he explained to her, then turned his attention to the phone. "Captain Hunford, please." A short pause followed. "Hey, Cap, this is Winton. Thought I'd better check in with you. Ms. Andrews is still with me... Yes, sir, I remember what you said. Look, when you see Kick, tell him I said thanks but I made my own arrangements. We're going out of town."

He listened to the reply, making a face at Robin, probably indicating his boss was not pleased with this turn of events. "Yeah, we'll be back by then." He clicked the off button and stuck the phone in his pocket.

"You didn't explain about the attack in the diner," she accused. "Why not? And why didn't you tell him about the man who stole my purse and tried to get at me?"

"Because he would say it was a random robbery at Dylan's. That's a rough neighborhood, anyway. Stuff like that happens all the time. Same with the purse snatcher. Could have been a crime of opportunity. The guy saw you enter the rest room with a purse on your shoulder. Not many people around. He went for it."

"Bull."

"Right. But you sort of had to be there to determine that, y'know? On the surface both incidents look pretty commonplace. Unrelated to what happened to your husband. You and I realize that's not the case, but Hunford might not see it that way. Neither would Kick."

"You don't trust either of them, do you?"

He sighed and stared out the window. "I need to think about it. We're dealing with something big here, Robin. Probably even bigger than murder. And to tell you the truth, I don't know who we should trust. Nobody but Hunford knew where I was taking you when we left the precinct. And only Kick knew we were headed for the coffee shop today. I know I shook our shadow before we got there."

The driver kept looking in the rearview mirror as if waiting for further instructions.

Eventually Mitch told him to take an upcoming exit where they ended their ride at a convenience store and gas station. Mitch paid the fare, then headed for the pay phone.

A few minutes later he rejoined her. "We'll need some toiletries and a couple of those T-shirts over there," he told her. "Why don't you pick out some while I get the other stuff?" He grinned. "Looks like it's your day to shop."

Robin did as she was told, wondering all the while where this was leading. Even if she asked him where they were going and he told her, it wouldn't mean a thing. She had no clue where they were now and wasn't acquainted with anything in this area.

He answered her unspoken question after he had paid for the items and they exited the store. "We're going fishing," he explained. "You ever fish?"

Robin slowly shook her head.

"Nathan will be here in a few minutes. He's taking us to the river. There's this fishing camp."

"The river," she repeated, trying not to scoff, entertaining some not so pleasant visions of camping in a zip-up tent on a muddy bank and slapping at mosquitoes. "What about the disk? Shouldn't we give it to someone?"

"I've got a friend, Damien Perry. He used to be with the FBI and still has contacts. When we get back, I'll give him a call. He speaks several languages. One of them might be Russian. At least he can tell me who we should go to with what we have."

"Who is this Nathan who's coming to get us?"

"Another friend. Lives a couple of miles from here," he said, his gaze on the road opposite the way they had come. "I arrested him once. He owes me a favor. That looks like his pickup now," Mitch said, pointing at a rust-colored vehicle in the distance.

"Oh, joy," Robin muttered darkly. In what way would a criminal repay having been arrested? However the man intended to reward Mitch, he seemed in a devilish hurry to do so. And drivers of these trucks traveled armed to the teeth, didn't they?

The dilapidated vehicle roared up to the station and parked beside a pump. The man climbing out was every yankee's nightmare, Robin thought. "My God, he's right out of *Deliverance*."

Mitch laughed out loud and took her by the arm, guiding her toward the three-hundred-pound gorilla. Sure enough, there was a three-tiered gun rack in the truck, though there was only one weapon visible. One seemed enough to Robin.

"Hey, Nate! What's happenin'?" Mitch greeted the man, slapping him on the shoulder, shaking his hand as if they were long-lost brothers. "Did I wake you up?"

The giant grinned, showing a missing eyetooth and others that looked in grave peril. "Naw, I was just cuttin' me a bear."

Mitch inclined his head to her and said in a mock whisper. "Nate's a sculptor. Uses a chain saw."

"Oh...well, that's...great." Robin wondered if there was a way back up the rabbit hole she had fallen into. "Hello, Nathan."

She tried not to stare at his hair. It was curly, long and caught up with a rubber band on top to keep it out of his eyes. It was mostly gray, though he couldn't have been much past thirty. His skin was pockmarked as if he'd suffered a terrible case of acne. Someone had broken his nose, flattened it, really. He wore a plaid flannel shirt unbuttoned and hanging loose over a once black, now gray, T-shirt with a horizontally stretched motorcycle logo on the front. Robin figured you could probably read a newspaper through the fabric it was so thin. His well-worn, dirt-smudged jeans rode low beneath his tremendous belly. She could imagine cleavage showing in the rear. The indentation of his navel, at the bottom edge of his shirt flirted with the open air. Scuffed, round-toed boots completed his outfit. He might have modeled for *Bubba Monthly*.

"Pleased to meet ya, ma'am," Nathan said, his voice surprisingly gentle and well mannered. He raked her with what appeared to be an appreciative look, though it didn't seem lecherous. His eyes were kind. "She a cop?" he asked Mitch.

"Nope, she's a friend." Mitch reached in his pocket, pulled out his wallet and handed Nathan a twenty. "For gas," he said.

Nate pocketed the money with a nod and proceeded to disconnect the gas pump nozzle from his tank. "The cabins is all vacant so you can have whichever one you want."

Mitch smiled at Robin. "How about that? We're in luck."

"Right. Lucky us."

While Nathan went inside to pay for the gas, Mitch walked her around to the passenger side of the truck and opened the door. Robin knew she had little choice but to get in and spend the duration of the trip sandwiched between Mitch and the chain saw sculptor.

"Hold that for me?" Nathan asked with a wide smile when he returned and opened the truck's door on the driver's side. Without waiting for her answer, he gingerly placed a cold six-pack of beer in her lap.

Robin politely declined when Nathan offered her a stick of chewing gum. He unwrapped several and folded them into his mouth, squeezed his frame behind the steering wheel and twisted the key with fingers that looked like dirty bratwursts. Nathan smelled of wood shavings and fish. At least there was no foul body odor.

"You like squirrels?" he drawled, popping the gum.

"Me?" she asked, looking up at him, and she did have to look up. He was very tall, even taller than Mitch.

"Yes, ma'am." His attention remained mostly on the road as he drove, but Robin was very aware of his interest in her.

"I don't really know," she replied to the squirrel question.

"I got one I'll give you," he said. "You'll like it."

Robin darted a look at Mitch, who wore a benign smile, as if nothing out of the ordinary had been said.

After jouncing around on rutted pathways through what seemed a jungle, they finally arrived at a grouping of modest little cabins built of cinder blocks, all painted chocolate brown. The shutters and woodwork were bottle green.

"We'll take the one at the far end," Mitch told Nathan. "Probably be here about two or three days. I'll send you a check for it when I get home. That okay?"

"Sure. Y'all need anything, just come on up to the house and get it. If I ain't there, I'll be down at Peggy's. Just go on in." He took the beer from Robin. "I'll bring that squirrel by in the morning. Got a little work to do on'er yet."

Robin nodded, wondering what one did to a squirrel to get her up to par. She dearly hoped he was talking about one of his sculptures and not the real thing.

* * *

The thick woods they had traveled through backed the row of six tiny structures and one large one that sat well away from the rest. Nathan's house, Robin guessed. He proved her right by heading off toward it with a backward wave of one hand, the other clutching his six-pack. Beside his front door a huge figure of an Indian stood guard. It had been hacked out of a log. Chain saw art had a certain rustic charm.

"What did you arrest him for?" she asked Mitch.

"Trumped-up charge of drunk and disorderly. He was planning to fight Peggy's old boyfriend who was due home that evening from a stint in the army. See, Nate used to be a boxer. If he had killed Tommy, it would have been murder." Mitch made a fist. "Lethal weapons."

"Did he resist arrest?"

Mitch laughed. "No. We got him drunk first. He went like a lamb. By the time he'd sobered up and we cut him loose, Tommy had said his hello to Peggy and left for...Montana, I think it was."

Robin didn't blame Tommy at all. Montana sounded good.

Mitch pushed open the door to the last cabin and entered first. "Looks okay. Come on in."

The place surprised her with its cleanliness. Plaid café curtains covered the windows, and there were matching spreads on the two sets of bunk beds.

"Indoor plumbing," Robin muttered as she checked out the interior of the boxy little unit Mitch had chosen.

One large room served as the living and dining area and contained a tiny kitchen set into one corner. Built into another corner of the square floor plan was a small bathroom and closet. She explored, opening the doors and checking out the cabinets.

Linens, paper products and cookware were furnished, but there was no food. "What do we eat?"

Mitch stowed the items he had bought at the gas station shoppette. "We have soup and crackers," he said holding up a can. "Beans," he added, "and cookies."

Robin rolled her eyes, stifling a cutting remark about his unhealthy choices. Secretly, however, she sort of anticipated eating what he had bought and was glad he'd left her no alternative. Especially for those cookies.

"Nate will have potatoes, meal, oil, soft drinks and whatever else we need. He keeps a sort of store with things people need to cook fish. Also has bait."

"Worms," Robin said, making a face.

"Want to go catch dinner?" he asked, thumping the cabinet door closed. "I'll borrow some rods. We can fish off the jetty."

"What's a jetty?" she asked, truly curious. "It's not a boat is it? Tell me it's not a boat. I do not like open water."

"Come on, city slicker, I'll show you," he said, holding out his hand. Reluctantly she took it and followed him back outside.

"All this fresh air," she said, taking a deep breath and then another. It smelled damp and vaguely like mildew, Robin decided, rethinking her need to indulge herself in it.

He walked her across grass splotched liberally with weeds and onto a long, weathered dock that stretched over the water and rested on stilts. Waves lapped at the pilings just below the surface of the boards.

The fishing camp was located on a section of bank that curved in, a sort of bay, that began with the dock, or jetty, and formed a semicircle that reached well beyond the far end of the camp where Nathan's house stood. She could just imagine Nathan and his screaming saw hewing out the trees and creating a clearing for this place.

"River's high," Mitch commented, looking out across the

expanse of water. The opposite side was not visible but hidden by thickly treed islands that blocked the view.

"This so isn't me," Robin mumbled to herself.

"I know, hon, but it'll do for a couple of days, won't it? It was this or involve family, which I didn't want to do."

"No, no, of course not. I completely understand. It's fine."

He went on. "Damien and Molly have little kids. I didn't want to go there, maybe put them at risk. If we'd gone to a motel, I'd have had to use a credit card. Easy to trace us, then. I was afraid somebody might be picking up transmissions from Kick's cell phone and would know we were at his house. I can't decide how else anyone would have known where to find us to get your purse."

Robin nodded. "Makes sense."

He laced his fingers through hers and turned back toward the cabin, walking slowly, looking at the ground as he spoke. "Let's stay here awhile just in case. If they're going to look for you at Kick's, they'll do it in the next day or so. When it's time for the inquest, it should be safe to head back and go to his place. Meanwhile, nobody knows where we are but Nate."

"And he wouldn't tell even if someone asked," she guessed.

Mitch shook his head. "No. Nate and I have been friends since we were kids."

Now that surprised her. "You're serious?"

He sat down on the edge of the porch and indicated she should do the same. "Nate's had a rough time over the years and looks a little ragged around the edges, I know. But he has a good heart, Robin. He'd do anything in the world for me just as I would for him."

This sort of loyalty and longstanding friendship was foreign to Robin, but she had to trust that Mitch knew what he was talking about. It gave her yet another view of him, this time of a man who had cultivated a very eclectic set of friends.

There was that former FBI guy who was also a lawyer, whom Mitch said would be glad to help him out. And Nate, who seemed to be on the other end of the spectrum, an undereducated ex-boxer who carved bears and Indians.

Yes, she was Alice, and Nashville was Wonderland.

"This will be fine," she told Mitch. "I can adapt."

"I believe you will." His beam of approval did strange things to her insides. She leaned against the log column that supported the porch and took a deep breath to calm her nerves. It was peaceful here and she imagined she would get used to the smell of fresh air.

Mitch absolutely reveled in teasing her. He liked to think it was to provide a distraction, so she wouldn't be worried about the disk and who was after it, but he knew better.

Robin was just so susceptible to jokes and so totally unpredictable about how she reacted to them.

"Nate modeled this one from life," he told her, resting one hand on the fierce, blocky statue of the bear that dominated a backyard filled with sawdust.

"He did not."

"Oh, yeah. Kept the ol' fella chained up over there by that tree. He finished getting a likeness, then turned him loose."

She looked at him askance, then surveyed the surrounding woods. "He let it go?"

"Sure did. Big mistake, too. The brute ate a fisherman who'd come up from South Georgia. Polished off his day's catch for dessert. Nate advises everybody to put food out in the woods every night to keep the bears from breaking into the cabins."

"You liar. There are no bears," she declared, her laugh a little nervous. "And, anyway, bears don't eat people!" A small hesitation. "Do they? I mean, I realize they must bite, but..."

He shrugged. "They *are* carnivorous. Check it out. This is

part of a wildlife refuge, and they say the bears are multiply-ing like rabbits around here." He walked over to the edge of the woods where the ground was clear and pointed down. "See there?"

Frowning, she peered down at the huge paw prints he had made earlier by adding "claws" to footprints Nate had left there. After a short perusal, she straightened and glanced to-ward their cabin. "Well, leave the food if it's necessary," she said, her tone matter-of-fact. She was walking fast, not run-ning, trying hard to conceal her haste in getting away from the bear signs. "But don't leave the cookies. Sugar can't be good for them."

Mitch hid a smile. She'd acquired an addiction to Oreos and rationed them like a smoker would the last pack of ciga-rettes.

The two days they spent at Nate's camp would have been perfect if not for his overactive hormones. Seeing her clad only in that tacky orange T-shirt when she was ready for bed made him...well, ready for bed. But certainly not for sleep. He knew he was going to be seriously sleep deprived when they left.

She, on the other hand, bloomed in the wilderness like a wild violet. The absence of makeup, the slight two-day tan and the couple of pounds she had gained gave her a healthy glow.

"There's an outdoorsy person in you," he teased, pinching her determined chin. "And she *likes* it here."

Robin angled her head away from his touch. "And she will be damned glad to return to civilization! Air-conditioning! Dishwashers! Restaurants!"

"You don't like cleaning fish?" he asked innocently, watch-ing with interest as she mangled her attempt at the chore.

Her glare should have slain him on the spot. Mitch laughed and took over before she sliced him up with the filet knife.

He could have stayed here with her forever and been completely happy. Well, happy if he thought they could *really* be together, which he knew was a fantasy. Staying three days was pushing his luck. Hunford or Kick, himself, would put out an APB on her if Mitch didn't return her as promised.

"We'll be in tonight," he told Hunford on the phone during his daily call in. But he didn't tell him exactly where they would be going. He stowed the phone and spoke to Robin. "I guess we have to go."

Did he imagine he saw a flash of disappointment in her eyes before she lowered them? Maybe it was only fear of giving up the safety of the camp.

"I should call Damien. We need to get that disk turned in."

She looked as if she wanted to say something about that.

"What is it?"

"Never mind. You're right, I guess."

But Mitch knew she had been about to suggest something else.

As if by mutual agreement, neither of them had discussed either the disk or the case since coming here. She had needed to get away, to get rid of some of that fear that kept her so tense.

Much as he would love to shield her from it and avoid it himself, he knew they had to go back and face the music.

"So, where to? Detective Taylor's house?" she asked.

"That's the plan. He did offer."

Chapter 9

Robin allowed Mitch to assist her out of the truck. "Good-bye, Nathan. Thanks for the squirrel." She clutched the small, carefully hand-carved animal to her chest and smiled at Mitch's friend. "I love it."

Nathan beamed, the gap in his teeth not objectionable at all, now that she was used to looking at him.

"Aw, it ain't nothin'," he said, ducking his head.

"It's something to *me,* Nathan," she said, meaning every word. The man did have talent. Mitch was right. Nathan was more than he seemed at first glance. A regular Gentle Ben. Bear guy. Eccentric artist and sometime pugilist.

She assessed Detective Taylor's house and grounds as Mitch made his farewell and waved Nathan off.

Then to her surprise, Mitch led her around to the back of the house, took a credit card from his wallet and promptly

pened a door with it. She'd read about people doing that and
ad seen it done on TV, but was stunned that a member of the
olice force had so little security at his own home.

It helped immensely when she saw Mitch open a metal box
ist inside the doorway and punch in a numbered code to shut
ff an alarm system. "Top of the line," Mitch told her. "In-
talled it myself for him." He flipped on the cold fluorescent
ghts.

"That was nice of you. I remember you discussing that
ilent alarm with the waitress at Dylan's Diner. Do you have
tock in an alarm company, by any chance?" she asked.

He nodded as he closed the little door on the alarm hous-
1g. "In a way. Pop owns one. I get discounts for friends."

She considered the sterile kitchen that looked as if it had
ever been used. Stainless steel everywhere. Extremely mod-
rn. No homelike touches, no curtains, no color.

They walked through the dining room and into the living
rea. Again, sleek lines, monochromatic, functional furniture
1at looked incredibly uncomfortable. She wished for the cab-
age roses and potpourri of the other borrowed apartment.
This gives me the creeps," she muttered.

She was unaware that she'd spoken out loud until Mitch
1ughed. "Me, too. As for the decor, Kick was...uh, dating...an
nterior decorator for a while there."

"Her first job, no doubt," Robin said. "I believe I like
Jathan's taste more than hers."

He chuckled again and tossed the plastic bag containing
1eir toiletries and extra shirts onto one of the Eames-style
hairs. "Well, make yourself at home as much as you're able.
have to make a call." He pointed to a corridor leading off
1e living room. "Find us a couple of bedrooms. Kick's is the
irst one on the right. I wouldn't open that door unless your
hots are up to date."

He flopped down on the sleek sofa and pulled out hi
phone.

Since he'd said that about the bedroom, she had to look
of course. She twisted the knob and peeked inside his part
ner's room. Just as quickly she closed the door. Mitch wa
right. Calling the room a mess would have been kind.

It made her wonder just what sort of man Kick Taylor wa
Definitely one who prized outward appearances and kept hi
slovenliness a closely confined secret. She would bet he too
his women to one of the other bedrooms when he brough
them home.

"Told you so," Mitch called to her.

Robin sauntered back to the living room. "You think yo
know me so well, don't you?"

"Better than you think. I knew you'd look," he quipped a
he met her gaze with one of amusement.

"All right. I admit to being curious. I simply wanted to se
how he *really* lives," she said in defense of her snooping
"That says a lot about a guy."

"Difference between Kick and me is that he likes to put u
a good front. In my case, what you see when you walk in th
door is pretty much what you get."

Yes, and that seemed very significant to Robin. Mitch Win
ton was an open book. True, she hadn't seen all the pages ye
but they were there for her to turn if she wanted to. Peopl
who deliberately hid their faults from the world made her un
easy. It was exactly what she did.

"How long has Detective Taylor been your partner?"

"Not long. He got a promotion and transferred over from Vic
a few months ago when he made sergeant. Why?" He frowned

"He seems very...eager," she commented.

"Yeah, I guess," Mitch said with a humorless laugh. "He'
outgrow that, believe me."

Robin feared that might not happen soon enough to help her. Kick Taylor had made it clear he believed she had killed James.

"He thinks I'm guilty," she said.

"Maybe not anymore," Mitch said. "He has to be wondering why somebody stole your computer and suitcase from the crime scene and is now chasing you around town."

"He doesn't know about the disk yet," Robin reminded him. "That might convince him I'm not the only one who could have done it."

"I'd like to run it by Damien first, I think." He looked at the phone and back at Robin. "I think that's our best bet."

Mitch made the call but got Damien's answering machine. Saying that you had a disk with several pages of Russian on it that people were willing to shoot you for was not a message to leave anywhere. He decided to try again later.

The name he had recognized on the disk really bothered Mitch. Rake Somers he had known for a long time. The man was crooked as a dog's hind leg, but no one had been able to pin anything specific on him.

Mitch had had one run-in with Somers soon after coming over to Homicide. A body had turned up down at Mose Landing, the victim a former chauffeur of Rake's who had just rolled over as a paid informant. He'd died wearing his wire. No doubt Somers had ordered the hit. But there wasn't a shred of proof linking him to it.

Vice had Somers under surveillance most of the time, but he always seemed to come up squeaky clean. It was rumored the feds were investigating him, too, hoping to implicate him in a highly organized shoplifting racket that covered three or four states. So far, no one had gotten lucky.

The killing of James Andrews *was* probably due to rage,

as Mitch had first suspected. Andrews refused to give over the disk with the numbers of the accounts he'd set up and got popped for it. Somers wouldn't have handled that personally, of course. If another body turned up, Mitch wouldn't be surprised. The shooter had made a bad mistake, not getting his hands on that disk first.

Until the firing board gave clearance, there wouldn't be anything official Mitch could do. About the most he could hope for was to compile enough information to clear Robin and redirect the suspicion where it belonged.

The pizza he had ordered and shared with Robin felt like fire in his stomach. Probably getting an ulcer.

Robin had excused herself to shower. Mitch looked up as she wandered into the room, toweling her hair, wearing the same clothes she had worn before. No makeup. That had been in her purse. Amazing how young she looked without that subtle mask of cosmetics. And how beautiful.

"Find everything you needed?" he asked.

She nodded and took the chair nearest where he sat on the sofa. "Did you figure out any of that?" she asked, looking at the page he was holding.

"Are you sure you don't know any of these people?"

"Never heard of them, I swear," she replied. For a while she was silent as if mulling over something. Then she sat forward and asked him earnestly, "Mitch, would you trust me to work on this? I mean, really work on it."

"What do you mean? How?"

"Instead of giving that to your friend or your partner today, get me a computer. All I need is a few hours. Maybe less. Let me see what I can find out?"

He looked down at the list and back up at her. "Something you haven't told me yet, Robin?"

"Maybe...there are programs I could access."

"Hack, you mean?"

Her shrug was as good as an admission. "I was just thinking that the bureaucracy might slow this down if you turn it over."

"And that won't happen if you do it yourself," he said, tongue in cheek.

"Well, no." She faced him squarely, her gaze intent. "You can watch over my shoulder. Give me a shot at it first?"

"Robin, be straight with me, please. Do you know something about this that you haven't told me?"

"No. But I've been thinking about something James mentioned casually—almost too casually now that I think about it—when he called me about bringing the disk. I thought then it was simply idle conversation, but now I'm not certain it was. He was planning a vacation." She raised one beautifully shaped brow and tilted her head in question. "Want to guess where?"

"Russia?"

"No. He mentioned George Town," she said with a quirk of her eyebrow. "That's in the islands. The Caymans."

"Numbered offshore accounts," Mitch said. "Well, that's what we suspected all along. No big surprise there."

"I know, but the only way James could have gotten the numbers is if he set them up *for* these people."

"Then he was to give the numbers to the individuals on the list. They wouldn't need to use their names, only the codes to access their accounts."

"Accounts he could easily access himself," she said.

"Maybe he did. So why was the disk in New York in the safety deposit box? Why not here in Nashville?"

She shrugged. "I have no idea unless he figured that was the last place in the world anyone would expect him to put it."

"In a locked box his wife had access to," Mitch guessed.

"Exactly. Maybe he was holding those numbers ransom or

something, trying to extort more money for himself. But first of all, we need to find out if these really *are* numbered accounts, don't you think?"

"Can you do that?" he asked, his suspicion mounting. Why would she want to involve herself this way?

"I can try. No promises. If I'm successful, this could establish that someone else had a motive to kill James."

"Besides yourself," Mitch reminded her. "All right, I'm game. We'll give it a shot and see what you come up with. What about the other file?"

"Nothing I can do about that," she told him. "I suppose I could get an online translation, but what if the information on it shouldn't be broadcast anywhere? I think we'd better leave that to your friend."

He'd been watching for a sign that she lied and saw no real indication that she was. No telltale fidgets or glancing away to the left or arms crossing over her chest. Her breathing looked even, regular, her eyes totally untroubled as her gaze met his. *Deliberately* met his, as if she knew it had to or he wouldn't believe her.

That bothered him. The cloak of composure she threw on every once in a while could probably conceal most anything she wanted to hide. He wanted to rip it off, get down to some honest feelings, at least, even if she wasn't keeping secrets associated with the murder. Now might be the best time.

He laid the paper aside. "First, I need you to tell me more about Andrews. About your marriage."

Her lips worked as she raked them with her teeth. Slowly, as if she were thinking, not rapidly as if his demand made her nervous. A tremulous smile replaced the tic, and her gaze softened. "James was...considerate."

"Considerate? He cheated on you, Robin," Mitch reminded her.

She shrugged that off as if it didn't matter. He had the feeling that it really didn't. She hadn't loved the man.

"You were more friends than lovers, even during your marriage," he guessed. Not a stretch, since she had all but said so before.

"Yes. Friends. I was coming out of a bad relationship. He helped me through that. A sort of attraction developed between us. Nothing earthshaking, but it was, I guess you'd say, comfortable. For both of us, I think. At least for a while."

Mitch resisted the urge to scoff. He just couldn't imagine marrying anybody on those terms. "So when he decided he wanted to get out of the marriage, he began to cheat? You said you thought he planned for you to find out?"

She looked sad, shook her head a little, but agreed with him. "He admitted that. The clues were pretty thick on the ground." Her small laugh sounded just a tiny bit angry. "Receipts for jewelry and flowers. He left them in his pockets where I'd be sure to find them when I took his clothes to the cleaners. Hang-up phone calls when I would answer. That sort of thing." She flipped one hand lazily as if she hadn't minded much.

"Was everything else...satisfactory? Sex, I mean." God, he hadn't wanted to ask that. *Why* had he asked that?

Her fake smile faltered. "Not really. Do we have to talk about this?"

"It's as good a time as any to get it out of the way. I don't like it any more than you do, but if I don't ask you, somebody probably will. The autopsy is tomorrow and the inquest will be held later this week. It's a sure bet it will be classified a murder and you will be asked about your relationship with the victim. In detail. So far you're the only suspect, though I don't think there's enough for an indictment. Be warned, that could change as the evidence comes in."

Fear rippled through her visibly before she could contai
it. Mitch felt like a heel, but he needed to learn more if he wa
going to help her. "Robin, look at me."

She did.

"Tell me what I need to know. I'll do everything within m
power to get this mess cleared up. If you don't, I can't help.

For a long time she just looked at him as if trying to se
whether he meant business. Then she gave a resigned nod.

Robin took a deep breath and tried to organize he
thoughts. How much would Mitch need to know? What wa
important and what could she safely withhold?

He sat on the sofa across from her, leaning forward, elbow
on his knees and hands clasped between them. The casual wa
he was dressed, the lock of hair that tumbled over his fore
head and his friendly encouragement could almost make he
forget he was a detective, that he still must suspect her o
being somehow involved in James's death.

Justifiably so, maybe, since he now knew she'd possesse
an excellent motive. She could hardly blame him for doin,
what he was trained to do. But it hurt to think he could stil
believe her capable of murdering her husband.

He looked sympathetic, maybe only a ploy to gain her trus
Or maybe he really did sympathize. So far he hadn't thrown he
any curves. He had been honest with her as far as she could tel

"You said you were in a bad relationship before you mar
ried James?"

She nodded and released a sigh, only then realizing she'
been holding her breath. "With Troy Mathison, a male mode
I had met six months before in one of the charity shows." Sh
interrupted her tale to explain, "I had done very little model
ing for about six years, only in special events like benefits
when my former agent called a favor."

"I see. Was Mathison a full-time model?" Mitch asked.

"Yes, and doing very well at it. Mostly magazines, catalogs, but only the occasional runway gig. He initiated our first conversation, indicated that we had a lot in common. It seemed we did at first. I soon found he was not quite as...congenial as he appeared. Our affair didn't last very long."

Robin rushed on, hoping that if she hurried through it, he would ask fewer questions. "After a whirlwind courtship, if you could call it that, Troy moved in with me. I'm still not sure how he accomplished that. I had always lived alone. Preferred it."

She forced a smile. "It didn't work out. He was self-centered, thoughtless, not at all the man I had thought he was. In less than two weeks I asked him to move out. He refused."

Mitch was frowning at her. "What did you do then?"

"Threatened to call the police. Troy laughed."

"And?"

"I called them and they made him leave. He was horribly embarrassed and angry that I followed through with the threat. He began to harass me, disrupting my life any way that he could. Even the restraining order didn't help."

"But James Andrews did," Mitch guessed.

"Yes. He lived in my apartment building. We had known each other for several years. Had dinner occasionally. I watered his plants and brought in his mail when he was away on business."

"Insurance?" Mitch asked, one eyebrow raised. "That took him away from home a lot?"

She had never thought about that until today. "I supposed the trips were business. I didn't ask and he didn't say. He looked after my apartment for me when I went to Florida to visit my mother. As I told you, James and I were friends. Neighbors."

"So you married him for protection?"

His question held a note of disbelief or censure. It was hard to tell. Mitch was wearing his detective face which revealed very little of what he was thinking.

"No, that's not true! Well, not precisely. He began coming over every evening, answering my phone, giving the impression to outsiders that he had replaced Troy, if you know what I mean. He even slept on my sofa when the calls began coming in the night."

"So you trusted him that much."

Robin bit her lip, unwilling to admit that she had slept with her bedroom door locked. "Eventually."

"He suggested the marriage?"

She nodded. "I refused at first. We didn't know each other quite that well. Then he began what he called his campaign to win me. It was...flattering."

How could she explain to Mitch that she had never actually been courted that way? Men had always just assumed she was fair game since she was a model.

"James respected me. He always said he liked me for myself."

Mitch smiled. His expression seemed forced. "That unusual?"

"In my line of work? Yes. When you appear wearing revealing clothes in fashion magazines and strut braless on the runway, some men just naturally assume you will hire out for anything."

He looked away, focusing out the window. "You make it sound like hooking or somethin'."

She sighed and shook her head. "Not that different. We're all selling *something,* Mitch. I was peddling my body, just in a different way. It's almost as degrading, sometimes as dangerous."

"That why you live like a recluse now?"

That hit too close to home to suit Robin. She didn't answer.

He took another tack. "Okay, so you finally took him up on his offer, married him and you moved in together. His place?"

"No, mine."

"You split the expense?"

"What does that have to do with anything? He was helping me."

She watched as he sat back and ran a hand through his hair, blowing out a breath of what appeared to be frustration. Robin liked it when he dropped out of professional mode and let her see the man behind the detective.

Strange how everyone had these masks they wore. She had grown so tired of hers, she had all but abandoned it in favor of seclusion so she could be herself. That must be why it slipped so often now. Practice was required to keep it in place, she guessed, and resented the necessity of it.

It was several minutes before he resumed his questions. "Did he ever discuss his work with you? Surely you talked about how your days went."

Robin thought back. "No, not really. We mainly spoke of art, the theater, the news, books. That sort of thing." Wasn't that strange? For the first time she considered how impersonal her conversations with James had been. Even sex between them had never gone beyond a minimum level of intimacy. Sad.

Her thoughts must have been reflected in her expression because Mitch leaned forward again, this time far enough to touch her hand. "Robin, I know this is hard. You want to take a break?"

His concern felt real. "There's very little else I can tell you. James *was* kind. He was my friend when I needed one. His affairs were as much my fault as his and only his way of exiting a relationship—a marriage—that was a mistake from the beginning. We did talk about that and agreed to part amicably."

"Big of you."

She decided to reveal something she had only recently admitted to herself. "You see, I could never give James what he deserved as a husband. It simply is not in my nature to love. It's not in me."

He laughed, a bitter sound. "Bull! The man used you, Robin. You trusted him and he used you. You gave him a home, paid his bills. Knowing his kind, I bet you a dollar to a doughnut he talked you into making a few investments, right?"

She frowned, her anger welling up inside her. She tamped it down. "Do you think I amassed what I have by doling it out to every man who bought me roses? I'm not stupid!"

"You refused to let him manage your money?"

"Of course I did. James said he had a degree in business management and assured me he knew what he was doing. However," she said, deliberately pausing to get his attention, "so did I."

"Bet he loved that," Mitch said with a smirk. It was almost as if it didn't surprise him at all. "Was he mad?"

"He was livid, but I..." The truth dawned as suddenly as her fury had struck. "That's it!" She grabbed Mitch's hand. "That's why he...I never made the connection before. Soon after that's when things started to fall apart with us."

Her breath came in short puffs as the time frame of his affairs fell into synch with their disagreement over her portfolio and liquid assets.

"Not so kind after all, was he?" Mitch grumbled. "I almost wish he was still alive so I could choke the bastard."

"I didn't kill him, Mitch," Robin vowed.

"Okay," he said easily, squeezing her hands gently, seeming distracted by all she had said. "Did he ever name a project, any specific deal he wanted to sink your funds into?"

"No. He just swore he could triple my investment. Do you suppose that's what he did with those men on the list? Invested for them?"

"Maybe. How much did he want you to fork over?"
Robin hesitated.

"Come on, honey. Do you think I'm after your little pot of gold? I've never taken a dime from a woman in my life. How much?"

"Half a million," Robin mumbled.

His eyes rounded. "Jesus! You have...?"

"No. He assumed that was all I had."

For a moment he was speechless. Then he croaked. "More?"

Robin nodded. "Close to two, but most of it's not readily accessible. Some is in a trust for my mother, some in stocks, the rest in a special account. I live on the interest."

"But you still work."

"Of course I work. I tried sitting around all day watching soaps or chatting online, but that's boring. I have to do *something*. And what I have saved isn't really that much when you think about it."

He shot her a look of profound disbelief. "Give me a minute here. This takes gettin' used to, okay? You want a drink?"

Robin nodded. "That would be nice. Do you think Detective Taylor has any white wine?"

He shook his head a little as he released her hands and got up slowly. "I'll go and see."

She knew she had irrevocably changed the way Mitch Winton saw her, and regretted the fact. He would treat her differently now. He would either keep his distance so she wouldn't believe him a fortune hunter, or he would pull out all the stops and go after her money like a mongoose after snakes. In any case, Robin felt she had lost something potentially valuable.

For a while she had been plain Robin Andrews, a woman from New York in a bad situation and needing his help. A woman he was attracted to in spite of himself. The only man with honest-to-God principles she had been close to since she could remember. But then again she realized she could be wrong about Mitch. She certainly had been wrong before.

* * *

Mitch braced one hand against the counter beside the re-frigerator and contemplated the bottle of unopened wine. *She was a millionaire.*

If nothing else, that sure let out ol' James's life insurance as a motive. But it also put Robin in the position to hire some-one to shoot him. If she'd done that, though, surely she would be flitting around New York with alibis up the wazoo, not stumbling over Andrews's body down here in Nashville, po-tentially incriminating herself.

Or maybe she had come to finish what her husband had begun and try to squeeze more out of Somers and the oth-ers. Some people thought they never had enough money. Mitch figured James Andrews must have either made in-vestments and/or set up offshore accounts for the people on the list, then got a little greedy and demanded more of a per-centage than first agreed on. The pages in Russian worried him even more. Foreign espionage? More likely, the Red mafia in New York.

Not that Mitch really believed Robin was mixed up in that. He only reminded himself once again that she could be, and that he had to recognize the possibility. Damned hard that was, too, since she raised his temperature several degrees every time he looked at her. He'd probably need blood-pressure medicine if she stuck around for long.

God, this was making him feel sick. He wanted her so bad he could taste it, but that was out of the question now.

Just when he'd given himself permission to ask if maybe he could see her again after all this was solved and settled, she pulled the rug right out from under him. Rich. Damn. And maybe playing him like a fish.

She'd just blown his mind completely with the news that she was wealthy. Models—good ones, at least—did make a fortune, he had heard. Weird that he couldn't recall having seen her in magazines, but maybe not so strange. He didn't spend a lot of time reading *Vogue* or whatever. Maybe she looked different now or had made most of her money on the runway instead of in the mags.

He guessed it didn't matter in the long run. She had no reason to lie about the money she'd made. It would be easy enough to check her financial situation and she would know that. Kick had probably done it already.

And where the hell was Kick, anyway? He should have been home an hour ago.

He yanked open several drawers until he found a corkscrew. "Just like at the country club," he muttered through his teeth, remembering the bartending job that helped put him through college. "Pour and serve and smile and listen." He splashed the wine in one of the stemmed glassed off the rack beneath an upper cabinet.

He sloshed a little bourbon into a highball glass for himself and carried the drinks back into the living room.

She sat right where he'd left her, hands folded in her lap, looking sad. What the hell did she have to mope about?

"Here you go," he said in as normal a voice as he could manage. "Merlot. I don't know much about vintage."

She took the glass. "Neither do I." After tasting it gingerly, she nodded. "Not vinegar. That's good enough for me."

"Is it," he said, not a question.

"You don't quite know what to say to me now, do you?" she asked. "It doesn't make any difference, you know."

"Right." He downed the bourbon and winced. Not a good vintage here, he thought. But maybe everything would taste nasty under these circumstances.

She leaned toward him. "Mitch, the money is just incidental. Two million is not that much really. Not when you consider it's probably all I'll ever make. Modeling pays well, sure, but it's an incredibly short-lived career."

He rolled his eyes. "Right, you're so over-the-hill now. Jeez, look at you."

Robin sighed with obvious frustration. "I'm still the same person I was an hour ago."

"So am I." He thunked down his glass, not caring whether it left a ring on the shiny surface of Kick's stupid ugly end table.

"Let's get on with this," she snapped.

Mitch stood, pacing in front of her, not looking at her. "Tell me about Andrews's friends in New York. Did you ever meet any of his associates?"

"We attended parties on occasion," she told him. "Three, I think, the whole time we were together. He introduced me to some people, but I formed the impression they were connected to the arts. He was big into that."

"Liked to show you off, huh?" he asked, noting as he did that she resented the question. He didn't blame her.

He saw her throat work. "It seemed so. I hated going out."

"You'd have even less fun here, I bet. No culture to the vultures."

She got up and marched right over to him, hands on hips and her eyes narrowed. "Are you trying to start a fight? I hate confrontations."

"Do you?" he snapped, almost glad to see her angry. "Didn't it even occur to you that it's normal to fight for yourself, Robin? You can't just stand around looking pretty and expect the best while you get pissed on! I've seen your courage in action. Why the hell didn't you show it when that creep was using you?"

"Don't do this!" she cried, virtually leaping up from her chair and beginning to pace. "What do you want from me?"

He grabbed her upper arm to stop her and got right in her face. "I want you to be yourself, Robin! I want to see who you really are for more than five minutes at a time!" His voice dropped to a whisper despite his fury. "I want that woman I've seen beneath the mannequin. Show me you're real. I'm sick to death of seein' that expressionless—"

She kissed him.

Mitch couldn't even think what he'd been doing, riling her up like that, but the feel of her tongue invading his mouth, the sound of her impatience as she deepened the kiss and the feel of her long, elegant fingers holding his face, tore coherent thought right out of his head.

Mitch slid both arms around her and grasped her to him as if she was his last hope of salvation. Damn, she felt great. Tasted sweeter than homemade jam and had him harder and hotter faster than he could ever remember.

He moved against her, fitting his body to hers in a dance that was likely to end in the bedroom if she didn't call a halt.

But he didn't want to stop, and she didn't want him to. Mitch slid his hands past her waist and down her slender hips, pulling her closer, holding her tighter.

"Well, well, well!" a loud voice crooned, forcing Mitch to release Robin and grab for his weapon. "What have we here?"

Chapter 10

"Makin' yourselves right at home, I see." Kick Taylor winked at Robin. "Mrs. Andrews. How you doin', ma'am? Gettin' a little help with your grief, there?"

"Shut up, Taylor," Mitch warned, resnapping his holster over the butt of his gun. "What are you doing here?" He glanced at his watch for emphasis, trying to hold his hand steady.

"I live here, remember? Where the hell have *you* been?"

"Out of town," Mitch replied. "Is your offer of hospitality still good or are you plannin' to give me a hard time?"

"Still goes," Kick said with a shrug. "But it's a good thing I wasn't a few minutes later, huh?" He looked at the drinks sitting on the coffee table. "I see you found the refreshment."

He motioned with both his forefingers. "Why don't you two just continue on with your business, and I'll come back in about an hour?"

"Knock it off already," Mitch said, less forcefully. No point in egging Kick on by overreacting. "It was just a kiss."

"And Niagara's just a waterfall." He shook his head and gave Mitch a wave of dismissal as he left the room. "You got a minute, man, we need to talk."

Mitch looked at Robin whose face glowed like pink neon.

"Will you excuse me?"

"Certainly," she murmured.

If she'd been able to turn off that blush, he would never have guessed their kiss had affected her at all. As it was, he couldn't really say whether it was actually the kiss or getting caught acting human that shook her up.

Well, he might not be piling in big bucks as a detective, but he sure knew how to go about solving that particular mystery.

Mitch decided not to tell Kick about the disk or the print-outs he had made from it just yet. If Robin screwed up and got caught hacking into places she shouldn't, or if not turning the information over was subsequently considered withholding or suppressing evidence, Mitch would take full responsibility, and Kick wouldn't have to share the blame. And Mitch still thought he should talk to Damien first.

He would give Robin her opportunity at cracking this. A few hours she had said. Then whatever she found or didn't, they would give it up and let somebody else figure it out.

"What you got so far?" he asked Kick. "Any red dirt on her shoes?"

"Lab report's not back." Kick busied himself digging around in the fridge for something, then straightened with a container of dip and set it on the counter. He opened an overhead cabinet and took out a bag of chips.

"She didn't do it," Mitch assured him.

"You think somebody's after her because she saw who did?"

"Maybe," Mitch said. "Or that she might know something

about what got Andrews killed. Could be something she doesn't even know she knows."

Kick shook his head. "That girl is yankin' you around. You better go on home and let me take over here."

Mitch saw he was dead serious. "Not a chance. She's not guilty, Kick. I'd stake my badge on it."

"Yeah, well, you have. And we know which part of your anatomy is making decisions, don't we?" Kick said with a frowning glance at Mitch's crotch. "Don't let her mess with you. Loosen her up a little and get her to talking, but *you* keep your mind on business. And call me immediately with whatever info you get out of her. This *is* my case. Whatever she's got, I want, and I want it yesterday!"

Mitch shifted, planting his hands on his hips. "Now who'd ever guess you'd been on the job for mere months?"

Kick grinned sheepishly and thumped the sack of chips. "Stuff it, okay? Just keep your ears open and your fly shut." He headed for the door.

"Where are you going?"

"I won't be back tonight. You know where I'll be." Kick smiled suggestively. "Call me if anything turns up I should know about. If she tells you *anything*."

Mitch leveled him with a look. He picked up the chips Kick had set out for him and nodded toward the door in a gesture of dismissal. "Thanks for the use of your place."

"Mi casa es su casa," Kick said. He saluted and disappeared out the back door into the garage.

"Okay," Mitch muttered. "We'll make ourselves at home."

Later that night Robin booted up the PC in Kick Taylor's home office. She felt uncomfortable using his personal computer since she hadn't asked. "Are you sure he won't mind? Maybe we'd better call him and ask," she suggested again.

"It would serve him right, but no."

"What do you mean?" She logged on, wondering why anyone would disable the requirement for using a password. That was the first line of defense. At least it was effective against casual curiosity. Just because a person lived alone did not mean his occasional guest might not get curious. She noted the programs visible on his desktop and wondered whether they were blinds like the ones on her computer, or whether his were for real.

"He's at his girlfriend's house," Mitch explained. "Besides, if we ask, we'd have to say what we're using it for."

"Oh. Okay." Well, it wasn't as if she planned to violate the detective's privacy or anything. She only wanted to get online. And she would be extremely careful not to leave any virtual tracks that might lead back here. Or to her own identity.

After a number of clicks, she was connected and into a database she frequented to check out potential clients before entering into contracts with them. What would Mitch, a detective, make of her resources? Robin wondered.

She entered one of the names from the list on the CD and the screen changed, filling with information on the man in question. "How the hell did you do that?" Mitch asked as if he hadn't watched her every move while she did it.

Robin shrugged. "It's perfectly legal. This is one I subscribe to. You want to print this?"

"Yeah, sure." He sat back in the chair he had dragged over beside hers and was shaking his head in disbelief. "Can you get that much on all of them?"

"We'll see. Read the names to me. That was the only one I could remember in full."

For each man she pulled up a file giving current occupation, age, marital status, address, credit rating and other financial information.

"This is great," Mitch commented as he riffled through the pages she had printed. "Is all of this current, you think?"

"I don't know *how* current," she replied. "Just a minute." She entered another site and began searching further. "This one's deceased," she murmured.

"Dead? When?"

She pointed at the date, then entered another of the names. All were dead within the last three months. All except Somers.

"Well, damn," Mitch muttered. "What should we make of that?"

Robin clicked a few more times to cover her tracks if anyone bothered to check who was checking. She then zipped right to another site, this one providing a few more details, including rather personal preferences most people would never publicize.

Other than a grunt of disbelief, Mitch made no sound as he read the collection of data she had pulled up on Somers and the others. When he had finished, he stared at Robin as if he had never seen her before. "This is more than we have in *our* files on Somers. I think we can safely assume who it is that wants the disk," he said. "The question is *Why?* Any common interests there?"

Robin hit Print. "Not any that are apparent."

"I can't believe you found all this," he said as he ran a finger down one of the pages. "No secret's safe."

"Even yours," she told him as she tapped the top page on the stack for emphasis.

He drew his brows together and pursed his lips, obviously lost in thought for a minute. "Checked me out, have you?"

She shook her head. "Of course not. If you remember, I haven't had access to a computer since we met, other than your sister's." His frown deepened. "And I won't do it in the future," she promised. "Your business is none of mine."

"Go ahead," he said with a lift of his chin. "They won't

have much, if anything, in there on me. I never bank, invest or shop online. Don't trust it."

Robin was tempted to show him. Her fingers hovered over the keys. No, that definitely would be a mistake.

"Go ahead or I'll go nuts wondering," he ordered. "That look on your face tells me you know something I don't."

She worried her bottom lip as she accessed another site and keyed in his name. Several Mitchell Wintons appeared, only one listed as living in Nashville. "There you are," she said.

"Ha! See? Name, address, phone and e-mail addy. Big deal." He had already gotten up from the chair and moved over to the sofa across Taylor's office when, unable to resist, she highlighted his name and clicked. A full page of information popped up.

"Hmm. Moderate interest in antique pistols, devotee of Cajun cuisine and a marked preference for the writings of DeMille. You want your grandmother's maiden name? Your current balance at the credit union? How much you owe MasterCard?"

He was back to her side in an instant. "What the hell... How did they get all that?"

She looked away from the screen before getting too caught up in his history. "You own credit cards. You do surf, even if you don't buy online. And your financial institutions' computers are vulnerable, more so than you—or they—believe. You've completed work applications, no doubt had at least one background inquiry."

"Not on the Internet!" he argued.

"Doesn't matter. Companies use their computers to file things. And they share, sometimes inadvertently. If I dig a bit more, I could discover your entire work history and any time your name has appeared in print for any reason. It's all there for anyone who's interested and knows their way around the Web."

He had propped his hands on the edge of the desk and was leaning very near. His gaze left the monitor's screen and locked on hers. "Are you? Interested?" he asked, his voice little more than a whisper.

Robin wanted to back away, but found she couldn't. His face was so close, she could see the individual hairs in his ten-o'clock shadow, the fine lines that creased slightly at the corners of his eyes. Such fine eyes, clear and blue. Deep cobalt in this low light.

The scent of his aftershave, barely discernible, combined with his own subtle essence and beckoned her even closer. His lips were slightly open. Waiting as though he anticipated a kiss. She was not going to kiss him again. No. But she couldn't seem to look away.

"Are you, Robin?" he asked, even more softly.

"Wh-what?" Her mind seemed blank, a slate waiting for chalk, a paper eager for pen. A heart anxious for...

"Interested?"

"Yes." The word rushed out on a shuddering breath before she could catch it.

Mitch's lips stretched into a smile. A gentle, happy smile she couldn't help returning, even when she knew exactly where those smiling lips were heading.

They touched hers, a mere brush of warmth to the left, then a return path to the right, lingering only a second, a tantalizing, mind-stealing second. Robin lifted her lips to meet his more firmly, seeking that elusive connection just out of reach.

Suddenly he was kneeling on the floor beside her chair, his strong fingers sliding through her hair, his palms anchoring her head as his mouth—that wonderfully mobile, beautifully sculpted mouth—gave what she sought.

Breath rushed in as he released her slowly, staring into her eyes, looking as perplexed as she felt. His hands trailed down the sides of her neck, slid over her shoulders, down her arms to encompass the fists she had pressed to her middle. She opened her fingers, and he laced his between them.

"You're making me crazy," he said, his smile now hovering just out of sight.

Robin felt uncertain. Did he want her to apologize for it? To protest? To give him permission? "What do you want?" she whispered, desperate to know.

"I want *you*," he said. A simple unvarnished declaration that was stamped on every one of his features. "I don't think... No, I know...that I've never wanted anybody this way. Ever."

Somewhere in her mind a faint alarm sounded through that lovely haze of desire he had roused. *You have heard this before,* it chimed.

Reluctantly she listened to that voice, heeded it, made herself draw away from him and turn in the chair to face the monitor again. "Let's take a look at that bank balance, shall we?" she said, her voice weak and unsteady.

His swift reaction told her how deeply her insult had cut him. "Sure," he snapped. "You do that." He was standing now, his back to her as he scooped up the pages they had printed. "While you figure out just how desperate I am to get my hands on your money, I'll see if I can solve this damned murder and get you the hell out of town."

"Mitch..."

But the door to the office slammed on the word and he was gone. Robin sighed, looked back at the monitor. She should log off now. Mitch Winton's business was no business of hers. It never would be now. She had made certain of that.

A part of her desperately wanted to take the risk, to see where this thing she felt for Mitch would take her. A good thing her brain was still in control.

Robin stared at the screen, not really seeing it. Instead she focused inward, her mind engaged in the poor choices she had made in men up till now.

Troy had swept her right off her feet with his fake charm

and very real good looks when she, of all people, should
know how misleading beauty could be. And James had played
on her need for someone to look a little deeper than her own
appearance. How ironic that he had done that and found a tall,
awkward child inside with a yearning to find love.

Robin reflected on how easily she had fallen into that relationship and how glad she was that she'd at least had the good
sense to protect herself financially before she'd met either man.

She wondered if James had put off the divorce, thinking
perhaps he could coax her into some sort of settlement. He'd
only mentioned it once, and then jokingly, when they'd separated. It almost seemed as though her continued goodwill had
meant more to him than a portion of her wealth. Perhaps he'd
had more money than she realized and didn't need hers.

Inspired by that thought, she quickly entered his name and
the statistics she knew about James Andrews into the program
she had already accessed to check out the others.

A quarter hour later she still followed the trail, printing as
she went. Now things were beginning to make sense. Robin
felt like kicking herself for not doing this before she had married James. But then, of course, she had respected his privacy
too much. And at that time she'd still had a modicum of that
worthless commodity called trust.

Mitch made the rounds of Kick's house, checking the windows and doors before turning in for the night. He would
spend the night on that awful leather sofa in the living room.
Couldn't afford to get too comfortable, even though he was a
light sleeper. He doubted he'd be sleeping, anyway, after what
had happened with Robin. And what had *almost* happened.

He should have heeded the captain's command and avoided
any involvement with her. Now Mitch had her believing he

was some kind of gold digger. The rotten timing of that kiss could hardly have left her with any other impression but that.

With a muttered curse, he automatically checked the security system and headed back for the living room.

Robin was sitting on the sofa waiting for him, a sheaf of papers spread out on the brass-and-glass coffee table in front of her. Her eyes were narrowed and her lips compressed into a firm line, disguising their soft fullness. She had her arms folded over her chest and her long legs crossed at the knee. One foot swung erratically, further betraying her anger. Not that she was attempting to hide it.

Mitch sighed and dropped into the chair across from her. No way could he explain what he had done. No way could he reassure her that he had no designs on her money.

"Okay. Think what you want to think," he told her. "No defense. I wanted to kiss you so I did. You want an apology, you got it."

"I think he had mob ties," Robin announced as if she hadn't heard him.

Mitch blinked. "Who?"

"James!" she said with a huff. She leaned forward and tapped the papers with her hand. "It's all there. Sal Andreini financed his education. James had a law degree!" Her breath rushed out in a shudder as she recrossed her arms. "This is my fault."

"That he had a law degree or mob ties?" Mitch asked. He knew very well that wasn't what she meant, but he needed a second to switch gears here. He'd been expecting her to light into him about the other issue, apparently forgotten now, or shoved aside for this old proof of betrayal. "So you checked him out."

"Finally!" she admitted with a furious nod. "He had even changed his name! Can you believe that?"

"Related to Andreini, was he?"

Again she nodded. "Nephew. He had absolutely *no* Italian characteristics! He didn't even look Italian. I still can't believe it!" She pushed up from the sofa and began to pace. "I bought every word out of his mouth! I was so *stupid!*"

Mitch got up, too, and reached out to touch her arm. "Hey, don't beat yourself up, Robin. You had no reason to think he wasn't telling the truth. He must have cared—"

She rounded on him, her eyes shooting sparks. "No! He never *cared*. You were absolutely right. He used me. I don't know how yet, but he did." Her throat worked as she swallowed heavily. Mitch thought she might be about to cry.

"Come here," he said roughly, drawing her into his arms. Mistake. But he didn't care. She needed a little comfort and he couldn't help but give it. When she would have pushed away, he gentled her. "No kissing, no ulterior motive here, Robin. Just a hug, okay? You need it and so do I."

He patted her back, feeling her give in and bury her face in his shirt. Her shoulders shook. "Now listen to me," he ordered, "James might not have been what he appeared to be, but he did what he could to get rid of that guy who kept bothering you, didn't he? That Troy whatever?"

He felt her nod against his chest.

"See? And I can't think of any benefit he would have gotten from doing that, or marrying you, a famous model, when one of his main objectives in life must have been to keep a low profile. Right?"

Again she nodded.

"So he must have been sincere in wanting to help you out. All that other stuff I said about him and your money was just my jealousy talking. Even if he *was* mixed up with the mob, he was still a man with feelings. And I can't imagine any man not wanting to play white knight to you, sweetheart."

She reared back, her palms braced against his chest, and looked up at him. "Why?"

"Well..."

"No, I really want to know. Why?" she asked again, seeming almost desperate for the answer.

Mitch knew he had to be careful here. He was not only answering for James Andrews, but for himself. "Because you bring out protective instincts, I guess. Not that you look defenseless or anything, but there's something about you that seems inherently good, Robin. Innocent. Any man worth his salt would do just about anything to preserve that. You're the sort of woman he would want to think well of him, to like and respect him, maybe depend on him a little. I'm sure that's what James had in mind."

"He *lied* to me," she insisted.

"Yeah, he sure did. But what else could he do if he didn't want you mixed up in whatever he had going, hmm?" He brushed a strand of hair off her brow and tucked it behind her ear.

"But he did involve me," Robin said sadly. "He called me to bring him the disk."

"Desperation, I bet," Mitch answered truthfully. "He must have been up against a wall, don't you think? His life probably depended on turning over what was on that disk."

"And I came too late to save him," she whispered.

"You can't blame yourself for that," Mitch said, taking her by the shoulders and giving her a gentle shake. "You had no idea what was at stake and he didn't tell you. How could you possibly have known?" He guided her over to the sofa again, urged her to sit and joined her. "Now why don't you show me all you found out about him?"

She'd discovered quite a lot. Mitch went over every fact she had unearthed. College records. Andrews had been no dummy, that was for sure. Hadn't graduated at the top of his class, but came close. Sure enough, one of New York's favorite crime bosses had footed the bill at the University of Virginia.

After graduation he had worked briefly for a small law firm in downtown Manhattan dealing with contract law. He had resigned in good standing after two years. Another two years with an investments and securities company. Again he had resigned. No record of any private practice or other employment. There was no record of any job with an insurance company. Apparently, Uncle Sal had put him to work for the family after the four years in legitimate trenches.

So what dealings did the Andreini family have with Somers down here in the South?

"What do you think it means?" Robin asked when Mitch had put down the printouts. "He was almost certainly working with his uncle, right?"

"All we can do is guess at this point. Maybe Somers and the others on the list provided some service for the Andreinis. James was probably in charge of the payroll. Say he electronically transfers the funds from his uncle's account and sets up offshore accounts for the men on the list. All he had to do then was to give them the account numbers. That way the money never comes stateside and won't need laundering. Maybe one of them got greedy and decided he wanted all of the numbers."

"This Somers man?" Robin asked.

"Must be. The others are dead."

Robin sighed and leaned back against the sofa. Instead of angry, she now seemed simply weary. "James probably would have come here to oversee whatever deal they had going with the Andreinis."

Mitch agreed. "Yeah, that makes sense. His uncle would want to keep an eye on whatever it was."

"But the Russian, Mitch? What does that mean?"

"Russian mafia's big in New York. Maybe they were collaborating with the Andreini family on something. It's already done, whatever it was. It's the payoffs that went south."

He patted her hand that rested on the cushion next to his. "Don't worry. We'll get to the bottom of it. You've helped a great deal by digging up this much. The D.A. will be ecstatic. The feds, too, maybe."

Robin smiled, but it looked a little wan.

"No, I mean it," Mitch assured her. "You know, I bet you could hire on with the Bureau here doing BIs. You're damned good."

She frowned.

"Background investigations," he explained.

"I know what a BI is," she said. "And I don't need a job."

"Oh." He had forgotten for a minute that she was independently wealthy and didn't need to work.

"I have a job," she told him.

"Designing Web pages," he said, nodding.

Robin cleared her throat. "Well, that's only a sideline. Something to feed my creativity. Actually, I have another occupation I suppose I should tell you about. You'll probably find out, anyway, since there are bound to be questions about how I acquired this much information on James and the others. Much of it you can buy if you know where to go, but some I, uh, got from unauthorized sources."

Damn, she intrigued him. To tell the truth, all she had to do was sit there to intrigue him, but this beauty had smarts he suspected he hadn't even begun to guess at. "Well? Exactly what do you do?"

She looked a little defensive. "I'm an intrusion tester."

A what? "The job title sounds interesting. You want to tell me what it means?"

"You'd call it a hacker for hire, I guess. Companies, institutions, agencies and so forth, hire people to test their accessibility. You see, the network administrators set up the systems, but they rarely test it to see whether they can withstand dedicated intrusion. They install proximity servers or firewalls, but someone has to check whether they work properly. Most of them don't."

Mitch laughed. "You actually get paid to snoop?"

"Paid quite well. I also track down those who do it without sanction. Which tonight, I guess, would be people like me."

He shook his head in awe and squeezed the hand that rested under his. "You're something, you know that?

Robin drew her hand away and looked at him. "I apologize for the accusation I made earlier," she told him. "I tend to get a bit paranoid about the...the money."

Mitch smiled. "It's okay. If I had that much, I would be, too. Please know that I don't have dollar signs in my eyes when I look at you, Robin. If you recall, I was mighty attracted to you before you told me you had it."

He could see that she wanted to believe him.

"I'm not very good with...people," she said, staring at her hands, fiddling with a small gold ring on her right hand. "I don't read them well at all."

"So you said. Well, I think you do just fine. My family liked you. I like you," he said, using his most ingratiating smile on her. "A whole lot."

She blushed and ducked her head. "Thank you." Her reluctance to continue was obvious. "I like you, too. But I think we should restrict our...whatever this is...to business."

For a minute he couldn't respond to that. Well, he *could,* but the response he had in mind wouldn't do. He wanted to take her in his arms again, this time to kiss her senseless, to shake her right out of that shell of insecurity. If insecurity was what it was. It could be she had a very real aversion to starting up something with a cop who she still might think had her bank balance on his mind.

She raised her gaze to his, awaiting his answer.

Finally he nodded, trying to hold his smile in place. "Okay. Strictly business for now. For the record, though, I would like to be friends when all this is over, if that's okay with you. Maybe call you sometimes and see how you're doing? Drop by if I ever get up your way and take you out to dinner?"

She brightened. As if she were six and he'd offered her a pony. "You would? I could show you the city! It's a great place!"

"Yeah, that'd really be something. I'd like that." He didn't have the heart to tell her he had already seen New York as well as a large part of the rest of the world. Besides, he wanted to see it all again. With her.

Mitch was torn between begging her to trust him and warning her not to offer her friendship so easily to a man she knew so little about.

This woman was such an ironic blend of sophistication and vulnerability. What the hell was he going to do with her? How would he resist her while she was here? And how in the world would he protect her when she left?

Chapter 11

Robin leaned forward and massaged the muscles in the back of her neck. Her eyelids felt heavy as lead. Maybe she could sleep now.

After Mitch had ordered her to bed, she had tried. An hour later, she had headed to the kitchen for a glass of milk, hoping that would help. Unfortunately, she noticed Mitch was sleeping on the living room sofa and she abandoned her quest. She didn't want to risk waking him. Then neither of them would have a good night's sleep.

Instead of going back to bed, she decided to do something productive. Feeling only a bit guilty for using her host's computer yet again without permission, she had gone into Kick's den, logged on and tried to find out more about what might have caused James's death.

The New York City, New Jersey and Nashville news

archives offered nothing helpful. Neither had a global search of arrest records. James had no priors under either of his names.

A couple of the men on the list had arrest records, but for nothing serious. No convictions. They were all businessmen, fiftyish, with seemingly nothing else in common.

"Don't tell me. You found out about my C-minus in Algebra."

Robin jumped, then swivelled in the computer chair until she faced him. "I couldn't sleep."

He handed her another glass of wine. "I know. I heard you wandering around earlier. See if this will help. Find anything new?" he asked as he handed her the glass.

"Nothing much. I was wide-awake, thought I would dig a little deeper and see what came up, but I don't think I got any facts that would add much to what we already know." She closed the program, backtracked carefully and logged off.

"What we already *guess*," he corrected in a wry voice. "It's two o'clock, y'know."

Robin shook her head and got up, set the wine aside and stretched. "I'm sleepy now. Thanks for the wine."

"No problem." His hot gaze wandered down from her face, growing intense as it traveled slowly over the tacky T-shirt she was wearing, hesitated at the top of her thighs where the shirt ended and then followed the line of her legs. "Oh, wow." His words were little more than a sorrowful murmur.

Robin resisted the urge to stalk past him and simply stood there, feeling gawky and woefully underdressed. Her hair was a mess, her breasts were too small and her feet were too big. At least now he'd seen the worst she had to offer.

Finally his eyes met hers again. He offered a sheepish smile and a shrug. "Sorry, couldn't help it. You just look so damned incredible."

He was the one who stretched credulity, but she wasn't about to comment on the width of his broad, bare shoulders, the trim line of his waist or the fact that he'd forgotten to fasten the waistband of his trousers.

She quickly looked away from him and focused on the picture beside the door, just to his left. "I guess we'd better get back to bed."

She heard his breath rush out in a short laugh. "Yeah. I could get ideas a *friend* shouldn't be entertaining. Some legs you got there, kid. You're the only person I know with pretty knees, you know that? Now some girls," he said with a negligent wave of his hand, drawing her attention back to him in spite of her resolve, "they have great thighs, curvy calves and cute ankles. Even pretty toes." He shook a finger at her legs. "You do, too. But I have never, *ever* seen one with knees that good."

Robin suppressed a nervous giggle. Mitch had turned back into the hallway with that last comment and was still shaking his head, muttering in disbelief.

"She could incite *riots* with those knees," Robin heard him say. "Gotta get that girl some baggy pants."

Robin followed him out and switched off the light, reassured that he would treat this attraction between them with enough silly humor to dispel it. She wished *she* could.

He made her laugh, something no man had ever done before. This wasn't the first time, either. Robin knew her sense of humor was underdeveloped. She had never felt the urge to giggle before, and it sort of unsettled her a little.

Still musing over that, Robin didn't realize he had turned around again in the darkened hallway until she ran smack into him. He grasped her shoulders, kissed her soundly on the forehead and turned her around. "Your bedroom's *that* way," he said, giving her a gentle shove. "Sleep tight, kid."

All these years she'd been waiting for a man to awaken that part of her she'd begun to believe was immune to desire. Why did it have to be him? Why did it have to be now? And why did the word *desire* seem so anemic to describe what he made her feel? She doubted she'd ever sleep again.

Mitch flopped down on Kick's break-ass sofa and braced his head on his hands.

Damn, that was close. He'd come *that* near backing her against the fancy wallpaper in the hall and doing his best— or worst—to claim that delectable body of hers. If he hadn't thought it would screw things up for good, he would have. He could have had her willing in less than a minute.

Her face betrayed every emotion she felt unless she was working hard to prevent it. But wasn't he actually the one who had suggested she drop that defense mechanism? That protective mask of hers?

She wanted him, too, Mitch knew without a doubt. The fact amazed him. Humbled him, too, but not enough to keep him from acting on it. No, it was her fear, her mistrust in his intent that did that for him. He couldn't make love to Robin with her thinking all the while he was putting the make on her for her money. Also, he worried that their being thrust into this situation of forced proximity might be causing the sustained level of lust.

Okay. He'd just have to deal with it. After all, he was responsible for her, wasn't he?

He exhaled sharply and sat straight up, bracing his hands against the seat of the sofa, feeling the tension within him ready to snap.

God, he wished he could run. Just go outside and run like hell until he was too exhausted to move. But then he'd just fall down somewhere and think about her, anyway. "Well, push-ups ain't the answer," he muttered. Not in his present condition.

Kick did have an exercise bike, Mitch remembered, thinking back to when he and some of the guys had helped his new partner move in here a few months ago. Maybe exhaustion would help him sleep. Or at least make him too tired to follow through on what he wished he could do.

He padded barefoot down the hall to the last bedroom and flipped on the light switch. There was no overhead light source, only a weird-looking lamp in the far corner that threw a weak fan of light on the wall and ceiling above it.

The cycle was top-of-the-line, as was the rest of the equipment Kick had in his little home gym. He wondered if Kick really was this body conscious or if he just collected all the toys for show. He stayed in good shape and had way too much energy. Maybe this is how he worked that off.

Quickly stripping down to his briefs, Mitch started his workout. A half hour later he had worked up a good sweat. His leg muscles were burning, and he was getting dehydrated, but his mind was still alert and filled with visions of the woman down the hall. Exhaustion helped more than he'd expected, physically if not mentally. He decreased the pace and wound down slowly.

When he got off the cycle and leaned down to pick up the clothing he had shucked, he saw her. She was standing in the doorway, virtually hugging the frame. The way she raked his body with that slumberous gaze of hers promptly undid any relief the workout had provided. He sprang to attention again at the sight of her standing there.

One long, slender foot rested on top of the other as she leaned against the molding in a sleepy, childlike pose.

"What's the matter?" he asked. "Still can't sleep?"

She raked her bottom lip with her teeth and continued to look at him from beneath those long, fanlike lashes. "I didn't want to be...alone." The last word rushed out as if she'd tried to hold it back.

Mitch dropped the clothes he was holding. She released the door frame supporting her and approached him warily, stopping a couple of feet away. No words were necessary. The rankness of her expression told him exactly what she wanted.

"Sure about this?" he asked softly, searching her eyes.

She nodded, reached down and clutched the hem of her t-shirt. He watched, spellbound, as she drew it over her head and trailed it on the floor. Breath caught in his throat. He didn't care. He needed her more than air.

Mitch opened his arms, closing them around her quickly when she came to him. He reveled in the feel of her. Her breath rasped softly but urgently as her hands gripped his back, those long graceful fingers sliding sinuously over his sweat-slicked muscles. Her small, perfect breasts bonded firmly to his chest by the dampness of his skin. His nose sought the silkiness of her hair, breathing in the sweet clean scent of her.

He traced her slender body with his palms, at last slipping them beneath the wispy silk that only half covered her bottom. Her skin felt smooth as satin as he caressed her, pulling her tightly against him, only half assuaging the ache she caused.

Vaguely he thought of a bed, though he wasn't sure they would make it that far. Instead, he backed up several steps to the padded exercise mat and lowered them to it so that they lay side by side. He trailed one hand from her hip to waist and then upward to feel, at last, one smooth firm breast beneath his palm. Almost reverently he lowered his mouth to taste her there, to explore the small tight peak with his eager tongue. He drew on it gently, then harder, his own body echoing the shudder that rippled through hers.

He smoothed his hand downward over her flat abdomen and lower to the nest of curls that surrounded his final destination. Heat enveloped his fingers as he pressed them against her, sliding one into her with a slowness and sureness of pur-

pose. Her resulting cry of pleasure almost ended his deter
mined attempt at gentleness.

She moved against him restlessly, pressing closer, her han
seeking, finding, drawing a groan from him as she stroked an
squeezed and pleaded with her touch. "Now?" he asked.

"Now," she answered, the word more demand than acqui
escence.

Mitch ravished her mouth, devouring her, loving her head
response, his mind completely focused on nothing but pos
sessing her in every way humanly possible. His body fitte
to hers in an automatic reflex. He sank within her as deepl
and surely as she had embedded herself in his heart.

Sheer undiluted pleasure coursed through him, obliteratin
any worries of how this would end, what would come of it. Ther
were no tomorrows, no yesterdays, only now, this moment ou
of time that would never be equaled again. Robin was his.

He drew back and thrust slowly, savoring the exhilaratior
providing and relishing the sweet slide of joy, the promise c
perfection just out of reach. Again and again, he gave an
took, offered and demanded, waiting only for her cue to de
liver all that he was.

Her pulse beat frantically beneath his mouth as he savore
her neck. His teeth grazed her upturned chin, and she crie
out, frantically seeking his kiss. Hot and wild, it went on an
on. The taste of her essence, sweet wine and his own swea
mingled as he claimed her mouth.

Her body undulated faster, meeting his every move and at
tempting to increase his pace. He executed a particularly deej
lunge and her breath hissed inward, her eyes closing tightl
as if she would capture the feeling and hold it.

The sight and sensation sent him reeling. With a groan o
surrender, he abandoned finesse and threw himself into mo
tion. He slipped one hand between them and touched her, des

perate not to leave her wanting. Her body grasped him, shuddered around him and forced him into a climax so powerful and prolonged, he thought he might die.

Mitch groaned, the last sound he was capable of making, and collapsed. *Damn.* He didn't think he could move anything if he tried. Even his lips. They must be paralyzed in a permanent smile.

Robin sighed beneath him. He felt the intake of air and the soft, replete sound of her exhalation. A wordless compliment if he'd ever heard one.

Mitch finally managed to roll to one side so that she could breathe more easily. She uttered a murmur of protest when he disengaged their bodies, as if she had wanted him to stay.

Only then did it strike him that he had made the ultimate mistake, the worst imaginable lapse of consideration a man could commit in this kind of situation. Never once had the thought of a condom entered his mind. If he'd had any energy left, he would have pounded his forehead and cursed his stupidity.

Why? After nearly twenty years of having sex, he had never—not one single time—neglected to protect a woman he had sex with. And now, with the very woman he loved, he had—

The realization hit him right between the eyes, as powerfully as a fist. *Loved.* He loved Robin. Oh, Lord. And while she might come to him looking for a little comfort on a sleepless night, he couldn't expect her, by any stretch of his fevered imagination, to love him back. Ever.

And even if she should, through some quirk of magic, decide she did, what could he possibly do about it? Ask her to marry him? Fat chance. Even with a prenup so she'd be sure he wasn't after her money, she'd think he only wanted her around as a trophy. *Hey, look at me, guys, I snagged me a model. A wealthy one at that.* God, he wished she weren't quite so beautiful. Or rich. Or mistrustful. He sure couldn't fault her for that. Not after she'd gotten mixed up with those two losers.

She also came across as a little insecure in some ways. Oh, Robin knew she was smart all right. And she had to know she possessed many other qualities in addition to her beauty. Trouble was, she didn't trust that any man would look beneath that facade to find the real Robin. Well, *he* had found her.

Now he just had to decide what to do with her.

Robin lay still and pretended she had fallen asleep. She really didn't want to open her eyes and look at him. What in the world had she been thinking? She hardly knew this man and here she was lying naked in his arms on an exercise mat in a stranger's house.

She felt his lips press against her temple, soft and warm and comforting. The splayed fingers of the large hand cradling her back caressed her skin almost tentatively. The other hand rested possessively on her hip. "Robin?" he whispered.

Reluctantly she answered. "Hmm?"

"We should go to bed. You'll get a chill."

She snuggled closer, still disinclined to face him. He would want an explanation, and she had no idea what to say, how to justify what she caused to happen.

He moved away a little, releasing his hold, but still touching her as if trying to soothe her. "C'mon."

She still refused to open her eyes as she struggled to sit up. He helped her as they got to their feet, then felt him fit the T-shirt over her head. Robin slipped her arms through the sleeves. When she finally forced her eyes open he had put on his briefs. He slid one strong arm around her, holding her at the waist. She might have been a sleepy child the way he handled her.

"I won't discuss this," she warned, feeling defensive.

"Okay," he agreed, his voice rife with understanding. And regret? Had she heard regret? No, she couldn't ask that.

"Don't patronize me," she said, hating the awkwardness she felt. He had been wonderful to her and here she was sniping at him. "I'm sorry. I didn't mean that."

"I know. It's all right," he told her, leaning once again to brush a soft kiss against her forehead. His hand rested lightly at the back of her neck.

Robin drew in a deep breath to fortify herself against his tenderness. All that did was inundate her senses with the scent of lingering aftershave, clean male sweat and sex. Mind-rending sex. Her head swam and she almost stumbled.

He tightened his hold on her, reached down and swept her right off her feet. Robin wound her arms around his neck and buried her face in the curve of his neck. When he put her down on the bed where she had tossed and turned earlier, she was tempted to hold on, to urge him to join her there for the rest of the night. Instead she snuggled deeply into the fluffy feather pillows and curled away from him, still unwilling to look him in the eye.

She had broken their agreement, the one she'd firmly insisted on herself. "Will you still be my friend?" The question escaped before she could stop it.

"Always," he answered, without pausing to think. "Go to sleep now." He rested his hand on the crown of her head for a second, then combed his fingers through her hair. "Don't worry, Robin."

She nodded, unable to speak. If she did, he would know she was about to cry. Robin didn't shed a tear, however. Not until she heard the soft snick of the door when he pulled it shut and she knew he was gone.

The next morning she showered, dressed in the clothes she had worn the day before and sat on the bed trying to read a dog-eared paperback she'd found in the nightstand. Anything to keep from facing the man she had seduced so shamelessly

Seduced. Hardly that, Robin thought with a smirk. There hadn't been much seduction to it, if any. All she'd done was show up and make it clear what she wanted. Yanked that shirt right off and made a perfect idiot of herself. Fine way to go about sealing a friendship. Now he'd think she was the epitome of the image she'd been battling all her adult life. Sex object.

Maybe that's what she was after all. She sure couldn't demand that Mitch respect her mind after last night. Even she doubted her intelligence now.

"Oh, get over it," she muttered to herself as she tossed the unread book aside and got up. Hiding out here in the bedroom was ridiculous. Certainly no solution. Besides, she was starving.

Determined to brave it out, Robin marched to the door, flung it open and almost ran right into Mitch. He was standing there balancing a tray on one hand, the other outstretched as if he'd been reaching for the doorknob.

"Morning. Brought you some breakfast," he said with a grin. "Hope you like your eggs sunny-side up."

Robin's gaze fell to the tray. Sure enough, there were two fried eggs, two slices of toast and a glob of jelly. Two steaming cups of coffee wobbled in their saucers. She backed into the room. "This...this wasn't necessary."

He brushed past her and set the tray on a small round table beside the window, then plucked up the art deco vanity stool and put it down for her to sit on. "There you go. Service with a smile."

She stared at him, then at the plate, unable to believe he had cooked her breakfast. She couldn't remember when—or if—anyone had ever cooked her breakfast, even her mother.

Even as a child, Robin had only been allowed fruit or low-cal yogurt to keep her weight below average. By the time she reached adulthood, the fare had become a habit. She had never eaten a fried egg in her life.

Mitch picked up one of the coffees and made himself comfortable on the bed. "Go ahead. Eat."

Robin sat down and picked up the fork. Tentatively, she cut a section of the white part and tasted it. A bit greasy, she thought as she chewed. She nibbled a corner of the buttered toast. "Very nice," she commented, since she knew he was waiting for her appraisal.

He got up and came over, taking the fork from her hand. "Like this," he instructed as he diced up the eggs and stirred them around. The half-cooked yolks spread over and coated the white making an unappetizing mess. He put the fork back in her hand. "There you go."

Robin considered refusing to eat, but Mitch looked so proud of himself for making it, she didn't have the heart. Well, she had certainly eaten worse-looking things, she thought, recalling sushi. And anchovies. And cottage cheese was not all that attractive now that she thought about it.

She scooped up a bite, determined to enjoy this even if it choked her. To her surprise it was delicious. Or maybe she was just so ravenous anything would taste good.

Nodding as she chewed and swallowed, with another forkful on the way to her mouth, she exclaimed, "Great!"

He beamed and resumed his seat on the bed. "Knew you'd like it. Much better with grits, but there weren't any."

"That's okay." She finished the treat, wishing for more. Jelly had always been a no-no. She spread it on the toast and wolfed it down. All of it. If she stayed in Nashville, she could just imagine herself at three hundred pounds in less than six weeks.

"You know I can't eat this way all the time," she said, taking the last sweet bite and reaching for the coffee. "Or even very often."

"Sure you can. Thin as you are, you surely don't have to worry." He set his cup down on the nightstand and leaned back on the bed, propped on his arms.

Robin laughed wryly. "Little do you know about the vagaries of weight control. I've gained almost ten pounds since I stopped modeling. And those added pounds were only due to less stress."

He frowned. "*Less* stress? What on earth could be more nerve-racking than what you went through with ol' Troy-Boy's stalking and James's fooling around?"

Robin smiled, feeling much more at ease, now that she realized he wasn't going to bring up last night's fall from grace. "Modeling is strenuous. It takes a lot out of you. People think we make outrageous amounts for just standing there in front of a camera or plodding down a runway and back. Believe me, it's hard work. We earn every penny and then some."

"You don't ever have to do that again, do you?" he asked, looking truly concerned. "Do you want to?"

"Goodness, no! I never wanted to in the first place." She made a face. "I had what's known as a dedicated stage mother."

His frown deepened. "I saw a special on TV once where this woman got her little girl all duded up and stuck her in every beauty pageant going. The poor kid looked downright miserable, pasting on that fake smile. Even had to wear a false plate to cover up the loss of her baby teeth. I wanted to horse-whip that mother."

Robin shrugged and sighed. "Well, Mom didn't go quite that far. I didn't begin my career until I was nearly nine. Some women live vicariously through their children, and I do think my mother was guilty of that to some extent. She's not happy that I retired when I did."

"Nine years old?" he asked, his voice nearly quavering with what appeared to be anger. "She made you work at *nine?*"

Robin smiled. "You might have seen me in your Christmas wish book cuddling Barbies. Of course you wouldn't have been looking at the dolls, I guess."

He grinned, but it looked totally forced, probably just for her benefit. "I didn't look 'em up in the catalog, but you can bet I peeped under their dresses when Susie and Meg left their dolls lying around. Wanted to see if they were anatomically correct. A guy thing, I guess."

Robin laughed out loud at the image of a mischievous little Mitch sneaking a peek at Barbie's undies. "That's priceless," she gasped.

His face softened. "*You're* priceless. I love to hear you laugh." Before she could grasp what he'd said, he rushed past it. "Did you play with dolls? Make kissy-kissy with Barbie and Ken?"

Robin blushed. "Don't all little girls?" Didn't every single one of them dress up their dolls and pretend weddings and happily-ever-afters? Of course, she'd had nothing to base her pretense on other than marriages she saw on television. Her mother and father had divorced when she was four, and she hadn't seen him since.

"You're an only child, aren't you?" he asked.

"Afraid so. Why, do I seem spoiled or something?"

"No, I just wondered what you did for fun. Who you played with. If you ever got your bottom tanned for mischief."

Robin sighed and pushed her plate back and forth on the tray. "No spankings. Not many playmates unless I happened to get a job that included other children. Even then, there was little time to play. I was homeschooled at first, had tutors later on, took the GED and managed to get into college. After that I lived with Mother and went part-time until I got my degree."

Mitch shook his head. "Missed all those beer parties and everything? Rough. You seriously need to play, Robin."

The thought tickled her. She wished there was snow outside so they could have a snowball fight or something. "I think it's a bit late for that. But I guess I did enjoy that fishing expedition. That counts."

She got up and picked up the tray to carry it back to the kitchen. "What's on the agenda for today?"

He brought his cup, sipping the rest of his coffee as he followed her. "We should probably hang around here. Kick will be home later and we could bring him up to speed about the disk. Damien's still not home, so I guess we'll have to trust ol' NPD."

"I suppose we should."

He ran one finger down her arm from shoulder to elbow. Touching her just to be touching, she thought. "It's Sunday and I usually go to my parents' house for Sunday dinner. Want to go?"

An automatic refusal rose in her throat, but Robin refused to voice it. She had already told Mitch she wasn't good at interacting with people socially. He hadn't listened then and he probably wouldn't now. Somehow that made her feel good. Besides, she hadn't done so badly with his mother and sister the last time, had she? He said they had liked her.

Mitch was close to his family, and she had no right to deprive him of their company just because she had a hang-up. "That sounds fine," she said, wishing she'd put a bit more enthusiasm in it. "Yes, let's *do* go," she added, smiling over her shoulder.

His delighted expression was reward enough for enduring just about anything. Strange how she kept courting that grin of his. It made her feel light inside. It was as if he were telling her she had done something incredibly wonderful.

A therapist would probably tell her she had a deep-seated eagerness to please and a profound need for praise fostered by some sort of early acquired neurosis. What the hell. Why pick it apart and ruin her mood? She wanted to go with Mitch.

If he didn't like her a little, he certainly deserved an Academy Award for his acting. And the man kept his promises. Hadn't he just proved it by not indulging in a post mortem of last night's insanity? Not one word or look or sly little gleam in his eye indicated in any way that he was thinking about what had happened between them.

It didn't come in a blinding flash or anything, but a tiny, unfamiliar glimmer of warmth slowly stole through her. She barely recognized it as the dawning of trust. Robin promised herself she would nurture it carefully and hope to God it didn't die.

Chapter 12

"What are you smiling about?" Robin asked Mitch.

"Just thinking about the kids. My niece turns thirteen today. We're sure to have cake and, knowing Paula, it *will* be chocolate."

Another five pounds, Robin thought with a sigh as Mitch pulled into the driveway. He had borrowed Kick's second vehicle, a small, sporty truck that looked brand-new.

Mitch parked, reached over and patted her hand. "Thanks for coming."

"Thanks for asking," she replied, her voice sounding sunny even to herself. "Shall we?" She opened her door, not waiting for him to get out and go around.

Never had she made a public appearance looking the way she looked today. In any other circumstance, she would have insisted on staying inside and hiding.

Her clothing was clean. She had run it through Kick's washer and dryer last night, but it was wrinkled. If the man owned an iron, she hadn't been able to find it. She realized she was wearing the same jeans and top she had worn the last time she had met the Wintons. Other than the T-shirt Mitch had purchased for her at that convenience store, this was all she had.

Also, her makeup had been lost with the stolen purse and her face was bare as the day she was born. Her skin was pretty good since she had always taken care of it. She had appropriated a bit of the moisturizer for men Kick had in his bathroom cabinet.

Her hair looked fairly decent after blowing it dry, but her nails were a mess with their week-old chipped polish. She rather liked her shoes, the neat pair of leather clogs she had bought for less than ten dollars. Well, she would simply have to do, whether she looked a fright or not.

Mitch escorted her to the door, then opened it as he had the last time they had come here. "You should knock," she said without thinking.

"Why?" He looked at her in confusion as if the thought had never occurred to him.

Patricia Winton waved at them from the kitchen door. "Come on through, you two. Everybody's out back."

Robin couldn't walk straight through the kitchen the way Mitch urged her to. She had to stop, inhale fully and close her eyes to savor the scent. "This smells the way heaven must!"

"Roast beef," Patricia told her. "I'll give you my recipe."

"Oh, I could never duplicate that. Not in a million years. If it tastes as good as it smells, I'll find myself dieting for weeks to come." She opened her eyes and smiled at Patricia. "Because today, I plan to eat my fill."

"Good for you!" Mitch's mother tossed him a roll across the island. "This girl's great for the ol' ego."

"I'd drink to that," he said cryptically, then shook his head as if dismissing the thought. "Got a beer, Mom?"

"Out back in the cooler," Patricia told him as she opened the oven. "Robin, grab that platter over there for me?"

And just that easily, she was fully incorporated into the effort that was a Winton birthday bash. She perched on a stool at the island and mixed potato salad. She folded napkins. She sipped the wine cooler Mitch provided and made appropriate comments while his mother kept up a running patter about the activities of the grandchildren she was raising.

"A piano recital? I always wished I could take lessons," Robin said truthfully as she straightened the stack of sturdy ironstone plates set out for the buffet. "Has Paula studied for long?"

"'Bout two years," Patricia said. "Since her big night is next week, we'll see if she'll give us a preview and play her piece for us this afternoon."

"Where is the birthday girl?" Robin asked. She had met the two younger children as they'd dashed in and out, but had yet to see the thirteen-year-old.

Patricia shook her head and clicked her tongue. "Puttin' on makeup. Susan gave her a set of it this morning, and the child's been back in the bedroom playing with it all morning. I shudder to think Paula's old enough to wear lipstick. She already thinks she's grown."

Mitch and his father entered then, both nursing a beer bottle and laughing at something one of them had said outside. Susan came in behind them carrying a handful of tools. "I fixed that gate so the kids can't open it from the inside. You can let Sheba out to play whenever you want to, Mama." The little Yorkie in question danced around her feet as if it understood.

Suddenly Mitch let out a whoop of laughter and pointed to the doorway leading off from the dining room. Robin turned to see what caused his merriment and saw a young girl dressed in hip-hugging jeans and a lacy, stretch tank top. Her face wore a thick mask of garish makeup and a profound look of hurt.

Robin automatically punched Mitch in the shoulder. "Stop laughing this minute. Can't you see she's practicing makeup for her recital? Floodlights leach out every smidge of color, and you have to compensate for that!"

Desperate to repair the girl's self-image, not to mention her heavy-handed application of cosmetics, Robin marched right over to her and stopped, shrugging helplessly. "I'm Mitch's friend, Robin. Would you mind terribly if I borrowed just a tiny touch of your powder? All my makeup was stolen when some jerk snatched my purse."

The girl frowned up at her as if Robin had lost her mind, but she said, "Okay, I guess."

"Robin's a model, Paula," Mitch said with authority. "Now, you listen to her about how to apply that goop or we'll have to put it away until you're older."

Robin turned around and shot him a nasty look. "And *you*, stuff a sock in it, Mitch Winton. Paula did just fine on her own." She turned to the girl. "Powder my nose for me and I'll show you a secret I learned in Paris about declumping mascara. Other than that minor smudge, you look smashing."

She followed the girl down the hall, noting the slump of her shoulders and the dispirited way she trudged. Moved more than she could stand, Robin slipped an arm around Paula's shoulders and leaned down to whisper. "You want to really wow 'em? I'll show you every trick in my book."

Paula sniffed and looked up. Though her mascara was running now, she was wearing a copy of Mitch's grin. "I had a problem knowing how much to use," she admitted, keeping her voice low. "Thanks for covering. The stage thing was brilliant."

Robin gave her shoulders a quick squeeze. "I was sixteen the first time I was allowed to buy makeup and try it myself."

"Sixteen?"

"Mmm-hmm. I worked pretty steadily, and they have people who do your face for you. You would not *believe* the mess I made when I tried to do it on my own. It's not easy the first time, is it?"

"No, it's not!" Paula laughed, Mitch's criticism forgotten. Robin's heart swelled with success. She had made another friend, and it hadn't been hard at all.

"That young lady's quick on her feet. I'm impressed."

Mitch nodded in his father's direction. "Yeah. I'm pretty impressed myself. You don't think I made Paula cry, do you? Maybe I'd better go back there and see. Robin's not really used to kids." He got up off the kitchen stool, and his mother shoved him down again.

"Don't you meddle. I have a feeling Robin might do a lot more good than you would."

Susan draped an arm over his shoulder. "Don't feel bad, bro. I was too chicken to offer Paula any suggestions this morning. She's not that keen on my advice since we had our little heart-to-heart about her boyfriend."

"Dinner's ready," Patricia said looking from one to the other. "All we have to do now is wait." She looked toward the door where Robin had disappeared with Paula. "I guess our girls could take a while. Anybody want another beer?"

Our girls. Mitch's smile felt bittersweet. In the back of his mind he must have had another reason for bringing Robin here today. Maybe he had wanted to see how difficult it would be for her to fit in with his family.

Had it been that hard for her? Was this all an act, a dedicated politeness on her part to pay him back for helping her?

He knew he would have the devil of a time adjusting to life in New York if the situation were reversed.

Their backgrounds were so different. He and Robin had nothing in common. Nothing but a murder investigation. And great sex. He bit back a groan, trying not to recall how perfectly they fitted, how incredible last night had been. How much he loved her.

"It just won't work," he said to himself.

"Don't be an idiot," his mother said knowingly as she pointed at him with a stalk of celery she'd been about to munch. "She's the one." His dad nodded. Susan wiggled her eyebrows and grinned.

Later, when they were headed for Kick's truck to leave, Mitch had to wonder if his family wasn't right. He couldn't imagine ever feeling this way about another woman. But did she feel the same way about him, or was it gratitude or hormones that prompted her to come to him last night?

He didn't speak until they were well on their way back to the house. She was smiling to herself, obviously happy with the way things had turned out today.

"Thanks for taking Paula in hand. She looked fantastic after you did whatever you did to her," he finally said.

Robin shrugged. "She's a sweet girl. Very open. Talented, too."

"And nuts about boys. Especially that jock, Ty Macomb."

"Ah, the studmuffin."

Mitch almost ran off the road. "The what? Did she actually call him that? I'll choke the—"

She interrupted him with a laugh. "No, no. That was just the impression she gave when she described him. We had an in-depth discussion about teenage male perspective as it relates to their current girlfriends' reputations. You needn't worry about her."

He relaxed a little. "Well, thanks again for whatever advice you gave. You might have saved the kid from getting too involved, pregnant or something."

Too late Mitch realized what he'd said, the subject he had brought up unintentionally. Or maybe he had subconsciously segued into it and not very well at that. He glanced over at Robin and saw the wry look she was wearing.

"*You* couldn't be. Could you?" he asked.

She turned her head so that he couldn't see her face.

"Robin, if—"

"I will *not* discuss it."

He rolled his eyes. "You can't just bury your head in the sand. If you happen to be pregnant, it won't just go away." But it could. If she wanted it to, it very well could end with no one the wiser but Robin and some doctor. "Robin, please tell me you wouldn't...?"

She turned to him, frowning. "No. I wouldn't. Leave it at that."

Like hell he would. The notion had grabbed hold of him, and wouldn't let go. Mitch realized that the thought of Robin carrying his baby didn't exactly cause any panic attacks. In fact, the idea intrigued him.

"That's not an event a woman needs to go through alone. Would you marry me?"

"Don't be absurd," she snapped. "I hardly know you."

He smiled. "Biblically speaking, you know me better than anybody ever has."

She huffed. "Get real. Like I'd believe you never had sex."

"Well, yeah, I have, but not that...well, not sex that was that...intimate, I guess you'd call it. Recreational is all." He hurried on past that gaff. "So, you know me *that* way and we're working on the social aspect like crazy, right? You're an easy woman to love, Robin. I'm half there already. More than half, actually. I'd say about—"

"Shut *up!*" she demanded with a huff. "If you don't, I'm getting out of this car at the next stoplight!"

"Okay, okay," he said, immediately sorry he had upset her. He was a fool to think she might not mind an unplanned pregnancy.

Mitch knew she hadn't given protection a thought, either, when she'd decided to make love with him. They were both to blame. He just wanted her to understand that he would be there for her if there were consequences.

Hell, he wanted to be there for her whether there were consequences or not and she ought to know that, too.

He made a final attempt. "But just for the record, I think you would make an excellent mother. Could you maybe forgive me enough to—"

He had just stopped for a red light and, good as her word, she popped her seat belt and opened the door. He reached across and grabbed her arm. "Wait! I promise. No more. I won't say another word, Scout's honor."

She slammed the door, crossed her arms and shot him a look that would curdle cream. That was justified. He knew he had rushed her. Her breathing seemed uneven and her movements restless. She was worried all right. Whether about the chance of being pregnant or his being in love with her, Mitch couldn't tell.

Mitch adopted a blank expression and carefully avoided looking at her for the rest of the ride. Anyway, his mind was too busy planning his strategic campaign.

He needed to get rid of all the outside interference before he could fully dedicate himself to winning her. But then she would be free to leave. It would have to be a simultaneous effort, he supposed. And he would have to work fast.

Robin was surprised, but not disappointed to find Kick Taylor still absent when they arrived at his house after dark. Her

mind was too tangled at the moment to deal with the expla-
nations and questions concerning the disk and what she'd
found out on the Internet. She might be pregnant, for heaven's
sake. Everything else automatically dropped way down on her
priority list of things to think about.

But she couldn't talk about it yet. Didn't dare dream such
a happy accident had happened to her. What would Mitch
think if she admitted she had considered the idea of becoming a mother long before she had ever met him? She'd even
gone so far as to check into artificial insemination. The only
thing that had prevented her going through with it was the fact
that she wouldn't know the donor. She couldn't let herself
hope now. That might jinx it.

They had entered by the front door since the batteries on
the garage opener seemed to have died. She watched Mitch
punch the code in the alarm system and reset it. "Where do
you suppose he is?" she asked.

"Kick? Oh, my guess is he's still at Charlene's. "I expect
he'll be home in time to hit the sack here. Workday tomorrow. You anxious to tell him what we've got?"

"I dread it. He won't be happy we kept it from him."

Mitch smiled at her. "He'll go nuts, but he'll get over it.
We'll dig in and get fortified before he gets here."

"Want something to drink?" he asked, leading the way to
the kitchen. Robin followed.

"Water," she said.

He handed her a bottle and helped himself to a soft drink.
"We should have brought home some of those leftovers."

Robin shook her head as she expelled a deep breath. "I
think I ate enough to sustain me for a week. It was the best
meal I've ever had, bar none. Your mother is a wonderful
cook." She smiled. "A wonderful person, just like the rest of

your family. I can't tell you how much I enjoyed being with them today."

"We'll do it again soon. You heard Mama insist," he said with a smile of pride, "and she'll be mad as hell if we don't take her up on it. Maybe next Sunday."

"Maybe. If I'm still here."

Though Robin had found herself fascinated and a little overawed by Mitch's family while she was at the Wintons', she now felt depressed and downright scared. They frightened her. *He* frightened her. She found herself wishing too hard for a way of life that was totally foreign to her.

As a child model, educated by private tutors and living at home while attending college, Robin was well aware that she lacked the experience to deal with men in general, and especially one like Mitch. She had never known unconditional love, which seemed to be the cornerstone of his family.

They were even willing to extend that caring to her, a virtual stranger. A murder suspect, for heaven's sake. What were they thinking? And yet they had welcomed her with open arms, perfectly content to accept her just as she was only because the son of the family smiled down on her.

Mitch himself offered her acceptance, maybe even love if she could believe him, not requiring her to do anything or be anything to earn it. But Robin knew nothing came without a price attached. The cost of letting herself love Mitch would be to relinquish the reclusive lifestyle she'd adopted, her insulation against being used. Could she give up that protection?

Was it wrong to crave more than this afternoon's taste of what a normal life was like? Could she dare risk feeling loved for herself alone, just once?

If she'd been honest with herself at the time, she might have admitted to knowing that Troy was not the one for her. He was an egotist who was used to getting everything he wanted, and his veneer of charm had been about as deep as a dessert plate.

James had cared. But it had not been love on her part or on his when they were together.

With Mitch it was different. At least her feelings were, and she badly wanted to trust him. More than she had ever wanted anything in her life.

She had surrendered herself to him physically already. No, she had practically thrown herself at him, Robin amended. No way she could deny that her emotions had gotten tangled up in that encounter. So had his, if he was telling the truth.

"Robin? You okay?" he asked.

She nodded, stopped wringing her hands. "Sure. I had a great time at your parents' house. Thanks for asking me to go."

Her entire body tensed further at his intense appraisal of her. "You're not okay. Look, I'm sorry if I upset you with all that about...what could happen. I just wanted you to know everything will be all right no matter what."

When she would have protested again, he held up both hands in a placating gesture. "Okay. We'll talk when you're ready to." His gaze slid to the refrigerator. "Sure you're not hungry?"

"No, and stop trying to feed me every time I open my mouth. I'm not *that* skinny."

"No, you sure aren't!" he agreed with a sly smile. "I think I see a little fat right there on your earlobe!" He tweaked it playfully with his forefinger.

Robin stepped away from him. "If you don't mind, I think I'll say good-night now." Mitch was too good to be true. She needed to get away from him, to ground herself in reality again.

He glanced at his watch. "At eight-thirty?"

She shrugged. Just being near him set her on edge. Not

only did she not know what to do with him, she couldn't decide what to do with herself. He was building her hopes too fast, too soon.

"Come on, we'll watch a little television and I'll fix us a snack later," he suggested, guiding her toward the living room. "You're not still mad at me, are you?"

In a way, she was. He had no right to tantalize her with offers of love and hope that she might share in that wonderful family of his for more than one afternoon. No right. She removed her elbow from his hand and hurried ahead of him, claiming a chair instead of the sofa where he might sit beside her.

"Well, I see I've got my work cut out for me if I want back on your good side," he said as he reached for the remote. He clicked on the small set, sat back on the sofa and stretched his long arms out along the back of it. "What'll it take, Robin?"

"A ticket home," she replied, forcing her gaze to remain on his. "I can't deal with this right now. I need to think."

He pursed his lips as if thinking about that. "*This,* meaning the investigation? Or is it *me* you have a problem with?"

"You," Robin admitted.

"And you won't even talk about it?"

"There's no point," she said, honestly wishing she could explain. "I don't want to discuss it because I really don't know what I can say." Not yet, anyway. He had put the idea of a child in her head and it wouldn't leave her alone.

"Let's try the truth. I made you uncomfortable when I mentioned a possible pregnancy resulting from what we did together. The fact is, it could happen."

"If it does, it would be my fault entirely. I should have—"

He held up a hand to stop her interruption. "Then I jumped right in there indicating I wouldn't exactly be traumatized if it did happen. That was clumsy of me. True, but insensitive, and sounded like I was being flip about it, which I wasn't. I know the impact a child can have on a woman's life and it's no small thing, I can tell you. All I was trying to do is reassure you that I do accept my responsibility. More than that, I would welcome accepting it, Robin. I love kids. I would especially love *our* kid. And I would love you. I already do, I think." He sighed and rolled his gaze to the ceiling. "Okay, I *know.* Sorry if that shakes you up. It sure as hell shook me when I realized it."

Robin realized her mouth had fallen open and snapped it shut. Then she laughed. She couldn't help it. The whole situation was so ridiculous. And astounding. He looked positively glum.

"It's not funny," he muttered defensively, punching the buttons on the remote with his thumb and focusing intently on the nearly silent television. Robin doubted he even saw the screen.

"No, it's not funny," she admitted. "It's just that I cannot imagine how you could think you love someone you've only known for a few days. Last night was just sex, Mitch."

A humorless grin played around his mouth. "For you, maybe."

Robin leaned forward resting her elbows on her knees, wishing she could make him understand. "I didn't mean to insult you. It was wonderful for me and you know it was, but a man your age shouldn't be naive enough to confuse sex with love."

"Naive?" His eyes narrowed as he questioned her with a look. Then he asked, "What exactly do you call love, Robin? Maybe respect and admiration? A need to protect? A feeling of possession while being possessed by somebody? All the emotions engaged while hormones go into gear? That feeling that's something like a strong magnetic force drawing you to another person? Are we on the same page here or reading different books?"

Oh, God, yes! Her eyes closed tightly on the prayer that he was serious. She might have replied, but the phone interrupted.

Mitch looked over at the digital display. "Kick's cell phone," he explained, then picked up the receiver. "Yeah, Kick?"

Robin watched as his brow creased and his mouth firmed into a grim expression. He listened for a long time without replying, then said. "Damn, Kick, it's Sunday for cryin' out loud. What are you doing at..." His eyes closed tightly and his jaw clenched. "No, don't come. I'll bring her down... Yeah, right away."

"What is it?" Robin demanded. "What's wrong?"

He bowed his head and rubbed the back of his neck as if it ached. When he looked up at her, she saw a mixture of regret and anger. "Looks like we have a bigger problem than defining love, Robin. The lab results came in Friday afternoon. Kick just got off the phone with Hunford and the D.A."

"And?" she prompted. She might have known. Just her luck.

"They think there's enough evidence to get an indictment. I'm supposed to bring you in."

Robin's heart nearly stopped. "But...but I didn't...I'm *innocent,* Mitch!" She couldn't go to jail. Not *now!*

He nodded. "I know that, but we don't have a choice here. You'll have to go in. I'll try to reach Damien again. He'll suggest the best defense lawyer." He stood and came to her, offering his hand. "Come on, we'd better go."

"What about bail?" she asked, walking hand in hand with him to the front door. Robin was thinking about escape. She had enough money to hide anywhere in the world until she knew...

"I'll be honest with you. Bail's not likely when it looks like murder one. Maybe a lawyer could argue for manslaughter since you didn't bring the weapon with you. I just don't know. You might have to tough it out until I can find the son of a bitch who killed Andrews. And don't you doubt for a minute that I'll find him, Robin," he told her with absolute conviction. "Soon as I can. Trust me."

Robin slid her arms around his waist and laid her head against his chest, wanting to weep at the moment of false safety his strong arms provided as he held her close. Mitch would prove her innocence. She had to trust him. There was no one else.

She could feel his reluctance to let her go when he took her by the shoulders and set her away from him. "We'd better go now before they send somebody else out to take you in."

There was nothing she needed to take with her. No excuse for stalling. She sighed and turned away, wiping the moisture from her eyes with her fingers. "What will you do with the disk and the information we printed?"

Mitch hesitated before answering. "I put the printout in Dad's safe this afternoon. The disk is in with Kick's music collection by the stereo. I want to let Damien have a look off the record before I surrender it. Like I said, Damien speaks several languages and might be able to translate at least some of it."

"You'll have to turn it in, won't you? Regardless?"

"Yes. I should bring Kick in on this, I guess, and see if I can get him in our corner before this goes any further. After I talk to Damien, maybe he and I can come back out here with Kick and go over what we have."

"Won't keeping the disk get you in trouble?"

"That's not important right now." He held her face in his

hands and looked into her eyes. "Robin, don't say anything when we get to the precinct, okay? Don't answer any questions. If they pressure you, tell them you're waiting for your lawyer. I'll have somebody down there within a couple of hours. Somebody good."

"I have an attorney in New York," she told him.

"No. You need the best defense lawyer you can get, not one who takes care of contracts and investments. Damien will advise us on this. He has a law degree himself, though he doesn't practice criminal law. He'll probably be glad to give us some help investigating, though, and being former FBI can't hurt. You hang tight and try not to worry."

He closed his eyes and grimaced. "But it won't be pleasant, Robin. They'll do a body search. Put you in a cell."

Mitch needed as much reassurance as she did, Robin realized. She forced a smile. "I'll be fine." But would she?

He raked a strand of her hair off her brow and kissed her forehead, his lips cool and gentle.

"Well, we'd better get on with it before I lose my nerve." She patted his chest, letting her hands linger a few seconds longer than necessary. "Let's do it. Should you use handcuffs?"

His pained expression grew worse. "God, no!" Then he hesitated, his jaw clenching before he added, "But they might when we get there. To take you to booking. God, I *hate* this!"

"It's all right, Mitch. I'm a tough cookie and I promise not to crumble." And she wouldn't, she promised herself. She would be strong and she would be cooperative. The police would have no reason to mistreat her if she went willingly and did everything they instructed her to do without protest. Then Mitch would know she was all right and would be free to concentrate on what he promised to do. He would do it, too. She knew he would.

Robin followed him out the front door and waited as he locked up, taking one last look at the house. Though it wasn't a place she would ever like to live, she certainly had spent the most incredible night of her life here.

He held her hand as they walked toward Kick's truck, which Mitch had left parked in the driveway. With the outdoor lights off, neither of them noticed the dark van parked beyond the truck until the door of it swung open.

Robin's first thought was that the police had been sitting out here waiting, not willing to risk her running away.

Without warning, Mitch shoved her sideways onto the lawn and followed with his body. She fell to the grass even as she heard the shot. Mitch landed on top of her, dead weight, knocking the breath from her before she could gather a scream.

Frantically she tried to move him. He didn't budge. Sticky blood covered her hands. Mitch's blood. *Oh, God!*

Scuffling feet approached. Two people, she thought.

They dragged Mitch off her and tossed him aside. She could barely see their outlines as she scrambled away from them.

Suddenly they seemed to be everywhere, holding her, grappling with her as she struggled.

The men dragged her toward the van. She screamed, kicked and fought for all she was worth, knowing if they took her away, she could not get help for Mitch. He might be bleeding to death right here on Kick's lawn.

Marshaling all her strength, Robin broke free of one man and kicked the other as hard as she could.

One drew back his fist and in her last instant of awareness, Robin tried unsuccessfully to duck.

Chapter 13

When Robin woke, she figured she hadn't been out for long. The vehicle she was in was still moving. Someone had bound her hands with duct tape and blindfolded her with a cloth.

Gas fumes filled her nose. The surface she rested on was carpeted and there was room to bounce around when the van hit bumps. She was in the luggage space behind the back seat.

Not that it mattered much. No way could she escape even if no one was watching her. She wriggled her wrists, but the tape held fast, almost cutting off the circulation.

This had to do with the disk and the information it contained. She had no doubt of that. These were probably the very people who had killed James.

Robin held still and tried not to panic. Okay. Mitch could

still be alive. If he didn't show up at the police station with her in a while, someone would come out there to Kick's house to get her. Probably Kick himself.

He would get help for Mitch. And if Mitch regained consciousness soon enough, someone might even try to rescue her. But what if he stayed unconscious until it was too late to tell what had really happened? What if no one found him before he bled to death? Somehow she had to get free to call an ambulance.

Keep your head, she warned herself. Don't lose it now. Mitch's life might rest on her finding a way out of this. Her own life certainly did. And maybe another little life no one knew about yet. But she couldn't allow herself to think about that or she *would* panic.

She used the next quarter hour or so to get her wits back and to determine that her jaw probably wasn't broken. All too soon the van stopped. Robin had no idea what to expect next. They might plan to dump her body in the river or something. Unless Mitch recovered and related what had happened, the police might think she had shot him, then disappeared. He had been taking her in for murder.

Maybe these goons had seen to it that Mitch was dead before they left him there. That thought was unbearable, so she promptly dismissed it. She had to believe he was still alive.

The back of the van opened and someone grabbed her legs and hauled her out. When they stood her up, she felt smooth pebbles under her bare feet. She had lost her shoes. Hopefully there on Kick's lawn where they would be found.

Two large hands grasped her elbows and half-dragged, half-led her across an expanse of a pebble-paved walkway. She heard a door open and they entered a building. The air was warmer. A house, she decided, because it smelled like a house; furniture polish, a spicy cinnamon air freshener or potpourri. There was a faint scent of cooked onions, too, which indicated there was probably a kitchen nearby.

Hands on her shoulders forced her to sit. The chair was straight-backed with carved spindles, its seat contoured, not uncomfortable, though she couldn't settle back in it because her hands were taped behind her.

"Where am I?" she asked, surprising herself at how utterly calm she sounded.

A man chuckled softly. "You don't want to know that. If you did, I would have to kill you, and I would regret doing that."

"You didn't mind having Detective Winton shot," she accused.

"No, not at all," he agreed. The accent was different from Mitch's in a subtly pretentious way, the voice itself higher in pitch. "However, dispensing with you would be such a waste."

"Because I'm a woman?" she asked, trying to inject a note of flirtation into her voice, "And you're such a Southern gentleman?" This had to be Rake Somers, she thought. As far as she knew, no one else had a vested interest in the disk. The other men listed on it were dead.

"No. Because you are delightfully droll. And resourceful. You've been having your wicked little way with the good detective and keeping yourself out of jail. I applaud your ingenuity, Ms. Andrews. It would have been so unfortunate for me if that disk had fallen into the hands of the police."

"What disk?" she asked.

He ignored her as if she hadn't spoken.

"Therefore, I've decided to cut you a little slack and let you live if you cooperate. That's the purpose of the blindfold. So you won't be able to identify me. See, you're perfectly safe if you comply with my needs."

Robin didn't believe him for a second. The blindfold was

to enhance her terror, not prevent her knowing who he was or where they had brought her. Or was he trying to give her a false sense of security? But she could be wrong on both counts. Maybe he wouldn't kill her.

He seemed to think she was crooked, so she might as well use that. God, she would use *anything* at this point. "Thank you so much. I admire a man with forethought. Do you need a partner?"

He laughed outright. "No, but I appreciate the offer. What you must do now is tell me where the disk is located."

"There is no disk," she said with a shrug. "I destroyed it rather than let the police have it. James told me to get rid of it if there were the slightest risk of anyone other than himself obtaining it."

Her head reeled with the unexpected blow. Her cheekbone was numb, and she thought she heard bells. She certainly saw stars. His fist had dislodged the blindfold just enough that she could see her captor if she lolled her head back a little. He seemed not to notice.

He was a heavyset man, close to sixty, with silvery hair and dark, narrow eyes. Distinguished. Impeccably dressed and carefully massaging the well-manicured hand he had used to strike her.

"Now, then," he crooned. "Let's have no more of those lies. Where is it?"

Robin took a deep breath, hoping to clear her head a bit more before she spoke. She needed to convince him that she was no threat if he let her go. Finally she replied, "I told you I destroyed it. But I know what was on it. For half of my husband's cut, I'll give you the numbers I memorized."

"That's precisely what got him dead, my dear. He was well paid before he set up those accounts. That was his job. Greed is a nasty vice, isn't it? You don't want to be guilty of that."

"I'm not greedy, but I want a little compensation. James left me with nothing." Robin knew she couldn't simply cave in here. Somers would see it as the ultimate weakness. He seemed one of those men who fed on that. "Can't we deal?"

"Repeat what was on the disk for me, and I will set you free. That seems fair to me."

Now Robin laughed. "Right. You'll simply let me walk out of here and risk me going straight to the cops? Get real. I want some insurance."

"Not needed. You had better hope the police don't know about the accounts. And they don't unless you told them. They'll believe it was you who shot your husband and later your lover, Detective Winton. The only sensible thing you can do now is run. I'll provide your transportation to the Caymans. Your husband's account there should take care of your expenses. But you won't access it until after I have transferred the others. You will give me the numbers. Now. And then you will tell me what else Andrews put on that disk, the information he threatened me with. Word for word."

"It was in code of some kind. I never knew what was on it. I just destroyed the thing the way he told me to. Burned it and buried what was left in Taylor's backyard."

All the while she was talking, her mind worked furiously. James had an account? His name hadn't been on that list. Though the reports of the other men's deaths indicated they were accidental, she would bet her last nickel Somers had arranged their deaths, then approached James for all of the account numbers. He would have been the only source. James had put something incriminating on disk to ensure that Somers didn't kill him, too. And the account numbers and names would have provided verification to the authorities if he ever had to turn it over.

"Well? I'm waiting," Somers said calmly.

"All right," Robin said. "Get me a paper and pencil. I'll write the numbers down for you. I'm sorry I can't help you with the other file he put on the disk. I got past the password encryption, but the entire thing was in code."

"What sort of code?"

"I don't know. Symbols of some kind. I didn't spend much time on it since it was nothing to me." She smiled. "But I figured the accounts might be important."

She hurried to add, "And you're right about my running. As long as I have funds, I'm willing to disappear."

He would kill her. He might let her live until they reached the Caymans just to avoid her body being discovered here. He probably would want to keep her alive until he saw whether the numbers she gave him were legitimate. If James did have an account there, this man would want that, too.

"You're thinking you haven't a chance of surviving, aren't you?" he asked as if he could read her mind.

"It did occur to me," she admitted wryly.

"Well, you're wrong, you know. I really don't want to kill you. If I intended to, you wouldn't need that blindfold. As long as you can't name me, you will be fine. There were five names on that list that I know of. I could be any one of those men. Or simply someone who knows them and was in their confidence. You needn't be afraid. Just give me the numbers. Recite them, and I'll write them down."

"And what happens then?" she asked.

She heard him sigh. "Then you will be given proper clothes and shoes for traveling and allowed to dress. Later tonight we will board a plane and go to retrieve the money. Fair warning, those numbers had better be correct. For your sake I hope your memory is infallible. I will also need the name of the bank, of course."

The name of the bank? Oh, God. Robin almost panicked.

There must be dozens, maybe hundreds of banks on Grand Cayman. But she had to run this bluff. Buy time.

"My memory's fine," she assured him. "Could I have a drink of water?"

"Certainly." Fingers snapped and in a few minutes, Robin felt the edge of a glass touch her lips. She drank, her throat almost closing with terror as her thoughts scrambled for a name.

What bank? Had James given her any clue at all? He had mentioned going to the islands, George Town in particular. Had he been trying to give her clues she might need if anything happened to him? Why hadn't he simply told her outright?

Because he might not have trusted her quite that far, Robin thought.

But the bank's name was what was critical now. Had he said anything else unusual? A specific name of something that could be the bank?

Damn! She couldn't think! She was as good as dead if she couldn't come up with something. Robin drank another swallow of water as if she were desperate for it. It took so little time to finish that glassful. And her mind was still a blank. "Could I have more?"

"I think not," the voice now snapped with impatience. "You're not by any chance stalling, are you, my dear?"

"You want those numbers or not? Give me another glass of water!" she demanded. Feigning anger was a lot easier than she would have thought.

The resulting blow was hard enough to knock her out. It didn't, but Robin let her head loll bonelessly to one side as if it had. She could feel the blood from her nose trail slowly down the side of her face.

How long could she fake unconsciousness?

* * *

Mitch had managed to stagger upright long enough to reach Kick's truck. He held his backup weapon in his left hand and was braced against the steering wheel, trying to get his head clear enough to drive when a car pulled up beside him. He watched as Kick parked, got out and ran toward him.

His partner opened the door and the dome light came on. "Good God, man, what happened to you?"

"Wh-what are you doing here?" Mitch shook his head. "Never mind. Somers has Robin. We gotta go after them. You drive."

"Somers?" Kick froze, staring at Mitch in the dim light of the truck's dome. "Okay, but first let's see how bad this is. Slide over," Kick insisted, frowning at Mitch's shoulder as he climbed in the driver's side.

"Went straight through, I think. Don't have time to—"

"We need to get you to the emergency room," Kick argued.

"Crank up this damned truck and get me out to Somers's place," Mitch ordered, his teeth gritted with frustration and pain. Only then did he realize he'd been pointing his pistol in Kick's direction all along, holding the gun in his right hand as he pressed the heel of that hand to the bullet wound in his left shoulder.

"How do you know it was Somers?" Kick asked.

"It was Billy Ray Hinds, his number-one gopher," Mitch explained. "Recognize him anywhere, even in the dark."

Kick cursed, twisted the key and geared the truck into reverse.

Mitch pressed even more firmly over the bullet hole just below his clavicle and leaned hard against the back of the seat to put pressure on the exit wound. The bleeding had just about stopped, he thought. The muscles of his left arm were barely working and he was beginning to shake. He transferred the weapon to that hand anyway.

Kick glanced down at the gun, then back up at him. "You just sit back there and try not to bleed all over my upholstery, okay?"

"Call for backup," Mitch ordered gruffly.

Kick pulled out his cell phone, punched a number on the speed dial and barked into the phone. "Winton's been shot, but he's ambulatory. We're headed out to Rake Somers's place on Willow Road. Need backup."

The other end of the conversation was not audible. Mitch thought it should be, given the relative silence and lack of road noise in smooth riding truck.

Nausea distracted him and he felt a little woozy, sort of disoriented. Something wasn't right about that call. He fought the urge to pass out and get away from the agony that knifed through his body like a sword thrust. If he gave in to the need, he'd be useless to Robin. Kick might not be able to handle this alone. Mitch let go of his wound long enough to lower the window and suck in a deep breath of cool night air.

He had to save her. Once Somers found out where the disk was, he'd kill her for sure.

"She got the disk with her?" Kick asked.

"Disk?" Mitch muttered. How did Kick know about that? Had he mentioned the disk? Should have maybe. But no, he hadn't. Mitch's mind cleared a little as he mentally swept away the cobwebs building in his brain.

"You're fading out on me, aren't you?" Kick asked.

"Not even close," Mitch told him, forcing his eyes to remain open and alert. Sheer anger at Kick's possible betrayal gave him strength.

"Why don't you put that away before it goes off? You're too damned shaky." Kick's short laugh sounded nervous. "You don't need to worry. I'm armed. I'll take care of things when we get there."

"Better keep it handy," Mitch said. He renewed his grip on the weapon and focused determinedly on Kick.

The drive seemed to last forever and the pain escalated with every bump in the road. Mitch prayed for strength. And he prayed even harder that he was mistaken about the suspicion that had suddenly grabbed him like a pit bull and wouldn't let go.

Mitch blocked out the pain as best he could and tried to concentrate on whether the suspicion was founded. Maybe he was in shock and that was causing paranoia. Getting shot could probably do that. Did he have enough reason to confront Kick and demand some answers? Now was not the time, but he couldn't afford to trust Kick at this point, either.

He used to work Vice. That would have thrown him into proximity with Somers at one time or another. Was Kick on the take? On Somers's payroll? It would explain Kick's wealth and Somers's brilliant success at avoiding arrest.

That could not have been Kick trying to get into Sandy's apartment that first day. But he could have phoned someone to go there, knowing it would take Mitch a while to get home from the precinct. Also, no one but Kick had known exactly where they would be when Robin's purse was stolen in the coffee shop.

It was possible that Somers had them followed, or by some stroke of luck had picked them up in transit. Mitch remembered thinking how improbable that had been, but hadn't seen any other way it could have happened. And Kick could easily have slipped Robin's suitcase and laptop out of Andrews's apartment before Mitch had gotten there that night.

As for the diner incident, Hunford might have told Kick Mitch was taking Robin home with him. Kick knew Mitch always stopped to eat there after he pulled night shift. He could have alerted Somers. Suddenly that was the only thing that made any sense.

If not for the purse theft and the thief going after Robin, Mitch would have given Kick the disk that day. Kick should have told Somers to wait until Mitch handed it over. But if Mitch was right and Kick had turned, he obviously wasn't calling the shots.

It was time to decide. Kick had parked to one side of the unlit driveway leading from the main highway up to Somers's house.

The pseudocolonial monstrosity looked cold and forbidding in the moonlight. The mansion was isolated by the wide sweep of manicured acreage surrounding it. Kick had parked far enough away that the noise of their arrival wouldn't alert anyone. And far enough that walking the distance would sap Mitch's flagging strength even further.

Mitch didn't know for sure this was where Somers was holding Robin. It could be anywhere, a warehouse downtown, a cabin in the woods, a deserted landing on the river. But Somers had no immediate family and no reason to avoid doing business at home. Taking Robin elsewhere would only make things more complicated than necessary for him. Mitch figured Somers would have instructed his men bring Robin directly to him. And this is where he was most of the time, reveling in his ill-gotten wealth.

Maybe Kick had been thinking along these same lines, but they had not discussed it. Why hadn't he questioned where they were going or if Mitch had overheard anything about where the kidnappers had taken Robin? Not a word.

He looked at his partner, realizing too late that his expression had given him away.

"You know, don't you?" Kick asked with a fatalistic shrug.

"Guessed," Mitch admitted. He had been holding the pistol trained on Kick all this time. "Somers got something on you?"

"In a way. I'm in over my head, Mitch. He goes down, I go down."

Mitch sighed. What now?

Kick turned to him. "Look, I was trying to get that disk without you or the woman getting hurt. I told him how it would be if they shot a cop. Every badge in Nashville would be on their asses in a heartbeat. If you'd have turned the thing over to me, they would never have come after it. Why the hell didn't you just give it to me, Mitch?"

"Did you kill Andrews tryin' to get it?"

Kick looked horrified. "God, no! You know me better than that! At least I hope you do. It was Billy Ray. He's real excitable. I know Somers was pissed at him afterward."

"How deep are you in this? You liable for anything else? Destruction of evidence on the homicide?"

"Somers wanted me on call that night. If anything went down he said I was just supposed to get the disk. That's all. I don't even know what was on the damned thing, and I don't want to know."

So that's how Kick had happened to be on call that night. Somers planned to get that disk and then ice Andrews. A homicide detective on the scene would have been mighty convenient. If Mitch hadn't shown up, Robin would have wound up charged with the murder. Or dead.

Mitch made a decision. He couldn't very well stop in the middle of this and haul Kick in on conspiracy to commit murder. He couldn't even subdue him at the moment.

"Help me save Robin. After that, I'll do whatever I can for you. Hell, you can even claim you were stringing Somers along, doing a little undercover off the record. If you don't put a good spin on it right now, tonight, this is murder and kidnapping and you're an accessory. Think about it."

Kick blew out a breath and leaned his head back on the

headrest. "Yeah. Okay. You're right. I know you're right. This is my only chance."

"Did you call for backup or did you alert Somers?" Mitch asked him.

"I called in help, man. You heard me do it," Kick insisted, looking outraged that Mitch would even question it.

Mitch knew they didn't have time to wait. God only knew what Somers was doing to Robin inside that house. Even if what Kick said was true and backup was on the way, they could arrive too late to do any good. But if Kick was lying and had dialed Somers, Mitch knew he could expect an ambush. Maybe Kick hadn't called anyone. There had been absolutely no sound at the other end of that call that Mitch could hear.

"I'm with you on this," Kick assured him. "You can trust me, Mitch, I promise. I want to make this right."

"I don't see any lights," Mitch said, careful not to question Kick's sincerity out loud. Privately he didn't need to question it. He knew Kick was only humoring him until they got inside that house.

"They'll probably have her around back in the family room. We should walk in from here." Kick got out of the truck as Mitch eased out the passenger side, keeping his weapon ready.

So Kick knew the place that well, did he? He had obviously been here before in his dealings with Somers.

Mitch's shoulder felt like hell, but he knew he had to do this and do it now. Robin was in there with those bastards, and God only knew what they'd done to her.

"Walk ahead of me," Mitch ordered. "Unload your weapon first."

"Trust me," Kick pleaded. "You're gonna need me in there, and I've gotta be armed."

"Unload. Now," Mitch repeated, moving his own weapon for emphasis.

Kick complied. He removed the clip and emptied it onto the ground. Then he led the way down the drive and around to the back of the house.

Mitch kept in step behind him, adrenaline kicking in at last. He knew it was temporary. This had to go down in a hurry.

The blinds were closed, but there were lights on inside. Mitch motioned for Kick to knock. "You try something, you die."

Kick nodded and rapped twice. "Mr. Somers? It's Taylor."

The door swung inward and Mitch saw the refrigerator-size Billy Ray step back. Mitch shoved Kick inside and rushed in behind him. "Freeze. Police!" he shouted. "Down! Face down on the floor. Now! Hands out, over your head. Back of the head. Do it!" Reflexes provided the swift intimidation he had learned at the academy and used over the years. The response was only partial. Somers refused to lie down and Mitch knew he couldn't force it.

The tableau in Somers's den was pretty much what he'd expected. The boss man himself had been standing in front of the straight chair where Robin sat. The roll of duct tape lay at her feet.

Somers had moved back and put his hands on his head, but was still standing. Billy Ray and the other goon—now spread-eagle on the floor—had been hanging around, enjoying the show, probably waiting to dispose of the body once Somers got what he wanted.

"Are you all right?" Mitch asked Robin, frowning at the swelling he noted on one side of her face, the trickle of blood from her nose.

She nodded, her breath rushing out with relief as he watched. The blindfold she wore drooped slightly over one eye. Mitch fought the urge to shoot Somers where he stood.

The hulk who had opened the door was looking up at his boss for instructions. Kick had grasped the back of a club chair to keep from falling when Mitch had shoved him inside. Now he straightened. "Want me to get their weapons?"

Mitch nodded. "Use two fingers. Left hand. Toss them over here on this chair. Don't try me, Kick. I'm not in the mood to be lenient." He watched the disarming without blinking. "Now down on your knees. Crawl over here and cut her loose. He had spied a pair of nail clippers lying in the ashtray on the end table a couple of feet away. He scooped them out and tossed them in Kick's direction. "Use those to cut the tape. Make one wrong move and you die."

He kept his weapon trained on Kick while he freed her. "Now back off. Get over there by Somers.

"Robin, call the police. Get me some backup," Mitch told her. He heard her pick up the phone and listened to the beeps as she dialed 911.

Her voice was a little shaky, but determined. "This is Robin Andrews. I was kidnapped and Detective Mitch Winton has rescued me. He needs police backup at the home of Rake Somers... I don't know the exact address. Look it up!"

"Willow Road," Mitch supplied.

"On Willow Road," she repeated. "And send medical help. He's been shot... Yes, he's conscious and holding the kidnappers at gunpoint. Hurry," she demanded, her voice much stronger now. "And don't forget the ambulance." There was a short silence. "No, I can't stay on the line and talk... Yes, I will do that."

Mitch heard her put the phone down on the table and, in his peripheral vision, noticed that she moved closer to him. "Get one of their weapons out of the chair," he told her. "Flick off the safety. Shoot if they move. Squeeze the trigger, don't pull. Fire and keep firing. Aim for the body. Head's too small. Got it?"

"I can shoot. I won't miss," she replied, her words emphatic and almost menacing. "Aim for the body," she repeated. Acting again, he thought, bless her heart. He saw by her grip that she'd never held a gun with the intention of firing it. He also had no doubt she would fire it now if necessary.

Mitch waited until he saw she had things covered. Then he closed his eyes for a few seconds and leaned against the club chair. He knew he was about to go down. A few more minutes, he prayed. Just until backup got here. He couldn't leave her to do this by herself. He opened his eyes. The room wavered.

"Steady now," he said, as much to himself as to her. "A little while longer. You okay, hon? They hurt you bad?"

"I'm fine, Mitch," she said, sounding breathless. "Don't worry. *Don't fall!*" Her last two words were almost a whisper, a frantic warning.

Mitch braced himself and forced his eyes open again. The few moments of rest hadn't helped, had only made things worse. He had to remain as alert as possible. Reduce the risk to Robin. That was when he realized that the perps were still unsecured. God, he was further out of it than he realized.

He edged toward the chair where Robin had been sitting. "Take this," he told Kick as he booted the roll of tape toward him. "Tape their wrists. Then pitch your keys over there and cuff yourself."

Kick coughed with disbelief. "Hey, man, I told you I was with you on this! Why are you treating me like one of *them?*"

"I told you I'd do what I can for you," Mitch said. "And I will, as long as you keep cooperating. But you never called this in, Kick. If you had, there'd be some cruisers out here by now."

Kick had picked up the duct tape and bound one of the bodyguards. Then he crouched over Billy Ray to tape his hands behind him. Suddenly Kick brandished an automatic. Billy Ray must have had it tucked in the back of his belt.

"Robin, drop!" Mitch shouted as he dived and landed on his right side. A bullet ripped into the carpet inches from his head. He rolled to his back and squeezed off a round, but Kick had moved.

Somers and Billy Ray both scrambled for the chair where one of the weapons still lay. Robin fired in their direction. Glass shattered in the bookcases behind them as the automatic belched fire repeatedly.

Somers toppled, but Billy Ray lunged for her from a kneeling position. Mitch sank three rounds into his chest. The ape crumpled to the floor.

Kick aimed then, but Mitch couldn't respond. His entire arm and hand felt like dead weight. The bullet thunked into Mitch's chest even as he made a belated attempt to roll and evade. He felt the entry a millisecond before he heard the shot. Paralyzed, he saw Kick's finger tighten again and heard an empty click.

He also saw blue lights flashing through the open doorway, heard the squeal of tires and then the thunder of footsteps.

Robin stood not four feet away. The now-useless weapon dropped from her right hand and bounced on the rug. Her eyes widened with horror as her gaze bounced between Kick and him.

Kick hurriedly wiped his weapon down with the tail of his shirt and lobbed the gun at Robin. Instinctively, she caught it to keep it from hitting her in the face. Gasping with panic, she attempted to maneuver it into firing position.

That was the last thing Mitch saw.

Chapter 14

The police burst in, weapons drawn, shouting the same warning to freeze that Mitch had used earlier. When they yelled for her to drop the weapon, Robin opened her hand and let the gun fall to the carpet.

Kick Taylor rushed forward, shoved her to the floor and twisted her arms up behind her back. He handcuffed her wrists, all the while reading her her rights. His words barely registered. Sirens screamed, moving closer and closer.

The entire room seemed to be swarming with uniforms. The noise level grew as more arrived. Her head ached and her stomach roiled. Robin turned her face to her shoulder and tried to block everything out.

She was so horribly worried about Mitch she couldn't think. She groaned when Kick roughly yanked her to her feet.

One of the police officers was bending over Mitch, and two

more were busy checking the others who had been shot—
Somers and his bodyguard.

"How's Winton doing?" Kick demanded loudly.

The policeman crouching beside Mitch moved aside as two
ambulance attendants rushed in carrying a stretcher and their
bags. The officer who had been examining Mitch frowned at
Kick and shook his head. Did that mean Mitch was dying?
Already dead?

"No!" Robin cried. She struggled to jerk out of Kick's
grasp and go to Mitch.

"Oh, no, you don't!" Kick snarled, his strong fingers biting into the flesh of her arm. "You're going down for this as
well as the murder of your husband!"

"What?" Robin had seen him shoot Mitch point-blank. No
way was he getting away with it. "*You* shot him! He trusted
you," she said looking straight into his eyes. "Mitch is your
partner. How could you have done that to him?"

"Shut up if you know what's good for you," he snapped.
His burning gaze slid away and his full lips tightened to a thin
line. "Murderin' bitch," he added.

"We'll take her in the cruiser, Sgt. Taylor," one of the policemen assured Kick. "You better ride separately." The cop
must fear what Kick might do to her if he got her alone in his
vehicle after she had supposedly shot his partner.

"Isn't that your truck parked down the drive?" the officer
asked, waited for Kick's nod and continued, "Why don't you
follow us?"

Reluctantly Kick nodded. "She's my collar. I don't want
anybody else horning in on this. You got that?"

The officer grunted his assent and took hold of Robin's
other elbow.

Kick definitely resisted letting go of her arm. Before he did,
he administered a bruising squeeze. "You'd be wise to keep

your mouth shut," he advised, his voice low and deadly, his teeth gritted. His glare was menacing, now devoid of the guilt she might have imagined scant moments ago.

The officer who took custody of Robin stood between her and the door until the medics carried Mitch outside. Kick followed them out and quickly disappeared into the darkness. Then she was propelled through the door and toward the waiting police vehicle.

Who would believe her if she told what really happened? She'd already been on her way in to answer one charge of murder when all this took place. The gun Kick had thrown at her, now bearing her prints, would match the bullet inside Mitch. No question she would be blamed.

Framed twice. Not a very believable defense. If Mitch died, she almost didn't care what happened to her, but she knew she had to care. She might not be the only one inhabiting this body of hers.

Damned if Kick Taylor would get away with this. She owed it to Mitch to see that he didn't. And damned if his sweet family would be allowed to think she had shot their son.

She strained to see Mitch again, but the attendants were already loading the stretcher into the back of the ambulance. The officer guided her roughly to the police car.

Her only hope rested with Mitch. And she knew that if he did live, *his* only hope rested with *her.* If Mitch didn't die from the wounds, Kick could not afford to let him regain consciousness.

She looked over her shoulder at the ambulance bearing the man who had saved her life, the man who had held her in his arms and loved her, the man who had shared his family with her and who had made her laugh. "Don't die, please," she whispered.

The police officer clamped one hand on her head and forced her inside the car.

Robin knew she had to get protection for Mitch at the hospital. He would be surrounded by the E.R. staff initially. Then he would surely go straight to surgery. That meant at least several hours of safety, hours that Kick Taylor would not be allowed near him. After that, Mitch would be all too vulnerable. A few moments alone with his partner and he would never wake up.

She leaned as close to the metal divider screen as she could and spoke to the officers in front. "Please, I need to see Captain Hunford as soon as we arrive."

"Yeah, right," one of the men said with a short, bitter laugh. "I just bet he'll be delighted to hear that."

Robin knew it was useless to relate Kick Taylor's guilt to these officers. She had seen the hatred in their eyes for a woman they believed had shot a fellow cop. But somehow she had to convince them to let her see Mitch's captain. Maybe she could instill enough doubt in his mind about Taylor to get a guard placed on Mitch.

She took a deep breath and tried again. "Look, I have information that will blow the lid off organized crime in Nashville. And I will not speak with anyone in authority except Captain Hunford. Tell him that."

One of the men issued a string of disgusted curses, and she heard the muted phrase *cop-killer.*

Robin sat back and tried to think of another tactic that might get her a few moments with the man in charge. She couldn't think of a thing. But then she recalled Mitch's interrogation when he had taken her in the night of James's murder. Captain Hunford had met them in the hallway afterward and he had come out of the room next door. Had he been watching? Surely to God, with the shooting of one of his detectives, he would be interested enough to observe Kick Taylor's questioning of her.

Two hours later Robin realized there might not be an immediate interrogation. Or any interrogation at all. She hadn't considered that possibility until now. Why would anyone bother to question her? They had evidence, probably enough to convict her.

Besides, it was the middle of the night. Sunday night. Hunford wouldn't be at work. Even if he decided to grant her a few minutes, it wouldn't be for hours yet. Not until morning.

She had gone quietly and submitted to every procedure so far without complaint. Three sets of fingerprints again. Local, state and FBI use, they'd explained. Three photos, front, side and at an angle. This was one time Robin was certain she didn't look up to par for a camera. Not that she cared.

She would be sitting in a cell in the county lock-up right this minute if it hadn't been so late at night when they had brought her in. They'd told her she would be kept in one of the holding cells here until morning when there would be a bail hearing. That cell was probably where the matron was leading her right now.

She had to do something. Time was growing short. There was no way to determine how long Mitch would be in surgery and when his partner might be allowed a short visit in the recovery room.

"You're allowed a phone call," the matron told her, guiding her into a room similar to the one where Mitch had questioned her that first night. There was a gray metal table and two chairs, a phone and a dog-eared phone book with the cover missing.

The guard closed the door, unlocked Robin's handcuffs and stood sentinel. "Well? Make it snappy."

Robin racked her brain for anyone who might be willing to help. She couldn't call Mitch's parents. They would be at the hospital by now and frantic about the survival of their son. A lawyer might help, but she didn't know anyone local.

Then a light dawned. Damien...Perry! Yes, that was his name. Mitch's friend, who would be able to suggest a lawyer.

If she could reach him, he might listen to her, or at least act on the possibility that she might be telling the truth. But Mitch had tried several times to call him about looking at the disk, and the man had not been at home.

She hurriedly paged through the phone book to the *P*s, relieved when she found the name. However, when she dialed the number and it rang four times, she only heard the answering machine. A deep voice with a slight British accent suggested pleasantly that she leave her number or try again later.

The prompting beep sounded and Robin blurted, "This is Robin Andrews. I've been arrested for shooting Mitch Winton, but I didn't. Mitch knows I didn't. The man who did is Kick Taylor and he can't possibly afford to let Mitch live. Get to the hospital right away and protect him. Please!" she begged. "Please be home. Please hurry! No one will listen to me! You've got to believe me! Help him!"

The matron had come forward and was prying the phone from her hands. "That's enough of that!" she snapped. "You want a lawyer or not?"

"Yes!" Robin cried. "I do! Let me call a lawyer. Anyone who can do something." She would dial the first lawyer in the book and demand that he inform Captain Hunford immediately that Mitch was in danger. "Oh, please," Robin pleaded, crying openly, not caring that her control had snapped. "I know you don't believe me, but please get someone to watch over him! Taylor will kill him if you don't!"

Anger at her helplessness drove her to rail at the guard. "If you ignore me, he could die! You want that on your conscience? On your record?" She read the woman's name tag. "Are you in this, too, Officer Aiken? How many of you on this force are working for Somers? How many dirty cops do you have in this town?"

The female officer was frowning at her as if she had lost

her mind. She wrestled Robin's wrist into one of the cuffs and snapped the other onto the leg of the heavy table. Then she left.

Robin slumped over the table, resting her forehead on her free arm, and struggled to regain her composure. She had to calm down and think of something else. *Someone* else who might do what needed doing. But who?

It seemed she languished there for an eternity, but she knew time was skewed and it was probably less than half an hour. They had taken her watch, and no clock was visible. She jerked her head up as the door opened. A rush of cold air whooshed in.

Along with Kick Taylor.

He looked grim and more than a little worried.

Robin strained at the cuff holding her arm. "You low-life bastard," she hissed.

"Want to kill me, too?" he asked softly.

"You leave Mitch alone," she warned. "Haven't you done enough? How can you live with yourself?"

"Looks like you've snapped. Two murders too much for you?"

"You shot him!" Robin accused. Though it didn't seem likely, she hoped to God someone was observing the way they did on the cop shows she watched on television. She prayed for it. "You shot Mitch Winton, and he saw you do it. *I* saw you do it. I'll scream it to everyone who will listen. You shot him and threw the empty gun at me knowing I would catch it without thinking," she accused.

"Ranting this way is pointless," he muttered.

"You were working for Somers. You knew about the disk and you stole my computer thinking the information was on it. You killed my husband. How much did Somers pay you?"

He had his back to the observation glass as he leaned his hands against the table across from her. "You better lawyer up, Ms. Andrews. You might even get bail." He mouthed the next words, "I hope you *do*." His gaze burned into hers. "Where is it, Robin?"

She didn't have to ask what he wanted. "Go to hell," she rasped, her voice hoarse now. "That disk is gone and the information's in my head where you will *never* get to it."

Taylor pushed away from the table and headed for the door. "They'll take you to a holding cell now. Rot there for all I care."

"That will take a while," she snapped. "And the more people I see, the more I'll acquaint with the facts. I told the officers who brought me in. I told Officer Aiken and I told Damien Perry. If you kill Mitch Winton now, someone will be looking into his cause of death very carefully, Taylor. If you go near him, they'll know you were responsible."

He turned, his manner too confident, too cocky and too relieved. "What makes you think he's still alive?"

Grief swept over her in a crushing wave. She could barely breathe. Her entire body felt boneless and her mind blank except for the overwhelming realization that it was too late. Too late for Mitch and too late for her.

Robin waited, knowing she had done all she could do. Mitch must be dead. Why else would Kick Taylor have come here instead of going to the hospital to await the chance to kill him? Still, she couldn't make herself accept that he was gone. Surely she would feel it inside her if that large a part of her world was gone forever.

The metal of the handcuff lay cold against the skin of her wrist. She sat up at the sound of the doorknob turning.

"Ms. Andrews." The voice was gravelly. The presence of the man she saw, a godsend.

"Captain Hunford!" Forbidding as he looked, Robin could have hugged him.

"I was informed you wanted to see me," he said. "Something about organized crime, I believe."

"Is Mitch dead?" she demanded, trying to search his eyes for the truth.

But he avoided looking directly at her as he ambled toward one of the chairs opposite her and sat down wearily. "Let's hear what you have to say."

"Is he *dead?*" she repeated, desperate to know.

He looked at her then, his gaze assessing her. "Not yet."

Robin exhaled sharply and pressed her hand against her mouth to stifle a sob of profound relief.

"What's this about a disk?" he asked.

"You heard? You were listening to Taylor when he was in here?" She knew he had been. How else would he know about the disk? Hope swelled within her.

The captain nodded once to confirm that he had heard. "I want to know what this is all about."

She reached toward him even though she knew he was too far away to touch. "Listen to me, sir. Please. Kick Taylor shot Mitch. Kick's somehow mixed up with Somers, and Mitch knows about it. If you don't put someone in that hospital to prevent it, I think Kick will try to kill him."

The captain gave her no assurance. "Tell me about the disk. Why is it hidden and what does it contain?"

Robin rolled her eyes. "God help me, I *want* you to have it! But I won't tell you a thing until you arrange protection for Mitch."

Hunford regarded her for a few seconds, then reached over and picked up the phone. She watched as he punched in numbers. His eyes never left hers as he spoke into the handset. "Put a guard on Mitch Winton at the hospital. No one but his parents and hospital staff allowed in to see him. I mean no one. Understood?" He hung up. "Satisfied now?" he asked.

Robin nodded, her shoulders slumping with that weight lifted off. "Thank you."

"I'm waiting," he said, drumming the fingers of one hand on the tabletop.

"The disk is at Kick Taylor's house. Mitch stuck it in with Kick's CD collection. It's in a case that says 'Classical Interludes.' On it is a list, including Somers, four other men who are now dead, and the numbers of their accounts set up in the Caymans which we think James arranged. There's more information on the disk that we couldn't decipher. It might say how they got the money. That's only a guess, but Somers was afraid it did, I think. They must have demanded the disk and when James wouldn't turn it over to them, they shot him. What Somers revealed to me while he was questioning me indicates that's what happened."

"Who shot Somers?"

Robin took a deep breath. "I did." She quickly explained the events leading up to it. Her kidnapping, the interrogation she endured, then Mitch's and Taylor's arrival and the shootout.

"And you?" the captain asked. "How were you involved?"

"James asked me to bring the disk to him. He had left it in our safety deposit box, but I don't know when he put it there. Somers and his people have been after it since the night James was killed. He must have promised them I was on my way with it."

"And the organized crime aspect of all this?" Hunford asked.

Robin hesitated, then shrugged. "I figured Somers must be up to his neck in something like that. How else would he have gotten a cop on his payroll?" She avoided his hawklike glare. "And...I thought that might be the fastest way to get you to talk to me."

Hunford got up and walked to the door.

"Wait!" Robin cried, leaping out of her chair, but the handcuffs wouldn't allow her to stand fully upright. "Don't you believe me?"

"I'll check it out."

"You're going to leave me here?"

"Ms. Andrews," he said patiently, "you have admitted shooting Somers. He has friends in this town who might love a little retribution when they find out. This is about the safest place you could be at the moment."

He rubbed a hand over his face. His features sagged and his eyes looked tired. "And, too, this is one of my detectives you're accusing, Ms. Andrews. But I *am* taking your accusations seriously. I'll see you in the morning."

"What will you do? Where are you going?"

"I'm going to the hospital," he told her.

Robin blinked hard, trying not to cry with relief as she sat down. "Thank you, Captain Hunford. I can never thank you enough."

There was no answer but the quiet closing of the door. Spending the night in jail seemed nothing compared to what poor Mitch must be going through. Or what he might have experienced if Kick Taylor had been allowed to see him alone.

Officer Aiken came back eventually, took the cuffs off her and moved her down the hall to a barred enclosure set in one corner of a room.

"Captain said to give you this," Aiken said as she handed Robin an ice pack. "For your face," she explained curtly. Robin took the small plastic bag of ice wrapped in a coarse hand towel and stepped inside the cage the officer had opened.

Outside the cell was another metal table and several chairs. Inside was a lidless toilet and a cot with a thin foam mattress and blanket. The entire place looked clean but bleak. Incredibly bleak.

Robin arranged the ice pack on her swollen face and lay down on the cot. She closed her eyes to block out the horror of her surroundings and tried to sleep.

She awoke with a start when someone shook her shoulder. "Ms. Andrews? Wake up."

Robin blinked awake and tried to move. Every muscle in her body felt like it had been beaten with a mallet. "Who...?"

"Damien Perry. Sorry I wasn't here sooner, but I tried to determine where things stood before coming over."

Robin sat up slowly, swinging her legs off the cot.

The handsome blond man had crouched in front of her. He reached out and raked her hair off the side of her face where it had stuck to the residue of blood. Her nose must have bled a bit more after she'd gone to sleep. With the fabric flap on the ice pack, she wiped at it. "How is Mitch?" she asked.

"Holding his own," Perry said. "He'll make it. How are you?"

Robin wiggled her lower jaw and winced. She felt her nose and wondered if it was broken. "All right. Have you seen him?"

"No, but I spoke with his sister twice tonight. The surgery's over, and he was conscious for a few minutes. The prognosis is good."

Tears rushed up and out before Robin could stop them. The stranger enfolded her in his arms and held her while she wept. She shouldn't allow it, Robin thought, even as she clung to him.

"There, there," he said, crooning to her as if she were a child. "Everything will be fine." He pressed a handkerchief into her hand. "I've spoken with the captain. He and I had a long conversation with the D.A. You're being released into my custody for the time being."

Robin stilled. "Then he no longer believes I'm guilty?"

Perry moved back and looked into her eyes. His were Arctic blue, yet his expression was warm. "He's inclined to think you shot Somers in self-defense, since it's obvious to him you were struck more than once. He noticed the tape residue on your wrists, which bears out your version of what happened. And Mitch would hardly be asking for you if you were the one who shot him."

"He asked for me?" Robin felt almost hysterical with relief. "Then he's well enough to talk?"

The stranger smiled. "Apparently. Hunford recounted all that you said to the D.A. The murder charge concerning Somers and that of the attempted murder of Mitch that Detective Taylor leveled against you when you were booked are being regarded as premature, to say the least."

Robin shook her head as she raked her fingers through her matted hair. "But Mitch was bringing me in for James's murder when all this started. What about that?"

Perry smiled as he stood and offered his hand. "Your prints were on the murder weapon, but the few they found were not located in a position where you could have pulled the trigger. The paraffin test proved you had not fired a weapon that night, Ms. Andrews. Even if you'd worn gloves, as Taylor suggested, you would have had traces on your arms or sleeves. Also, no gloves were found at or near the scene. There were no blood spatters on you, consistent with shooting someone at such a close range. Mitch included that in his report. Taylor suppressed it."

"But they had enough other evidence…."

Perry frowned. "Yes. It seems some of the facts reported to the D.A.'s office were doctored a bit. Details left out, that sort of thing."

Robin's breath caught as she stifled another wave of tears.

Perry's brow creased with concern. "I'm sorry. I've upset you further, haven't I?"

"No, no," Robin protested, shaking her head vehemently. "It's just that I didn't expect anyone would go to so much trouble...for me."

"Mitch must have told you I'm a friend of his. And I have a suspicion that you are perhaps a bit more than his friend. Am I right?"

Robin nodded, feeling her face heat. "Yes. A bit more."

"Good for him. So," he said, taking both her hands in his, "shall we get you out of here and over to the hospital where you belong? Susan has sworn to beat me about the head and shoulders if I delay. Come on. The paperwork's done. All we have to do is get your things."

"They only took my watch and ring. Leave them." Robin left the cell as fast as she could. Damien Perry didn't argue. He swept her out with a haste that made her wonder whether Mitch's condition might not be more serious than he'd led her to believe.

Her continued questioning on the way to the hospital never shook Perry's adamant assurances that Mitch would recover in no time at all. The man proved maddeningly patient with her.

She couldn't help but notice, however, that he drove his Jag as if it were the lead car in the Grand Prix.

Chapter 15

The waiting room outside the Intensive Care Unit was packed. Mitch's entire family filled half of it. Then there was the captain, two other detectives and a tall, attractive redhead Perry introduced as his wife, Molly.

Mitch's mother rushed forward and took Robin's hands. "Oh, you poor baby! Look at your face! I'm *so* glad you're here now. He was asking for you."

"He's conscious?" Relief flooded through her. "How is he?"

"Groggy. In and out." Patricia Winton's red-rimmed eyes betrayed her worry. "Dr. Fleming said the surgery went well. There was only one bullet still in there, but they got it out. No permanent damage that they can tell yet. His vital signs are improving right along, but he lost an awful a lot of blood."

"I'm type O-positive," Robin declared in a rush.

Patricia patted her hand. "All taken care of for now, but we'll tell them in case he needs more." She reached out to Damien and squeezed his arm. "Thank you so much for bringing Robin. And I don't know what we would have done without your sweet Molly. She's kept us sane."

Damien smiled serenely and leaned to kiss Patricia's cheek. "Mitch will be fine, Pat. He's tough as nails."

She held on to him. "They're moving him to a private room as soon as his blood pressure stabilizes," she said hopefully. "The nurses have been trying to clear us out of here."

Mitch's father put his arm around his wife and led her back to one of the chairs. "Come on, Patty. Sit down and take it easy. You're lookin' a little peaked." He tossed Robin a smile. "When you go in there, you tell Mitch he'd better perk up or else."

Susan joined them, looking Robin over with a frown. "God, you're a mess! Come on, let's fix you up a little before you see him." She grabbed her purse off one of the end tables.

Robin looked to Damien Perry for permission. She was in his custody, after all.

He gave her a little nod, then raised his voice to speak to the others in the room. "Now that Mitch is past crisis, why not go down to the cafeteria and have something to eat? I'll stay here and page you there the moment there's any further word."

Everyone agreed and began filing out of the crowded room.

When she and Susan reached the rest room down the hall and Robin looked in the mirror, she almost fainted. Her nose was swollen and the skin around her eyes was bruised. Dried blood caked her nostrils, the corner of her mouth and the bottom edges of her hair on one side.

"Wash your face and hands," Susan ordered as she dug around in her bag for something. "Use some soap and get that blood out of your hair. You can stick your head under the hand dryer."

She plunked a hairbrush on the sink and fished again. "Here's some powder base. Not your color, but it'll do. Maybe help conceal those shiners. Daub on this lipstick. Smudge some on your cheeks while you're at it. You look like a corpse."

"Thanks." Robin said and began scrubbing.

"So who worked you over?" Susan asked, her keen gaze narrow and intense.

"Somers. I feel like hamburger meat."

"You look like it, too, not that Mitch would mind how you look. Well, he would, but only because you were hurt. I just don't want him to leap up off that bed and go try to kill somebody." She grinned. "Time for that later when he's healed a little."

"Somers is already dead," Robin told her, halting in her attempt to disguise the signs of her ordeal, her voice dropping to a whisper. "I shot him."

Susan's worried frown melted into an expression of compassion. She rested a hand on Robin's shoulder. "Oh...honey, I'm sorry you had to— No! I'm not sorry," she admitted suddenly, the fierce light shining in her eyes again. "Good for you. Now, get that face fixed and go see your man!"

Robin rushed through the ritual application and swept the brush through her hair. "Not much improvement," she commented as she tucked the tail of her blouse into the belt of her jeans. There were drips of blood on the fabric that covered her chest.

Susan quickly shed her long-sleeved T-shirt and handed it over. "Here, switch. He doesn't need to see that blood on you."

Robin changed hurriedly, pushing up the sleeves as she

glanced in the mirror again. "I won't win any contests, but at least I won't scare him to death. Thanks so much, Susan."

"What are sisters for?" she said with a grin. "You'll owe me. Name your first kid Susie."

Impulsively Robin hugged her. She couldn't ever remember being moved to do that to another woman. A little unsettled by her unaccustomed effusiveness, she laughed and shrugged. She wanted Susan for a sister. Could that possibly happen?

"He'll be okay, Robin," Susan assured her. "You'll see."

Together they hurried back to the waiting room. It was now empty except for a couple who had not been there before and Damien Perry, who sat thumbing through a dog-eared copy of *People Weekly*. He stood immediately when they entered. "No news yet."

"Oh, for goodness sake, sit back down, Damien," Susan said with a roll of her eyes. She nudged Robin with her elbow. "He must have been raised in a palace. Royal manners, you know." Her attempt at a British accent was atrocious.

Damien sighed. He also remained standing.

"Do you think I could see Mitch?" Robin asked hopefully.

"I know Stevens fairly well. I'll ask," he said, seeming glad to have something to do besides sit and wait. In a few moments he returned. "I'm sorry, Robin. Stevens says Captain Hunford left strict orders. No one but his parents and the staff. It's for Mitch's protection, he says."

Robin kept an eye on the door to ICU, noting the unimpeded entry of a man who appeared to be a doctor. He was wearing green scrubs and a mask and seemed in a hurry.

The worst thought occurred to Robin. "Damien, no one's checking the identity of the staff! The officer didn't even blink when that doctor buzzed himself in."

Damien whirled and headed directly to the door of the unit

and punched the buzzer. Robin was right behind him, ignoring Officer Stevens as he jumped to his feet and protested. "Mr. Perry, I told you—"

The doors swung open. Two beds were occupied. Most of the personnel were at the far end of the unit and busy setting up the machines to monitor a patient who must have just arrived. Only one was attending Mitch. He held a syringe in one gloved hand and the tube to Mitch's IV in the other. He was about to inject it. Robin screamed, "No! Kick, don't!"

She would have run at him, but Damien grabbed her by the arms. The action gave Kick time to bend one leg upward and snatch a gun from his ankle holster.

He placed the weapon against Mitch's temple. "Stay back. I'll kill him."

Hearing the commotion, the nurses attending the other patient turned. Two started toward Kick. Damien ordered them back. "There's no way out but past me, Taylor. Give it up."

Kick dropped the syringe on the bed and reached up to pull the mask from his face. The gun in his other hand remained steady pressed against Mitch's head. "We'll see about that. You," he said to Robin, "get over here. Now!"

Damien increased the steely grip he had on her arms. His voice sounded reasonable, without a trace of anger. "A hostage is not the answer, Kick. Put down the weapon and come quietly. Killing Mitch won't help you now. Everyone already knows all that he could tell us."

"Let her go. Get her over here," Kick insisted, his eyes wide, frantic. "Don't and I'll blow his head off."

The desperation in his voice chilled Robin's blood. The man was cornered. If she could offer him a way out, at least he wouldn't hurt Mitch.

"He'll do it, Damien," she said in a near whisper. "Let me go with him and get him out of here!"

"No! Taylor, put down the weapon," he commanded. Robin wondered what the hell Officer Stevens was doing behind them. Probably gawking. In all fairness, he couldn't shoot at Kick. Any shot fired would endanger the people at the far end of the room.

Robin relaxed her shoulders and arms as if she'd given up the struggle. Damien's grip automatically gentled. When it did, she jerked away from him and dashed out of his reach.

"Turn around!" Kick demanded the instant she was free of Damien. Back toward me."

Robin stopped, spun around and did as he ordered. She felt a strong arm encircle her neck and the cold kiss of the pistol barrel against her head.

She didn't worry that Kick would shoot her right now, since she was his only ticket out of the hospital. But when he no longer needed her, Robin knew he wouldn't hesitate to kill her.

She realized she made a good shield for him. She matched him in height, though not in strength. "You can do this, Kick," she assured him. "You can get away, clear out of the hospital. Just take it slow. Don't panic."

"This can still work," he muttered to himself. If he hadn't heard her words, at least her tone of voice must have been reassuring. He was making plans. She could almost hear the wheels turning in his head. But he hadn't moved from Mitch's bedside yet and that was her objective.

Damien and Stevens blocked the only doorway leading out of the unit. Both were armed now, their stances indicating they were merely waiting for an opening, a clear shot. Even Robin knew better than to hope for that.

Kick must also realize they wouldn't take it even if the opportunity presented itself. There were too many civilians in here to risk a shootout. She had visions of oxygen tanks exploding. And of bodies falling everywhere as they had in the hail of bullets at Somers's house last night.

She risked a glance at Mitch. He lay there looking so vulnerable she wanted to weep. But his eyes were open now. His gaze flicked to his left hand and back to her. With two fingers he gave the syringe Kick had dropped on the bed a little push toward her. She moved her right hand slowly, groaning and twisting slightly to distract Kick as she picked it up.

"Be still," he barked, tightening his hold.

"Hard...to...breathe," she gasped. His choking grip on her eased a bit and she sucked in a deep breath. "I'm ready," she muttered, hoping to prompt him to leave the room.

He took the cue. "Everybody move over there! On the far side of the room away from the door! Now!"

The barrel of the pistol remained firmly against her temple. Robin knew if she jabbed him with the needle now, he would squeeze that trigger reflexively. She had to wait until he relaxed a little. Until he felt safer. Maybe in the elevator. At least in there no one else would be in danger. She hoped.

Robin positioned the syringe in her hand, her thumb on the plunger, uncertain what effect it would have if she did use it. Who knew what was in it? Obviously something that would have killed Mitch. That could be just about anything, given his weakened condition. But somehow, she didn't believe Kick would have risked using it without the absolute certainty that it would kill and kill quickly, allowing him to sneak back out of the hospital undetected.

He might have gotten the scrubs and mask without much trouble out of the laundry somewhere, but surely he would have caused a stir if he'd tried to obtain anything lethal from a source within the hospital.

No, he would have brought this in with him already prepared. Probably a street drug, a whopping dose, Robin fig-

ired. As a cop who used to work Vice, he would have access
to that.

The question was, how quickly would it work? Fast enough
to prevent his shooting her? Even if he relaxed the position
of that gun for a few seconds and took it away from her head,
would he still be able to shoot?

She would have to disarm him somehow, or else convince
him that she was no threat.

"Buzz us out," he ordered. Robin did. He snarled at Damien
and Stevens. "If these doors open again before we're off this
floor, I'll shoot her," Kick warned them. As he edged sideways
with her out of the ICU doors and allowed them to close, the
elevator chimed. He whirled around keeping her between him
and whoever stepped out.

Captain Hunford appeared, both hands occupied with cups
of coffee. His tired eyes flared at the sight of Kick holding
her at gunpoint.

"Taylor!" he exclaimed. His gaze flew to the vacant chair
where Stevens had been keeping watch.

"Get in there with them!" Kick ordered, his voice grating
with desperation. "Do it now, Cap, or I'll ice her right here."

Hunford nodded and did as he was told. He pushed the button with his elbow and buzzed himself into the unit. His worried gaze collided with Robin's, but he kept silent.

She remained docile as Kick walked her to the elevator and
they entered. "Punch Lobby," he said.

Robin did. She knew she was on her own now. Hunford
would call downstairs. There would be officers or security
guards there when the elevator opened, she had no doubt. But
they would be able to do no more than Damien, Stevens or
Hunford had done. If she didn't get her act together and figure a way out of this, Kick would escape and most likely kill
her once he didn't need her as a hostage.

Well, years ago she'd thought she might like to try acting
Now seemed an excellent time to try her skill. Hadn't she
spent most of her life pretending a confidence she didn't feel
Presenting herself as a whole different person than who she
really was? She could almost hear Mitch telling her to go for
it.

She could literally smell Kick's fear, and his greed was obvious. If she could allay the one and feed the other, this migh
work. She had to *make* it work.

"You might want to put the safety on, Kick," she said
calmly. "If you accidentally shoot me, you'll never get those
account numbers I memorized. All that money is just waiting."

"It won't do me any good now," he snarled. "So just shu
the hell up."

"Now's not time to lose it, Kick. You're too smart for that,"
Robin said, hiding her terror and pretending exasperation
"All you have to do is steal us a boat! Believe me, I can get
you all the way to the Caymans if you can find a craft capable of the trip." She thought his arm loosened a little.

"C'mon, boats are my thing," she lied. She didn't know
port from starboard. "And this is your *only* chance at tha
money. Think! We can be rich, Kick. Somers is dead. My husband's dead. Who's left to care about the accounts? Work with
me here."

She allowed a short laugh to escape. Actually it was a pre
cursor to hysteria, but she thought maybe it sounded non
chalant enough to fool him. "I thought I had Mitch convinced
to go after it, but he was just playing me. Planned to turn me
in all along."

The elevator stopped, the round light at the top blinked *L*
for lobby. Robin still had her hand on the panel. She pressed
the door-close button and held it.

"What do you say?" she asked. "There's close to eight million, only one of it mine. My price for the numbers is your clicking on that safety so I don't wind up dead if your finger twitches. I want to live to spend *my* million."

His silence told her he was considering it.

"Show of faith, Kick. Click it on, and we're in business."

"They'll be waiting when the door opens," he argued, his voice breathless with fear, his every muscle taut against her and around her neck.

"They won't know the difference if it's on or not. I'll act terrified. We can pull this off if you don't wimp out."

After a couple of seconds she heard a click. "Okay," he said. "But you screw me, lady, and I'll blow you away."

"Okay. Give me a second," she said, her tone businesslike as she could make it. She could do this, she told herself.

Mitch expected her to do something and, by God, she meant to do it. "Let me take a deep breath first and flex my neck a bit, then we'll go for it."

He moved his arm out well beyond her neck to allow it, but the gun still rested against her hairline. She prayed he actually had put on the safety.

Robin drew in the deep breath she'd requested, then spun within his grasp, surprising him, releasing the button on the panel as she dropped to her knees. She stabbed the syringe directly into his groin and mashed the plunger with her thumb.

His gun dropped to the floor as he grabbed himself with both hands, screaming and doubled over. Robin scrambled sideways and threw her body over the pistol to keep him from getting it.

She clutched the gun close to her chest and curled herself over it, rubbing her thumbs along the smooth metal while her fingers squeezed it in a death grip.

The doors slid open, and the elevator immediately filled

with cops. Robin clenched her eyes shut and curled into a ball.
Someone stepped on her leg and stumbled. The noise level
deafened her. Officers or guards shouted as the struggle ensued.

Kick alternately gagged, screamed and cried as they
dragged him out of the elevator. She might have added a few
groans to the melee herself. All she could think was that she
had the gun. She had to hold on.

Chapter 16

"Ms. Andrews?" Hands pried at her arms, trying to pull them away from her sides. Someone tugged at her ankles. She couldn't unfold. Her body felt rigid, every tendon locked in place. She shook silently, her breath huffed in and out in short unfulfilling gasps, and her eyes wouldn't open.

"It's all right now, ma'am," a male voice assured her in almost that same deep drawl Mitch always used. "We have him secured." The words registered somewhere inside her brain, but her muscles refused to respond.

"He's passed out, see?" the voice told her gently. "You can get up now. I'll help you. They're taking him away. He's cuffed and not even moving. Fainted, maybe."

Dead, maybe. Robin knew she should tell the officer that

Kick Taylor might be the victim of whatever lethal substance he would have used on Mitch. But she couldn't seem to form words.

It was over now. Mitch was safe. She had done it.

She heard the deep voice again, at a distance and not so gentle now, as it summoned someone outside the elevator. "Hey! Get a doctor over here. This lady's in shock!"

So I am, Robin thought with a shudder. Shocked as hell to be still alive. It was ridiculous to lie here in a heap like a frightened child when Mitch was clinging to life by his fingernails up on the third floor.

Slowly, forcing herself to unwind and get to her knees, Robin checked the safety on the weapon she held. Sure enough, it was on. She very carefully laid it down on the floor of the elevator. Her prints were on that one, too, now. For someone who knew so little about guns, they certainly seemed to land in her hands often enough these days.

"Ma'am? Are you okay now?" said the man who had been trying to assist her. He was a heavyset guy in his late twenties—she would guess a beat cop.

She glanced at his name tag. "Yes, Officer Marks, I'm fine. You probably should see about that weapon there," she said, pointing to the gun on the floor. "I'm going back up to the ICU."

He scooped up the pistol and took her by the elbow. "I'm sorry, ma'am. You'll have to come with me."

She couldn't break free. He had the gun now. She was fresh out of syringes and her muscles felt like Jell-O. Robin didn't even have the strength to protest verbally.

"Don't worry, Ms. Andrews," he said gently. "I'm one of the good guys."

Robin devoutly hoped so.

* * *

Mitch awoke with a start. The bullet holes had obviously been plugged with salt. He felt as if he'd been worked over by a wrecking ball. "Where's Robin?" he grunted.

"It's about time you came around. I swear you'd sleep through a tornado." Susan leaned over him and stuck a straw in his mouth. "Drink some of this. Sorry it's not coffee."

Mitch took time to drink the ice water, but only because his mouth was so dry he could hardly talk. The simple act of sucking on the straw exhausted him. His eyes kept closing, but he knew he had to fight that. He had to know about Robin.

"She's okay," Susan said as if she'd read his mind. He hated when women did that, but in this case it was convenient.

"Where is she?" he rasped. "Is Kick—?"

"Kick's taken care of. Robin's safe. She's with the FBI."

"God, no. Not the witness program?" He'd never find her.

Susan shook her head. "No, nothing like that. It's all Damien's fault, and don't think I didn't ream him out about it! Apparently Robin told him about the disk with the Cyrillic on it, and they're holding her for questioning. They think her husband was spying."

"She's innocent," he said, barely able to utter the words.

"Sure she is," Susan agreed. "It'll be all right, Mitch."

"She's alive," he mumbled, a huge weight rolling off his chest. He hadn't lost her.

"She's alive," Susan repeated. Mitch hung on to those words as morphine from the IV rushed through his veins.

When he fought his way out of the fog again, she still wasn't there. Damien was. "Where is she, Perry?" he demanded.

"New York." One thing about Damien, he told it like it was. "A couple of the agents flew up with her to check out the rest of the contents of her safety deposit box. That's much faster than going the usual route, getting a court order to open it. She agreed to do it."

"Comin' back?"

"Of course," Damien said. Maybe he wasn't telling it like it was.

"What day is it?"

"Tuesday."

"What week?"

Damien laughed softly. "Same week, Mitch. You haven't been comatose, just under the influence. They eased off on the painkillers this morning."

"No joke," Mitch grumbled, wincing as he shifted, trying to find a more comfortable position in hell. "Tell me everything."

Damien sat near the foot of the bed. "First off, Robin refused to cooperate in any way until the surgeon himself assured her that you would recover fully. She insisted on seeing you, and did, but you were totally sedated by then. It took three of us to subdue you once Kick Taylor took Robin out of the ICU. Remember?"

Mitch didn't. The last thing he recalled was pushing the syringe toward Robin and watching her grasp it, the only weapon he could offer her against a nine-millimeter. "Did she use it?"

"What? The syringe? Oh, yes." Damien exhaled, brushing a hand over his face. "Kick's dead. Massive dose, pure uncut. She injected all of it. A fraction would have done the job."

Mitch hated that Robin had been forced to take a life. Two, actually. The encounter at the Somers house came back to him full force. At least Robin would be safe now.

"She must have been glad to get out of Nashville," he said more or less to himself.

Then he looked and saw Damien watching him with a worried frown. Mitch tried to smile, to alleviate that worry. "Knowing Robin, she would feel responsible for causing everything, even my gettin' shot." He couldn't really blame her for wanting to put it all behind her. "It's not as if we have much of a history to work with. Or anything in common. Just two people thrown together, dodging bullets."

"And you neglected to duck," Damien said, getting up from the bed. "I'm leaving now. Your parents will be here in a few minutes. Try not to look as though you're awaiting the coroner, will you?"

"Yeah. Thanks, Damien."

He paused at the door. "Mitch? She really had no choice but to go."

And Mitch had no choice but to go after her. First thing on his agenda once he got untangled from all these damned tubes.

Robin waited in the outer office of Special Agent Nick Olivetti. One of the junior agents kept her company. Actually, he guarded her to keep her from disappearing downstairs, out the door and into the crowded streets of New York. He chewed antacid tablets and pored over a magazine while she anticipated the next interrogation. No rubber hoses and blinding overhead lights for these guys. All very civil. "How was your husband connected to the Russians?"

There had been many questions, but they all seemed related to that one. Variations of it. Repetitions of it. On and on it went. Robin had no earthly idea James even knew a Russian. But then, she had known nothing of his background other than what he had chosen to tell her, until she found the information on the Internet. He could have been an international spy for all she knew. She would not have found that on the Web, even with her resources. How many times must she tell them she had no knowledge of his activities?

The door to Olivetti's office opened and he beckoned to her. "Ms. Andrews, we have a few more questions."

Wearily she got up and went in. She plopped down in the chair he indicated, forsaking any attempt to remain aloof and impervious to his badgering. She threw up her hands. "Look, I simply can't give you what you're looking for. Arrest me, offer me deals, browbeat me until I collapse, but I cannot give you any more information about James Andrews."

He tossed a paper onto the desk in front of her chair. "Do you read Russian, Ms. Andrews?"

"For the thousandth time, *no!*" she exclaimed, exasperated. "A bit of French, enough German to order food, two courses of Spanish to graduate college. That's it."

"Look at it. There is what was on the disk you provided. Another page of it in the envelope with the copy of your husband's will that was in your deposit box. That envelope is addressed to you. Tell me what that means. Why would he leave you something written in Cyrillic if he knew you couldn't read it?"

A good question—she would grant him that. Robin pushed out of the chair and leaned over the desk until she was almost nose to nose with the creep. And he was a creep. He had short, slicked-back hair that reminded her of a 1930s gangster and beady, black eyes that drilled holes in her nerves. He even wore a pin-striped suit, for crying out loud. And a very ugly tie. After three days of this constant haranguing, she hated the sight of him.

If she had learned anything at all during her little adventure in Nashville, it was to stand up for herself. She was sick of being what everyone ordered her to be, arranged for her to be, expected her to be. Well, no more. She had stood up to killers and survived, hadn't she? The worst this legalized goon could do was arrest her, and he obviously didn't have enough proof against her to do that.

"Has it ever occurred to you to get a damned translator, Olivetti? Or is the Bureau so strapped it can't afford one?"

He didn't back down an inch, but she'd known he wouldn't.

He was a hardass if she'd ever met one. Robin doubted she'd tell him anything even if she did know something. Mitch Winton should give courses to these guys on how to interrogate people. They could use a little charm.

"We have *tried* to translate it, Ms. Andrews. It is in Cyrillic, but it's also in code. The words make no sense. You have to have the key to this. You *know* his code!" he insisted. "Now *look* at it." He pushed it forward with a jab of his finger.

Robin sat back down. She took the page and did as instructed. No one had shown it to her before. Mitch had printed out what had been on the CD, but she'd never really studied it.

All she saw here was a pageful of characters totally unfamiliar to her. Strings of letters that meant nothing. Just strange characters in a peculiar font she'd never have recognized, unless someone told her it was Cyrillic, as Mitch had done.

Suddenly something clicked. *Font!* Maybe that was the key. She raised her gaze to Olivetti who was still glaring at her. "Get me a computer," she ordered. "And the disk. I have an idea."

He led her down the hall into an office equipped with a number of computers. In moments she had the disk, which she slipped into a CD drive. She opened the file with the page in question and paused. If this didn't work, she could be stuck here in New York forever going round after round with the FBI.

She selected the text and changed the font to Courier.

"Damn."

"See? Still unreadable," Olivetti commented.

Robin sat back in the chair, stared at the screen and then at the letter to her that had been left with James's will. They're not the same," she commented.

"Yes, we *know* that," he told her, his impatience growing.

Still unwilling to give up, Robin opened a blank document in the word processing program, changed the font to Cyrillic and hunted and pecked the initial line of it, the shortest line, until she had the right characters lined up.

шШСчПСрхупЦч. She highlighted and switched to the English Courier font.

The first letters read TSERAEDNIBOR, Robin Dearest each word spelled backward, all caps, no spaces. Robin whooped and grabbed Olivetti's sleeve. "There it is! That's all he did! He reversed the words and ran them together. He changed the font. No punctuation, no spaces."

Olivetti frowned, shaking his head in disbelief. "But...but that's *too* easy! Too simple."

"Because he thought *I* was simple. You see, I work with fonts a lot since I do Web pages. He knew that and figured I'd try that first." She got up from the chair and offered it to him. "Here, you do the grunt work and mail me a translation. I'm out of here."

"No, you're not. We're not done," he said. "If he implicates you in any way in anything, we have to—"

"All right, all right, don't waste your energy. I'll stay." What could it take him, twenty minutes? An hour, to reverse the spellings and figure out where the spaces went? "I suppose I should see what it says. The one page is obviously personal."

"Yes, I know, but I have to—"

"Relax, Olivetti. I know you have to translate and analyze it. Go ahead." She couldn't resist the dig. "Now that I've broken the big bad *code* for you."

Robin observed his excitement as he summoned another agent to decipher the disk document on another computer while he doggedly typed in and translated her letter from James. She didn't even bother to listen while he explained to the other agent what *he* had discovered.

She didn't look over his shoulder while he slowly keyed it in. Truth was, she was too antsy to stand still. Pacing, glancing out the window, counting the minutes until she could get out of there, Robin thought about what she would do when they said she could go.

Would Mitch want her to come back to Nashville? She could call his family again, as she'd been doing several times a day, and get updates on his recovery. Did she have any right to read anything serious into the intimate encounter she'd had with him? He had admitted an attraction. She had acted on it and initiated the sex herself. Maybe he had only been accommodating?

No, Mitch hadn't taken it that lightly. Had he? How could she be certain? She had so little experience with men, it was impossible to tell.

A little voice inside her whispered. *He said he loved you. He was willing to have a child with you. He risked his job for you. He took a bullet for you. What more could you ask?*

Robin hugged herself as she stared out the window into the rain and thought of the sunny days that could have been idyllic if not for the threat imposed by Somers. It was autumn here already. She missed the heat. That wonderful, steamy Southern heat, not all of it due to the weather. She missed Mitch.

"Here, read it," Olivetti said. Robin turned, walked over and took the printout from his hand. His gaze met hers and fell away, but not before she noted the glint of apology. "I added the spaces and punctuation," he said.

Dearest Robin.

There is a disk in the box that you must deliver anonymously to the authorities in the event of my death. Let them figure out the simple code, as you will have done with this letter. I have used code only to discourage those with a cursory interest who might inadvertently see it. The disk contains detailed information that will blow apart a very widespread and lucrative enterprise involving insurance fraud.

You need not know the details, only that the others

involved were most likely instrumental in my death if I succumb other than to natural causes. I will warn these individuals that this hidden disk is my insurance and if I am killed, it will go to the appropriate agencies. Deliver it for me as a final favor to one who loved you. Be well and happy and please accept my apologies for all the pain I caused you during our marriage. The separation I forced was to protect you. J.

Robin dropped the letter and turned away from Olivetti. The other agent began a whispered conference.

A few moments later she felt a hand on her shoulder.

"Ms. Andrews? Robin. I'm satisfied you had nothing to do with this. You're free to go. I'll have Johnson drive you to your apartment."

She nodded, not even curious about what the other document had contained. She didn't want to know and didn't think Olivetti would share that information even if she did. At least she knew now that it wasn't dealing with international espionage.

James must have been truly desperate to have asked her to bring that disk to Nashville. Clearly Somers had called his bluff. With the other men on the list dead, James would have known Somers meant business. She would always wonder whether James might have turned the disk over in time to save himself if her plane had not been late. Probably not. She would have met the same fate as James. Almost had.

No mention had been made of James's uncle, so Robin felt certain this enterprise was one James had entered into, perhaps to prove his initiative to the Family, or to make his own way without their involvement. That can of worms she would *not* open.

If the FBI discovered his connection to the Andrienis, she could plan on a very long stay in New York while they inundated her with a whole new set of questions.

It was then Robin realized that she had made her decision to leave New York days ago. And that it had nothing whatsoever to do with any investigation and everything to do with a certain detective who might or might not need her.

"So, you'll be around if we need to ask you further questions?" Olivetti asked, when Robin was almost out the door.

"Absolutely not. I'm leaving as soon as I pack."

"Where are you off to?" he questioned, offering the first real smile since she first met him. "We need to know."

"Nashville," she admitted.

"Nashville?" He actually made a face.

"Yeah," she answered, drawling the word as Mitch always did. "Y'all come on down one of these days and I'll take ya fishin'."

He laughed. "That is undoubtedly the *worst* Southern accent I've ever heard in my life."

Robin winked. "Improves with practice, so I heah. 'Bye, now."

Mitch plunked his glass of iced tea on the end table and pushed the crocheted afghan off his legs. "Hell, it must be ninety degrees in here and you're trying to cover me up? Get out of here and get a life, Susie. I can take care of myself."

His sister was driving him nuts hovering. Granted, he was not a good patient. The nurses had probably uncorked champagne the minute the elevator door closed and they knew he was gone.

Despite that, he couldn't seem to make anybody mad at him. They immediately excused any bad behavior as resulting from his wounds. A rousing good cussin' match was what he needed, but Susie could get the best of him, and he refused to give her the satisfaction.

"Please, Sue, go home, huh? Leave me to suffer in peace?"

She walked behind the sofa and ruffled his hair. "Ohh, Mitchie's in a baaad mood! Whassa matter, baby?"

He knew very well what was wrong with him and so did she. Robin had been gone for more than a week. Eight days, to be precise, and he wasn't yet able to go after her. That was what was wrong.

Mitch clenched his eyes shut and prayed for patience. There was none to be had. "Get out of my house, Susan," he ordered.

She stayed at a safe distance and smiled sweetly. "Soon as my shift's over."

The doorbell chimed. "God, more company, just what I need."

Susan skipped across to the door. "Might be my relief now," she said happily.

Everyone he knew had been here, taking turns at force-feeding him chicken soup and trying to keep him wrapped up to his eyebrows and sweltering. His price to pay for coming directly to his house instead of recuperating at his mom and dad's where the treatment would have been even more intense.

"Whoever it is, tell 'em to go away. And you go with 'em," he called to Susan.

The stairs creaked as she hurried down them, and Mitch heard the front door open. Then, silence. No voices to indicate who it was. Maybe just a delivery. He heard her return up the stairs, her tread slow, measured.

"Susie?" he asked, afraid something was wrong.

"Susan's gone."

Mitch's eyes widened. "Robin?" The name tumbled out in a disbelieving whisper as she appeared in the open doorway.

He struggled to rise, but she ran to him, preventing it. She sank to her knees in front of him and looked up. "I had to come."

Mitch reached out, touching her hair, her stubborn chin. "I wasn't sure you would. You didn't call me."

"I called every day and spoke with your parents or Susan. Didn't they tell you?"

"That you asked about me," he replied, "but you didn't call *me*, Robin. Why?"

"I didn't want to talk to you," she admitted. "Not until we could do it face-to-face. I needed to see what you were thinking."

Mitch raised an eyebrow. "Why does every woman in the universe think she can read a man's mind?"

"You don't exactly have what you'd call a poker face," she told him. "Do you want me here, Mitch?" She looked at him then, examining his eyes as if she was looking for a lie.

Mitch took her hand in his. "What are you talking about, do I want you here? You make me love you like crazy, then skip out? You think I'd let you get away with that? Hell, no. I was coming after you."

"You're sure about the love thing, Mitch?"

"Come up here and kiss me. I'll show you how sure I am about the love thing."

"No. As much as I'd like that, you aren't up to it and we have some issues to settle."

He rolled his eyes and nodded. "Ah, *issues.* Well. We could settle them all if you'd climb on up here with me." He dropped his voice an octave and made her promises with his eyes. "I want to taste you, Robin. I want to breathe you in, fill you up, hear those little sounds you make when I do. Kneeling at my feet is not how I want you right now."

Her smile was slow and seductive. "No?"

Now he wasn't so sure. "You're teasing, right?"

The smile grew wider, and her palms slid slowly over his bare legs, caressing muscles that grew tenser by the second.

"The issues first, all right?" she said, sitting back on her heels and removing her hands.

Well, damn. "I love you. That one's settled," he declared, trying to focus on what he was saying and not the sensations she'd just discontinued. "I want to marry you, if you'll have me."

Her swift intake of breath and wide eyes told him she hadn't been ready for that. Maybe hadn't even considered it. She swallowed hard and looked away, staring out his window at nothing. "Marriage is a huge step."

"Right, one I've never taken. See, all my life I was waiting for you. Now you're here. What's the problem?"

"I don't know, Mitch. We're so different."

"Ah, playing devil's advocate now, aren't you? You really want to. You just want me to convince you. How's this? I'll move to New York. They could use another cop up there in the Big, Bad Apple, don't you think?"

"You'd do that?"

"Absolutely. Hunford's about ready to fire me, anyway. Says I can't take orders worth a damn."

"What about your family? I can't believe you'd leave them just like that for a woman you scarcely know."

He lost the smile and told her seriously, "Oh, I know you, Robin. And they'll understand. They're well aware that I love you. That I would do anything, go anywhere, just to be with you. If marriage scares you, we can delay it, bypass it altogether, whatever. I just don't think I can be without you."

Her silence drew out interminably. "What is it, hon?" he asked, reaching for her hand, needing the contact more than anything. "Something's in the way. Let's have it."

"Trust," she said simply, the word hardly audible. "Love is important. Essential," she admitted, "but so it trust. I've worried so much about you, Mitch. About Kick's betrayal and

how you would take it. You were such a trusting man before
and I am so afraid you might have lost that. I saw him shoot
you point-blank. That had to affect you. Will you be able to
trust people ever again? It's one of the things I...I love most
about you."

She loved him. Mitch wanted to do cartwheels, drink a
fifth of Jack Daniel's, kiss everybody on the planet, take
Robin to bed. But now was not the time to celebrate. She was
seriously worried.

"What you're asking is if I'll trust you, right? I trust you
with my life, Robin. You saved it, remember?"

She sighed and closed her eyes. "What I'm really saying
is that I don't want you to be like me, Mitch. It's a horrible
way to live, without trust."

"You don't trust me?"

"Well, yes, I trust *you,* and I know you won't hurt me,
but—"

"What about my parents? Susan? Trust them?"

"Of course, but—"

"Damien?"

"Yes."

"But no one else? Not yet, anyway, right?"

She nodded, looking so sad it made his heart hurt.

"Then why the hell are we going to New York to live?" he
asked. "Your friends are all right here! You want a fancier
house, we can find one. Of course, you might have to help foot
the bill. I'm not wealthy like you are. I do, however, have a
pretty good retirement fund and almost five hundred in sav-
ings."

Suddenly she laughed. "You poor man, you *are* after my
money!" And she didn't seem at all worried about it. "But we
do have to go to New York."

He nodded, trying hard to look enthusiastic about the move. "Whatever you want."

"Not to live," she told him, her grin impish and provocative. "But there's this small shop in the Village where they sell antiques? Well, the last time I was there they had this lovely oak cradle...."

"You're *not!*" His grin threatened to split his face in two.

"Well, yeah, if you can trust those little kits."

Mitch slid off the sofa and joined her on the floor, taking her in his arms and kissing her until he could barely draw breath. He could taste her relief, her joy and the love she found so hard to admit out loud. It was there, all right, invading all of his senses with its sweet fog of lust.

"Mitch?" she whispered, her hands roving again, this time with earnest intent and serious consequence.

"Yeah, hon?" he rasped, his own hands busy.

She drew back and looked directly into his eyes. Hers were shining. Her smile enchanting. "You are the richest man I know."

"Oh, baby, tell me about it!" He couldn't think of a thing he wanted that he didn't have this very minute.

* * * * *

Silhouette® Desire

Meet three sexy-as-all-get-out cowboys in Sara Orwig's new Texas crossline miniseries

STALLION PASS

These rugged bachelors may have given up on love…but love hasn't given up on them!

Don't miss this steamy roundup of Texan tales!

DO YOU TAKE THIS ENEMY?
November 2002 (SD #1476)

ONE TOUGH COWBOY
December 2002 (IM #1192)

THE RANCHER, THE BABY & THE NANNY
January 2003 (SD #1486)

Available at your favorite retail outlet.

Silhouette®
Where love comes alive™

SPECIAL EDITION™

From *USA TODAY* bestselling author

SHERRYL WOODS

comes the continuation of the heartwarming series

The DEVANEYS

Coming in January 2003
MICHAEL'S DISCOVERY
Silhouette Special Edition #1513

An injury received in the line of duty left ex-navy SEAL Michael Devaney bitter and withdrawn. But Michael hadn't counted on beautiful physical therapist Kelly Andrews's healing powers. Kelly's gentle touch mended his wounds, warmed his heart and rekindled his belief in the power of love.

Look for more Devaneys coming in July and August 2003, only from Silhouette Special Edition.

Available at your favorite retail outlet.

Silhouette®
Where love comes alive™

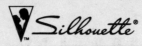

COMING NEXT MONTH